THE FINAL SENTENCE

NICOLE ANNBURY

Edited by Meg McIntyre (Phantom Pen Editorial)

Cover Design by Miblart

www.nicoleannbury.com

ISBN: 979-8-9929047-0-3 (Hardcover)

ISBN: 979-8-9929047-1-0 (Paperback)

ISBN: 979-8-9929047-2-7 (Ebook)

First Edition: June 2025

CONTENT WARNING

The Final Sentence contains some themes and depictions that might be sensitive to certain readers. Please go to my website for a full list of content warnings.

nicoleannbury.com/books

To Chase, my best writing buddy.

PROLOGUE

The groan of a floorboard alerted her to danger. She wasn't alone. Her thoughts raced as she tightened the blankets to her chest, unsure if she should move, afraid of who was sneaking up beside her. It was finally happening to her, a survivor, soon to be the victim of an intruder. She had been here before, but on the other side, viewing the dead body. And now she might be the next victim.

The creaking floor signaled more movement, and she was grateful to her older apartment for warning her of the impending threat. She knew she had to protect herself, to live through whatever was about to happen. She reached for her stun gun under her pillow, her hands shook vigorously, as she was thankful she kept it close by. The room was still pitch-black in the early morning hour, even darker than normal with the moon hidden behind overcast skies. Her heart raced, the adrenaline and fear making reality seem like a fantasy. Unsure of where the intruder was except close by, she took aim with the stun gun in hand, ready for defense. She could sense a presence getting closer, the hair on her neck frozen. She was still unable to see anyone, but she knew she had to take charge and press the trigger.

The room flashed and buzzed like a million cicadas in the deafening darkness. Her breath seized for a brief second when she saw the intruder was wearing a mask—just like the one she saw secured around her dead aunt.

CHAPTER 1
2018

Margot's grief was piercing and hot, digging deep into her chest as she sped past the welcome sign to Cape Ivy, Missouri. Her hometown sparkled and charmed, but also dimmed and lied. It was pouring some of the heaviest rain of the year, and loud thunder boomed right as Margot turned on Henderson Street toward her parent's house. After being away for two years, she found her birth city much the same with an added fast-food restaurant on Kingsway Corner. She parked and mustered the strength to face the weather and the pointed questions from her parents. She had loved her childhood home, a restored Victorian house that her parents had taken great care to return it to its 1920s glory. As she darted toward the concrete stairs to the wrap-around front porch, memories surfaced of the spot where she'd sought refuge after finding Nadine dead.

Margot squinted as the rain splashed from above and below, leaving her with soggy jeans and a mascara smear across her face. *Maybe I should just check into my hotel room.* She hadn't cared about her appearance until she'd reached the covered porch, but now that she was going to see her parents, the anxiety of confronting her past settled nicely into her throat. She wondered what she looked like after the downpour, considering the inside of the house was so pristine and she now felt like a soaked blanket. Margot waited outside and debated whether to leave. She hadn't notified her parents of her return, as she had barely spoken to them since she left a year ago. She glanced through the mosaic window in the front door, which allowed her to see her reflection. Margot was naturally pretty, with long auburn hair, pale blue eyes, and a natural pout. She rarely wore makeup, preferring just a hint of gloss and mascara. Though Margot had lived through enough for a lifetime, her twenty-three-year-old face thankfully didn't reveal it.

As Margot knocked on the front door, a breeze brought a strong floral scent from the gardenia shrub her mom planted years ago. The overpowering smell didn't mix well with the bitter coffee she'd gulped down just minutes before. She knocked again, studying the living room's large chandelier and its cascading prisms of bouncing light as she waited for someone to greet her. After the second knock, no one came, so Margot waited on the front porch chair until the rain dissipated.

The last time Margot entered her childhood house, met with a vanilla scent from a burning candle that permeated the front foyer, she returned to grab her last box full of keepsakes. The day had been sunny and warblers were chirping, but Margot's mood didn't match—it was much heavier. Grief weighed heavily on Margot's heart, an ever-present burden to carry around, even when she wanted to forget. Her puffy eyes had made it difficult to see in the bright light of day, not that she ventured out in it much. At that point, the shock of Nadine's death was still too powerful and overwhelming. "I'm sorry for your loss," was all she could remember. Margot had hoped leaving Cape Ivy would help her forget about everything that had happened on that July day.

The clunk of heavy shoes warned Margot of life inside. In Margot's haste to shield herself from the rain, she hadn't noticed that there were now two front doors on the porch. Just as she spotted the new door, she heard a lock come free. An unfamiliar face peered back at her. "Oh, hey. I didn't hear anyone out here," the man said, surveying Margot.

Margot's eyes darted around, trying to find an address marker. "Um... Hi. I'm looking for my parents. Do they not live here anymore?" Margot said as she finally realized the single-family home must have been converted into a duplex.

"Hmm. I don't know. But I doubt my neighbor Phil is your dad. I moved in last year, so I'm not sure," the twenty-something guy said. He scratched his head of untamed chin-length brown curls and narrowed his green eyes at Margot.

They moved without telling me? I guess that serves me right. Payback is the therapy of choice in the Mays household.

"That sucks that your parents bolted on you. Do you need a phone or anything? I was just about to run an errand, but I can hang a little longer. I'm Carter, by the way." He flashed a thin grin.

"Oh, no. I won't bother you. My parents didn't know I was coming to town, and I'm trying to figure things out since I've been gone for a while. I'm Margot." *That didn't sound weird at all.*

Before her return to Cape Ivy, she had left for a new city. She knew it was running away, but she felt she had no choice. Margot needed a reprieve from the constricting pain that came with sorrow. She spent her days hiding from everyone in a rented room with furniture that wasn't her own. She floated through the days, clinging like a rogue thread begging to be pulled, only to unravel unsatisfactorily. Her parents didn't understand why she ran, as their grief wasn't the relentless kind she dealt with.

An online troll had disrupted Margot's life a year into her escape from Cape Ivy, when she'd found her own face staring back at her with the caption: The Masked Niece is Revealed. Someone had been following her and posting pictures of all the little things that had become familiar and safe. The front door of her apartment, red with an old Christmas wreath from a big box craft store. Margot getting out of her car, the picture zoomed in on the face of a woman she still didn't recognize, even if everyone now thought they knew her.

Margot knew the pitying stares of onlookers as she walked into a room. The first time she'd felt the stun of eyes upon her was when she walked into a college class after summer break, where the sorrowful gazes didn't falter. Her aunt's death was front-page news, the top story on all the news outlets with titles like Dead Aunt Found by Niece. The headline was so cold, she didn't quite believe it was her until the images continued to flash, some lingering longer than others.

Margot had feared the day when she would be recognized. In a recent crime report on local news station KFCI-13, Cape Ivy's own Loni Smart had taken a deep dive into some unsolved cases, which stirred up dusty interest. After the exposure, knocks at her door from reporters—both professional and amateur—ignored phone calls from unlisted numbers, and rushed glances from strangers became her new normal. Even when she posted as sadgirlxx on her favorite blog, *Death Toll*, the other online chatters flooded her with their own questions.

In some ways, she was glad that her hidden existence was coming to an end. She could stand in the sunlight rather than hiding in the moon's darkness. Although she had trepidation about stepping foot in her hometown, she'd grown tired of hiding. Maybe she could help solve her aunt's murder now that she was back home. The only connections she had left in Cape Ivy were her aunt's grave and her parents, although their relationship had been strained. With her dead aunt's inheritance thinning out and Margot's sudden fame, she knew it was time to return home and face the pain she'd been forced to stop running from.

A voice pulled Margot from her thoughts. "Margot Mays. I recognized you because your face is all over the internet," Carter said, beaming.

"Yep, that's me. Maybe I've made a mistake coming back here," Margot said, feeling lightheaded. Her stomach churned like an approaching tornado and the burning bile of terrible coffee and sweet flowers in the air became too much. She attempted to throw up over the front porch railing, but she just dry heaved.

Carter grabbed her before she stumbled. "Let's get you inside out of the elements. Just until you feel well enough to drive again."

Margot agreed as the anxiety of being back in Cape Ivy overcame her. "I won't stay long. I just need to catch my breath." Margot drank the water Carter brought her. She closed her eyes and took small breaths, but when she opened them, Carter was smiling and staring at her. She noticed his shy smile, one corner of his mouth raised. He still had some boyish charm—a face that probably helped him out as a kid. His eyes shimmered as he kept a protective distance from her.

"I'm still in shock that *the* Margot Mays is in my apartment," Carter said, shaking his head.

"That's me. Freak show, much? I should leave and let you get to your errands," Margot said. She attempted to stand, but the room spun wildly.

"I promise I'm a good guy. I was a Boy Scout and everything." Carter chuckled. "Here, I'll open my front door so you feel safer. Besides, those errands can wait." He propped a chair to hold the door open. The heavy rain had faded to a mist.

Margot oddly didn't feel nervous around Carter, but it could be because of her newfound illness. "Just give me a minute and I'll be gone." She looked around the room. Overused modern design elements had replaced all the prior Victorian charm, likely by a flipper for some fast cash. Although Carter's only decor included a hand-me-down couch and box store lamps. "When did they split the house into two homes?" Margot asked, attempting to sit up on the too-soft couch.

"I really don't know. Phil was here before me, so maybe he can answer that. I'm a student at Ivy University and the rent checked out for me," Carter said, using the nickname college students used for the State University of Missouri–Cape Ivy campus.

College was a point of contention with her parents. They'd begged Margot to get an education, but after seeing a dead body, she didn't feel motivated to continue her studies toward any degree, much less get out of bed.

"Cool. What are you majoring in?"

"Criminology. I'm in the graduate program."

"So that's how you knew my name so quickly. Glad to know you haven't been stalking me." Margot laughed.

"Oh, I don't even live here. Now I have you cornered," Carter said, staring without the smile he possessed earlier.

Margot's heart dropped into a stomach full of bile. "I, um..."

"Margot, it's a joke! Stalkers don't tell you who they are until the end, when they try to gaslight you into believing it was all your fault,"

Carter said with a laugh. "Besides, I saw all the commotion about you on *Death Toll*."

Margot was confused. Her senses told her that Carter was safe, but his words chilled her. "Maybe we cut out the sarcasm until I know you better."

Carter leaned toward Margot. "I was hoping we'd get to know each other." His face turned serious. "So you thought your parents lived here? Sounds like you lost track of them?"

"Yeah, you could say that. Trauma has that effect on families." Margot pursed her lips.

"You grew up in this house? Which one was your room?" Carter asked, looking around.

"At the back end of the house." Margot darted her eyes around the oddly familiar yet unfamiliar place.

When she first moved into her bedroom at ten years old, she'd been happy that it was on the ground floor because her parents' room was on the top floor, where Phil apparently lived now.

"Would you mind if I take a look at it?" Margot asked, looking toward the hallway.

"Not at all. Are you feeling well enough to walk, or do you need help?" Carter quickly got to his feet, ready to assist.

When Margot stood, she no longer felt dizzy. Without answering Carter, she walked through the living room, passing the hallway closet where she used to curl up with her books and read through the night, pretending it was her own private getaway. At the end of the hallway, she saw the large bay window that looked out on a giant oak tree full of wrens and sparrows. A gentle breeze blew the orange and red fall leaves. The Monet vibes gave her a sense of serenity that she would expect to feel in a yoga studio or at an artist's retreat, making her feel more comfortable sitting with her deepest grief. It was the perfect spot for a writer to sit and enjoy nature and write about the beauty of our world. Or, as Margot knew, the beauty in the surrounding nature, but the ugliness in the people who inhabited it.

Margot sat down on the edge of Carter's bed and took deep breaths. She could feel her heartbeat slow down, a sense of peace blanketing her. She remembered Nadine's many visits to the house and the way Margot would dart to the front door to see her favorite person. Nadine was home to Margot—her confidante and the person who loved her the most. Margot's mom, Stella, wasn't the affectionate type, devoted to rules and more focused on her work than giving her daughter the love she wanted. Margot felt alone when she wasn't with Nadine, who'd doted on her and was a great escape from her routine home life.

A cell phone notification interrupted Margot's thoughts. She pulled out her phone and read the message from the *Death Toll* app: Margot Mays is in Cape Ivy!

"Just checking on you and making sure you're OK?" Carter asked with a safe distance between them.

"Yeah. It just feels weird to be back in this house. This room holds a lot of sad memories I had been stuffing away. But it looks like my presence back in town is front-page news," Margot said, sighing.

"I'm sorry. If I can do anything to help, just ask."

"Thank you, but I need to go. I guess I have to break down and call my parents to find out where they moved to." Margot huffed.

"I hope you find them. Hey, would you want to hang out sometime? I mostly spend time at the university library, but I don't mind being a soundboard for you if you need a friend."

Margot considered his words and eventually agreed to meet. "Do not tell anyone that I came here!" she said before she walked back toward the front door.

"I promise. I'll guard this secret with my life." Carter winked.

As Margot walked to her car, the faintness now gone, she was ready to visit a very important part of her past.

Nadine was my best friend. I'm determined to do everything I can to solve her case.

Back in her car, the rain dissipated and the sun slowly inched out from the clouds; there was no rainbow to be found, but it was still a warm welcome after the embarrassing encounter she just had. Steam slowly rose from the hood of the car as she turned the ignition and navigated toward Lorimier Cemetery. Even though her car didn't have GPS, it knew the route by heart, and she parked in front of the flaming red maple tree in Missouri Park. Although the rain had drenched the ground, Margot needed to be close to where Nadine's body was buried. She trudged toward the grave and spread out a blanket, sitting next to a headstone that read Nadine Chastain.

"Nadine, I've finally returned home. Although, I still don't know where my parents went, but I'll figure that out. I can't believe it's been two years." Margot felt awkward talking to a headstone, but she had been withholding her words for too long. "Now that I'm back, I'm going to do everything I can to get justice," she said, brushing away a fallen leaf that landed on the headstone.

Police had released no suspects in Nadine's killing, but Cape Ivy, Missouri, wasn't without its share of murder. With a population of roughly 500,000, it was the largest city for miles, located two hours south of St. Louis. Many came to Cape Ivy with big dreams, but of course, most didn't make it. It was a mix of big and small town, college and run-down. It was on a major earthquake fault line that kept people on edge, as if the killer on the loose wasn't enough. The city presented itself as a beautiful city of roses with Gothic and Victorian houses and landmarks. The popular rose garden and its sundial brought families from all over, but no one knew what lurked beyond its allure. Cape Ivy had lots of beauty, but even more skeletons. Now, Margot was part of the ever-growing stories and secrets that lay within the city confines.

Margot had visited Nadine's grave a few times after the burial. After she moved away, she always wondered if someone was paying their respects. But as she now talked openly, visitors bowed their heads in sympathy as they walked by. In Margot's dreams, she visited Nadine many times. Sometimes she had cried, yelled, and begged for some kind of sign or answer, but none had ever come. Nadine never gave her any clues or answers in her dreams; there was only a lifeless body where love had been.

As the wind picked up, stirring the rain from the leaves and leaving droplets on Margot's hair and face, she looked to the sky and let the rain softly dampen her resolute face. Before walking away, Margot turned to the headstone and asked, "Who did this to you?"

CHAPTER 2

2003

"You won't ever amount to nothin', just like your bastard daddy. Now go to your room and don't come out until I say. I don't want to see you for the rest of the day," Sandy said, pointing to Jack's bedroom.

Deep in the outskirts of Cape Ivy, Jack Moore lived with his mom, Sandy, and his aunt, Kathy, in a dilapidated house, with their relationships not in much better shape. There was no adult "man of the house" to be found—he'd left twelve years ago when he'd learned he'd knocked Sandy up. She was a reluctant single mom; her sister Kathy convinced her to keep Jack as a financial commodity. Since Sandy didn't have any workable or reputable skills, Jack was her check to pay the bills.

"You heard your mama. We need more prayer around here. That boy is full of the devil and he showed it today by dumping that crap on that little girl's shoes," Kathy shook her head.

That morning, Jack had set his plan in motion to stop the teasing he had been enduring when Emily, a girl in his class, took a liking to him. As most eleven-year-old kids like to do, his classmates had mercilessly tormented Jack about Emily on the school bus. Each day, he could feel his face getting redder and hotter, and he just wanted to run away. But he quickly learned that if he was mean to her, it would all end.

Jack waited out Emily's stop, which was a mile up the road from his own. Emily cheerily hopped on the bus and bounced toward the back, near where Jack sat. But this time, Jack was prepared. Just as she was about to sit next to him, he faked getting sick and "threw up" all over her pretty sparkly shoes with a special concoction he'd brought from home. He had rummaged through the garbage and found the ingredients to create a mixture of leftover egg juice, grape jelly, and soda and shook it until it had the perfect thick and sticky consistency.

Emily screamed and ran to the front, asking the driver to take her home, but he told her he had to finish his route on the street first. She had to sit with this vile stench for a little longer. Emily sat up front and loudly cried because her feet were "smelly and ugly." Other students saw her and her stinky feet as they entered the bus, including her best friends who got picked up next. Jack laughed and laughed while the other boys joined in; the girls just patted Emily on the shoulder and let her know it would be OK. He was thoroughly pleased. Emily would never give him one of her smiles again, and he would never have to worry about that fever returning to his face. A reputation was born.

Jack knew his mom didn't want him. He lost track of how many times he was told he was useless and that his mom's life would have been much better without him. His Aunt Kathy was ultra-religious and had scolded Sandy into doing the Godly thing rather than getting the abortion she'd wanted. Sandy had Jack because Kathy convinced her that an abortion would eventually send her to Hell. Jack never met his dad, who left before his son's heartbeat was barely a month old.

Kathy was a strict disciplinarian, and her punishments became more severe as Jack grew older. She would withhold meals, or make Jack stand in the corner for hours at a time, or make him stand in the bathtub while she poured hot water over his feet. Kathy repeated bible verses during the punishments, asking Jack to repent for his sins, but all he could do was cry out in pain. Sandy never intervened; she left most disciplinary actions to Kathy. She only spoke up about the errands Jack ran, like picking up her groceries, and only cared about making sure that Jack stayed out of her way. Jack hated his dad for choosing to impregnate his mom and ditching him for a life of Hell with Sandy and Kathy.

Jack was eleven years old when Kathy moved out of the house he shared with his mom, allowing him a lot more freedom and fewer beatings. He still suffered beatings when Kathy came to visit, but certainly not as frequently as when she'd lived with him. Kathy had initially moved in to help Sandy, who was incapable of caring for a child. That was the first thing Jack and his mom ever agreed on—she was incapable of caring for any living thing, including herself. Kathy started dating a man named Paul after they met at church, and they moved into his house in Vance Town, which was a few towns over.

Jack first met Paul after Sunday school, which Kathy required him to attend. When Kathy and Paul found Jack fighting with other kids on the playground, Paul quickly snatched him by the arm and dragged him to his car.

"Listen here. You will not behave like that on the property of the Lord. You better be grateful I didn't whip your ass in front of everybody. Never let me see you fighting ever again," Paul said, only inches from Jack's face.

Paul was short in stature, with thinning hair and a crooked nose, likely from a well-deserved beating, Jack assumed. Jack could feel Paul's hot breath that smelled of coffee and donuts, and all he wanted was to punch his yellowed teeth, but tears escaped his eyes.

"Don't be a sissy! Quit your cryin' and go to your room once we get back home," Kathy said in disgust, her bleached hair showing an inch of poorly covered gray at her part. A permanent sneer rested on her lips.

During Jack's final appearance at church, they held a revival with snakes, music, and dancing. Jack was both scared and overwhelmed, feeling awestruck. He had never been to a concert before. There were people thrashing about, saying they were "wild for the Lord" as they collapsed to their knees, arms raised and crying.

The revival brought several churches together, so it was a packed house, and people ran into each other like it was a mosh pit for Jesus. "Rise up and declare your faith by coming to the altar and professing

Jesus as your only Lord and Savior, or die in the lake of fire for eternity," the preacher urged the youth.

Jack took off running in the other direction, met by many hands on his shoulders. He dodged them and kept running until he eventually reached a large oak tree in the woods. He didn't know how far he was from home, so he debated trying to walk, unsure of his destiny to die in a lake of eternal fire. Jack just knew he had to get away from the crazed eyes of the pastor and wanted no part of his performance.

In the dark, his mind played tricks on him, as every tree reached for him and every noise was a church member coming to bring him back. Eventually, Jack came upon the forked road, Mountain Road, and he knew he was going the right way. Thankfully, he never slept on the van ride home like his church-mates; otherwise, he wouldn't have known whether he was headed in the right direction.

When he finally made it home, he tensed up as he turned the door-knob, bracing himself for Kathy's wrath. But he was surprised to find that Kathy wasn't there. Jack immediately went to his room and shut the door. He crawled into bed and waited for Kathy to bust it open, asking why she didn't hear the church van drop him off. But she never asked, and he never told. The next day, Kathy moved out, and Jack never returned to church again. One of the first things Jack did was feign illness when the church van arrived to pick him up for Sunday school. After several attempts, they just stopped showing.

Since Kathy left and Sandy had few rules—mostly to leave her alone—Jack made the old dilapidated shed outside his own getaway. Every "man" needed his privacy, and Jack's was the run-down shed that stood roughly thirty yards from the house, with a patched roof and an obvious termite problem. The bottom of the eroded structure allowed for small critters to take shelter during the colder months, and Jack had scared away many a raccoon and opossum, who quickly scurried to safety in the vast unknown of the woods. Inside the shed, the floors were uneven and warped from too many rainy days, which caused waterlogged wood beams to rot away. Jack laid down plywood that he found during one of his many bike trips to the local grocery store—a decent temporary fix. It was such a pride and joy for Jack that he would sleep in it if it weren't for the poor insulation. After staying out there overnight once and waking up with many mosquito bites, he decided that was enough for him. He determined that having a bed was a better trade-off, and escaping to the shed first thing in the morning was a suitable compromise.

The shed was where Jack kept his most prized possessions: his beautiful collection of butterflies pinned to the wall. He caught many living butterflies—plain ones like the cabbage white, or rare ones like the zebra swallowtail, or majestic ones like the milkweed monarch. Jack had found a book at his school library on butterfly species, checking it out again and again because he found them fascinating and easily manipulated. He loved how he could catch and control something so delicate. He was powerless in this world, yet he found something that he could dominate and, as its wings beat furiously against his grip, he'd take a straight pin and push it right through its thorax. The genuine beauty for Jack was to watch its wings beat faster as it tried to escape from the wall, but Jack knew from experience there was no escape—he only wished that he could tell if they were screaming.

One weekend in his hideaway, Jack heard car tires on gravel, which usually meant Kathy and Paul were visiting. Jack's stomach immediately ached knowing he'd have to see them. But instead of going straight inside the house, they went to see what Jack was doing in the shed and saw his butterfly collection.

"What on God's green earth is happening? This is the work of the devil!" Kathy said in complete shock, taking in Jack's "work of art."

There were at least fifty butterflies. All were long dead, just pinned and defenseless for all to see. Kathy and Paul's eyes darted left and right to the monarch and cabbage white, their mouths open, and finally to Jack's stone-cold face.

Paul violently grabbed Jack's arm and dragged him toward the house, with Jack's feet digging into the dirt along the way, making him lose his right shoe. Jack tried to escape, but he was no match for Paul's strength. Paul slammed open the front door, which startled Sandy, who sat on the worn-out sectional. "What the Hell is going on? Why are you barging in like the damn police?" Her head spun around, showing the graying that Kathy tried to cover up in her own hair. Sandy had a firm jaw that she pushed out even further when she concentrated.

"Your son is the damn devil and I'm about to beat it out of him, that's why. Do you know what he's doing out there in that shed? You need to get off your ass and pay more attention or you'll have a damn murderer on your hands!" Paul paused to stare at Sandy. "This boy is out there killing butterflies and you have no control. Someone's gotta be the man of the house and teach him right from wrong." Paul removed his belt as he directed Jack to lower his pants and underwear.

Jack's eyes searched the room, meeting his mom's as he pleaded with her to make it stop. "I promise to be a good boy. I won't hurt butterflies anymore, and I'll do my chores without making you angry." He cowered in fear, his shoulders slumped as tears welled in his eyes.

Jack's pleas were futile—neither woman would ever come to his rescue. Paul repeated his order for Jack to take down his pants, which Jack continued to refuse. A smack across the face sent Jack to the floor. Then a foot was against Jack's lower back and the next thing Jack knew, Paul had raised him up by his neck, standing and exposing Jack from the waist down to all three adults in the room. Paul grabbed both of Jack's hands and told Kathy to hold them high in the air and to not let go—the beating began.

The only sounds heard were Jack's wails and Sandy's laughter. Her deep belly laughs were just audible over Jack's screams, and they continued long after Jack's beating ended. She laughed so much she was weeping tears. As soon as she stopped laughing, she'd start up again, her squared jaw vibrating up and down. Mocking Jack's howls would get her going. Jack could barely stand, and a stream of urine he could no longer hold pooled at his feet. Paul and Kathy stared at his vulnerability. The leather belt cut Jack open, and Paul's aggression and strength left welts in his wake. It would take several months for the marks from this beating to heal, although Jack would not get out of grocery duty. He would wince in pain from bathing, walking, and especially riding his bike. That night, Kathy and Paul set fire to the shed, and that was the end of the butterfly shrine.

It was one of the first times that Jack truly felt a sense of loss.

CHAPTER 3
2018

Through the drizzling rain, Gemma watched as Margot kneeled next to Nadine's grave, a spot Gemma knew well. She had visited occasionally, hoping to run into the infamous niece. Once she heard Margot was back in Cape Ivy, she knew Margot would find her way here. Gemma held her umbrella at eye level to disguise her gaze from several headstones away. She watched Margot walk toward her car, bowing her head against the rain. If she knew she was being watched, she showed no sign of it as her stride did not quicken. Gemma followed behind, widening her steps until she was inches away. *Should I tap her shoulder? No, I don't want to frighten her. Maybe I'll carefully get in front of her.*

Two more quickened big steps and Gemma was at Margot's car, where they met face-to-face. Gemma's heart fluttered facing her. "Margot, hi. I'm onyxheart on *Death Toll*. We've chatted a few times. I'm really sorry you've been exposed like that," the dark blond with thick black glasses said as she stood with rain soaking her boots.

A crease appeared between Margot's eyebrows as she looked Gemma over. "Oh, yes. I know who you are. Um, hi, onyx?" Margot said, shrugging.

"You can call me Gemma. Did you just get back to Cape Ivy today?" Gemma asked, although she already knew the answer.

"Yes. Although it's already been a shit show. My parents moved without telling me and the guy living in my old house is also on *Death Toll*." Margot shook her head.

"No way. Who is it?" Gemma asked. *I already know this, too.*

"He's drcrime. Do you know him?" Margot questioned.

Gemma smiled. "Yes, I know him. We meet at the library sometimes to chat about true crime. Maybe you can join us?"

"Well, he also invited me to the library. Honestly, it's a lot to handle returning to this city, but it would be nice to have a social life," Margot said.

Gemma handed Margot the umbrella and retrieved her phone from her purse. "Give me your number and I'll text you mine," Gemma said, typing on her phone. She noticed the slightest hesitation in Margot's movements. "It's OK. We only know each other online, so I'm sure it's hard to know if you can trust me. I know this is odd meeting like this." Gemma waved her arms around the cemetery.

"Yeah. It's a lot to take in. I don't really like giving my number out, so maybe I'll just message you later on *Death Toll* to schedule a time to meet. We can invite Carter—I mean, drcrime." She gave a short laugh.

"Certainly. I totally get it. See you soon. And welcome back to Cape Ivy." Gemma smiled as she turned her head to watch Margot leave in her car.

Back inside her own car, Gemma believed the meeting had gone as planned. She wanted to get as close to Margot as she could—really connect with the crime victim. *Death Toll* was a starting ground for her own obsession with true crime, as stories about murder dominated her internet searches. *I hope I didn't appear too desperate.* After growing up as a loner, meeting friends had been difficult until she became engrossed with all things death. Her own story was one of isolation, and she'd recognized the slight shift in Margot's voice when she spoke of her parents. Family problems were a dominant shadow that followed Gemma through her youth.

Gemma arrived back home and put on her comfiest clothes, settling on her couch. "The following contains graphic accounts of violence and may be disturbing for some audiences." Gemma couldn't recall how many times she'd read or heard that same line, as she never missed a new documentary, podcast, or article about a true crime event. She pressed play on the latest episode covering the Crimson Spree Shooter. As she massaged her neck, she sunk into her oversized couch, hanging on every word of the episode.

"Bryan Norris was the Crimson Spree Shooter, named because of the color of the truck they eventually found him in after a lengthy standoff and even lengthier body count. The following three episodes will detail the tragic events of that day. New Berlin, Missouri is an old German town south of Cape Ivy, complete with an aged cemetery and tavern. The steins are full of American beer and the pretzels on the table have long since grown stale, unlike the recent trauma that still grips the townsfolks' memories. An out-of-towner could never know the pain New Berlin attempted to bury with their annual Oktoberfest and the many, many prayers and Hail Marys spoken at St. Mark's church in hopes of cleansing them of that awful day. With a small population, the actions of an enraged man affected almost everyone—either by blood or in passing, no one escaped the knowledge of what had been done."

Loud banging on the front door spooked Gemma and the remote slid to the floor, the TV pausing on a still shot of the killer. Gemma stood staring back at the face on her screen when a second knock sounded, her head snapping in its direction. She opened the front door to find the grocery order she'd scheduled and let out a deep sigh before hauling the bags inside. *Damn it, they gave me the wrong juice again.* Gemma shoved the food into the cabinets and refrigerator.

Back at the couch, she fluffed a pillow for her back and pressed play. "Like many families, the Norrises lived modestly on a single income, with the wife at home raising their child. The American dream still existed around there even as the stereotypical facade had so long ago shattered elsewhere. However, when the wife became unhappy, tragedy overtook them and the entire town. Bryan was the hopeful offspring of parents Barb and James, who struggled to conceive. When their Christmas baby was born at a hospital near Cape Ivy, the devoted parents felt like they won the lottery. Online searches revealed the happy, smiling faces of a maturing family."

Gemma thought of her own family life. She'd moved from one house to another, never spending more than one consecutive holiday in one place. She'd lived in this apartment the longest she'd ever lived anywhere. It was a great comfort to her, and after signing a new one-year lease, she didn't have any plans to move. Thankfully, a former foster parent of hers owned the building and kept her rent cheap. Her modest one-bedroom was plenty big, yet small enough to shield it from prying eyes. Gemma was private and had learned to keep her pain to herself, with the help of a few therapists along the way. These walls saw little of anyone else, except the occasional delivery driver who came just past the threshold.

"Bryan met Aimee in high school, where the point guard and cheerleader began their fairytale. Straight out of high school, they had a daughter and seemed to live the American dream. However, Aimee developed wanderlust with visions of her own career. She grew tired of being at home and wanted some excitement, which an affair provided."

The many notification dings on her cell phone distracted Gemma from the show as she quickly checked the recent chatter on *Death Toll*. It was abuzz with post after post about Margot's return. The responses ranged from support to crucifixion.

"I knew sadgirlxx was Margot! I just didn't want to blow her cover."

"I hope she isn't the next victim."

"She has a lot of nerve showing her face after she ran away."

Damn. Margot needs me in her corner. Although, I guess I'm just as guilty for approaching her at the cemetery. Gemma sighed, turning her phone on vibrate.

"What Bryan learned as his daughter turned five years old was that Aimee's affair was fully developed. It was a blow to his ego, especially since Aimee's beau was his friend and work supervisor, which created another set of problems. In the manufacturing world, you become brothers. At least, that's what Bryan thought. However, most brothers aren't expected to sleep with their sister-in-law or betray their brethren. In some ways, the shock of the affair was equally painful to the loss of his best friend. Bryan learned of the affair by chance, but his next moves were calculated."

Gemma closed her eyes to the forming headache. She often experienced them when she watched a screen for too long. However, she persisted, as there would be an online discussion on *Death Toll* about this series and, since a few members were local, it was big news. She could admit that true crime had consumed her. She'd grown accustomed to her boxed-in life regardless of what a typical twenty-one-year-old should be doing.

"Aimee's journals would later reveal how disappointed she was in how her life was turning out—a planned dream life for some, but for her, possibilities dwindled each day. Some would now say it's because she wasn't rooted in the area and that out-of-town values didn't belong around there. Aimee was originally from another town just north of nearby Cape Ivy, which some folks in New Berlin considered suburban, which sounded like a bad word. The couple's disagreements often became full-blown fights, with Bryan sleeping in a tent behind the house occasionally, his favorite firearm secured beside him. We later learned from a next-door neighbor that Aimee was fearful because of threats he'd made when they were fighting. She had no reason not to believe him.

"When Bryan invited over a few work buddies, she noticed a confident man that others surrounded. The man with an enticing laugh who always had a story to tell. Sean was extroverted and his gregarious smile and laugh drew her in, giving her a drunken buzz. Without him, the gatherings would be stale and boring. He wasn't an overtly attractive man, with a shiny bald head and waistline that protruded from his pants, but he made up for it with his personality and charm. The way she laughed when she was near him intoxicated Aimee. She could forget about her boring life and drop the charade of happiness that New Berlin folks expected of her. A laugh turned into a hug, and a hug turned into passion."

Gemma thought about Aimee's need for an escape. For Gemma, true crime gave her the escape she craved. When she watched documentaries or listened to her favorite murder podcasts, it gave her a break from the unrelenting thoughts she'd grown to live with. Her inner monologue was dark and reclusive, but therapy was helping her break out of the shell she'd created. She'd always been told she was overly sensitive, called an empath, and she would agree given that she had taken on the burdens of those closest to her in life. Although, as Gemma grew older, her sensitive nature turned more cynical, and she often assumed the worst in others. So many people had disappointed her over the years, stifling the part of her that wanted a connection. She wanted closeness, yet she pushed people away because she feared they could hurt her.

"It only took one time for both parties to be hooked. Whenever one mentioned they should stop and to 'think of how this will affect Bryan,' the other would laugh and say 'he'll never find out.' Of course, colossal lies like this have a way of getting out. Aimee never considered that her five-year-old daughter would have a watchful eye. Aimee thought leaving her in the living room would be sufficient for her time with Sean. She could have never known that her daughter would tell of her escapades to set Bryan off."

Gemma bit her lip as she replayed her interaction with Margot. *I really hope I didn't scare her off.* She knew from experience that when people entered her own life, she questioned their motives. In some ways, the confined walls of Gemma's existence were a comfort to her.

Because she was the only person she could fully trust.

CHAPTER 4

2018

A library was a great place to get lost in your head, even if murder consumed those thoughts.

As she entered the historical building with Greek architecture, her steps echoed inside the massive rotunda. Margot's eyes misted over in awe. The campus library was a place she'd initially fallen in love with when she first toured the university. However, after discovering Nadine dead, her campus life completely shut down. Now that she smelled the faint scent of lemon, she inhaled with a big grin. She'd always hoped to return to see this majestic carpentry, and once she learned Gemma and Carter wanted to meet here, she agreed. Plus, if they turned out to be weirdos, she would be in a public place with an easy escape. It also allowed her to gather books on killers, the FBI Behavioral Analysis Unit, and the police academy's crime scene practices, which would become her new normal. *No guy will approach me now.* Margot laughed to herself. She planned to surround herself with books on criminology to understand the killer's mind and hopefully uncover her aunt's murderer.

"Don't worry—I'm just planning to solve murder cases, not become one." Margot smiled at the librarian, checking out her books.

The stuffy librarian peered at her over wiry glasses and gave her a thin smile.

"I've seen an increase in these types of books being checked out. True crime definitely seems to be a hot market these days. I must admit, I have become interested in the past year," the librarian said as she scanned the books.

"There's certainly no shortage of cases out there. There are many books on our most famous serial killers, like the Zodiac Killer, the Killer Clown, and the Milwaukee Cannibal, but I'm also interested in the less notorious ones. The killers that creep into our small towns, that get little to no notoriety, that go undetected—just like my aunt's killer has," Margot's voice cracked as she looked down at the stack.

"Oh, dear. I am so sorry. Your aunt was murdered? I would think reading about these killers would bring back horrific memories, then?" The librarian frowned.

"Actually, it's giving me purpose." Margot collected her books from the counter and headed to the area where the group had planned to meet.

As Margot turned the corner, she noticed Gemma and Carter at a secluded table. The two appeared comfortable with each other as they gently laughed and pointed to something in a book Gemma was reading.

"Margot! I'm so glad to see you again." Carter grinned.

"Hi, Margot. I'm glad I didn't scare you away the other day." Gemma twisted her lips.

"Oh, no. I mean, I rarely talk to strangers in a cemetery, but it's nice to put a face to the person I've been chatting with." *Unlike my aunt's killer.*

"I'm jealous you two were online friends. I guess my drcrime posts didn't lure you in," Carter said.

"Yeah, the name isn't all that original." Gemma snickered.

Margot set her stack of books down and sat at the oak table. She looked across at Gemma's book stack, which was nearly identical to her own.

"Hey, my professor is going to give a speech next month about her work capturing the Bandana Rapist. Do you guys want to come with me?" Carter asked, reading from his laptop.

Simultaneously, both women said, "Yes!" Dr. Williams had a reputation as a prominent figure in the true crime world and was now a professor at Ivy University. She'd previously worked as a profiler and assisted local authorities with capturing Cape Ivy's last serial killer.

———

After their initial meeting, the three often sat together like that for marathon study sessions, sometimes several times a week. They eventually named their group the Crime Three, which rhymed with the recent documentary from their area that everyone was talking about. Although neither Margot nor Gemma were in college, they behaved like they were cramming for a degree. When it was time for the library to close, Margot would make the short drive from the Ivy University campus to her newly rented downtown apartment. She much preferred this apartment to the one she'd lived in before returning home because this one didn't have any neighbors.

———

Margot walked up to her second-floor apartment above the Old Town Pharmacy on Broadway Boulevard, nearly dropping the many books in her arms. She opened the door, plopping her heap of research onto the couch, and let out a deep sigh. Margot didn't know if all the studying would lead her to uncover Nadine's murderer, but she hoped this research would give her the brain power to understand the killer and get one step closer to revealing him. Margot wouldn't have characterized herself as a true crime aficionado prior to Nadine's death, but it had certainly consumed her identity ever since.

After changing into sweatpants and T-shirt, Margot poured a glass of wine and spread out her books on the bare hardwood floor of her scantily decorated apartment. She didn't have Nadine's flair for decor; rather, she lived minimally. It pleased Margot to find thrift store goods, including her retro faux leather sofa and a Persian rug she'd picked up from a clearance sale. She organized her books and paperwork based on years of murder—she believed that would be the easiest way to keep track.

Margot knew about serial killer fandom, and it disgusted her. She could never understand how women became obsessed with these killers and wrote them in prison or showed up at their trials, as if the killer would spare their life should they get acquitted. She knew several on *Death Toll* who were the exact type—the ones who were obsessed with Helter Skelter, or had the Lady Killer bite mark tattoos, or had traveled to visit the Torture Doctor's Murder Castle. Margot initially joined the site out of boredom after coming across it in an article she'd read. However, once inside the chat, it became a bit of an obsession, which she knew was becoming unhealthy. As far as she knew, though, most of the people there were mere spectators to murder and never knew how it felt to be on the other side of it. Others were armchair sleuths who thought they could put the crime pieces together.

While Margot was in hiding, she could live the sheltered life that came with the aftereffects of trauma. But now she was out in the open and exposed, like a groundhog scurrying out of hibernation. Margot downed the rest of the wine and let out a deep sigh. The trolls and media hadn't found her new apartment or learned of her library routine, but she knew it was only a matter of time. People's curiosity doesn't go away because the victim tells them to. For now, she needed to study and block out all the noise, with the sole purpose of figuring out who the killer was. Margot had long since resigned herself to missing out on the typical life of a college student—the sororities, parties, and obligatory all-night keg fests. But it was worth it to get closer to whoever killed her aunt. Margot considered herself stuck somewhere between post-high school life and adulthood.

Margot had many lonely days when she moved away, but now that she was back in Cape Ivy, meeting Carter and Gemma had allowed her to throw herself into research with people who wouldn't judge her Google searches. The guilt came on like a wave and she'd slump her body in regret when she thought about her old friends. She knew she had been the "bad friend" by ignoring messages from her high school friends who asked to get together. They were there during her hardest times—fights with her mom and later Nadine's murder. Margot had learned how to shut everyone out, and she had paid for it by spending her evenings alone, which sometimes meant missing out on the fun of her youth, often crying about the past. But just as quickly, Margot would tell herself to "snap out of it," courtesy of Stella, and then she'd be back to her no-nonsense self and studying once again.

Since returning to Cape Ivy, Margot lived with the constant fear that the killer was at the grocery store, behind her in the checkout line, or posing as the mailman, who could easily spy on her. Right after the murder, she was anxious about who he could be, but now she actively searched for him, always looking for this faceless killer who left no clues. Margot did not know what hair color, physical build, or age to look for, and that was the most frustrating part. She had conjured up an image of what Nadine's killer could look like, but she couldn't know if it was the real man. She envisioned him to be fairly muscular because he needed to hold down his victim, as he not only put a mask over Nadine's head but also pinned her to the bed and bound her hands and feet.

As far as other physical traits, Margot sometimes saw him as dark-haired and other times lighter—his face was often blurry to her, much like Nadine's image slowly became. As time went by, the once vivid image of the woman she loved so much was falling deeper into the corners of her mind, where it became harder and harder to picture. Margot's only wish was that she could have saved her.

CHAPTER 5

2003

After the humiliation of being beaten and losing his beloved shed, twelve-year-old Jack roamed the countryside near his home. The country had some perks, as there was a lot of anonymity living near so many trees and so few people. Jack felt much more at ease alone with his thoughts, which became more sinister each day. Visions of revenge against Paul and Kathy occupied the forefront of his mind. He wanted to kill them, but he relished the idea of torturing them first. Some days, it was with a sneak attack with an ax to the back of their heads. Other days, he would locate a gun and slowly murder them with non-life-threatening wounds that would bleed them out.

These thoughts brought glee to Jack who savored the thoughts of the day he could pay them back for what they'd done to him. His mom wasn't off the hook, but at least she let him roam around the neighborhood, and she didn't care too much about what he did.

Roughly two miles down the gravel road near their house was the diversion channel, a tributary off the Mississippi River to prevent flooding. Although, around this area, people used it to fish and go swimming, and some even used it to bathe. Jack noticed an older man wearing overalls with a scruffy beard, likely in his late fifties, who walked around with a rifle taking shots at wild turkey. "I'll get you next time, motherfucker!" he yelled at them as he missed. Jack didn't know who this man was and had a general distrust of adults, so he spied on him for days while he hid in overgrown bushes. Eventually the man noticed Jack, pointed a rifle to his head, and told him, "You have two choices, kid: confess your sins, or prepare to die." Jack didn't know what that meant, but he certainly wasn't ready to die.

"I'm sorry, sir. I was just watching what you're doing, and I just wanted to hang out or something, that's all." Jack's lips vibrated in fear.

"Who are you, and where do you come from?" the man growled.

Jack introduced himself, and the man eyed him up and down suspiciously, pointing the rifle at Jack's chest. "You ain't no thief, are ya?" he laughed at the kid's fear.

Jack was terrified, nearly peeing his pants. "No, sir. I haven't touched anything."

The man snickered at him. "Good. I didn't want to call the cops on a kid. I hate cops. Was one once, ain't no more. My name's Louie."

"Maybe you can teach me to use that gun?"

Louie stared at Jack long and hard. Then he finally laughed and said, "Maybe, kid. We'll see how I feel about you later."

It took a few weeks for their bond to be sealed, but eventually, they became inseparable. Louie told Jack to call him "Uncle Louie" should anyone stop by, because "people get the wrong idea if a grown ass man hangs out with a little kid."

"I ain't gonna get accused of being a pedo. I already spent time in prison for other shit. Ain't gonna get shanked for touching boys," Louie told him. "No fuckin' way, kid."

From that point on, Uncle Louie was the closest "family" member Jack had. He was Jack's mentor in everything as Jack grew older, from hunting and basic repairs to plumbing and how to outsmart the police. While Louie was in prison, he had become a valued member of the Aryan Brotherhood and, as a former cop, he provided valuable insider information to inmates. He passed that information on to a growing Jack, who learned the many tricks of the trade.

In his time as a cop, Uncle Louie was a crooked one, landing himself in prison for planting false evidence and making fake reports. Now Louie lived on social security in a rundown trailer on the edge of town and declared that he "lived off the grid."

"Now, if a cop ever talks to you, only give them short answers or none at all. I saw too many men in prison for yappin' too much and gettin' their words all twisted, and now they got life. Best to keep shut," Louie directed Jack as they worked on one of his junk cars.

Louie's yard was full of what most passersby would consider junk, including rusted out old cars and appliances he used for parts for his side job fixing up broken stoves, lawnmowers, and car engines. Louie was very handy. He was a much better mechanic than he ever was as a police officer, and an even better con man, which suited him well during his prison days, as he could finagle the hierarchy system behind bars. Louie began a cash hustle of handyman work once he got out of prison, and eventually Jack tagged along.

Jack learned so much from Louie—how to change a tire, how to repair a blown dryer fuse, how to fool a lie detector test. Jack saw Louie as his hero and thought he could do no wrong. He often daydreamed of Louie coming over during one of Paul's visits and beating Paul bloody as revenge for whooping Jack. The dream always ended with them killing Paul together. Jack craved that revenge; he wanted Louie to rescue him.

Once, Jack told Louie about the beatings, but all Louie said was, "Sometimes you gotta take your beatings like a man, kid." Jack's master plan of seeking revenge was ruined and he nursed the familiar feeling of rejection—yet another adult denying him pleasure. Louie told him, "I can't get myself back into any trouble. Gotta walk the straight and narrow here on out. Can't go back to the clink. Sorry, kid."

Jack's heart dropped in his stomach, realizing that the revenge he had dreamed of wouldn't happen, but Louie still gave him a way to escape. He continued to practice his skills with firearms, hunting, and fishing and became very skilled at handiwork as Louie's apprentice.

"You ain't half bad, kid. You're a quick learner. These skills will help you find a job someday."

Jack had never considered his future, but he enjoyed these odd jobs working on broken machines. He was also interested in a new skill he learned when they went out to the countryside one day. Louie taught him about the art of being still and patient when hunting, especially with deer. Patience was required to sit and wait for the deer, which could take hours. Sometimes he'd get lucky with a buck or an entire family; other times, he'd wait all day and nothing would arrive. He'd just spend all day with his thoughts, consumed with violence and revenge.

As Jack got older, he took Louie's advice more seriously. By sixteen, he was no longer interested in the child's play of pinning butterflies—his thoughts had become more focused on hurting women. Jack blamed his aunt and mom for everything that went wrong in his life, and they became the reason for his profound hatred toward women. Plus, the thrill of watching a human female squirm as she was about to die seemed like ecstasy in Jack's mind. He fantasized about sneaking up on women and grabbing them from behind, snapping their necks or strangling them. The goal was to catch them off guard before they saw him and screamed. For Jack, the element of surprise was alluring. As he walked around the grocery store, he'd see a woman shopping and consider following her to her car and assaulting her. But he also knew that they would catch him if he did something like that in public. For now, Jack honed his stalking skills by climbing trees and peeping into houses, feeling invisible and, for the first time, powerful. Jack was in total control—he had human victims who were completely unaware that they were being watched.

Jack's first Peeping Tom experience happened in the woods near Louie's. He came upon a house he had never seen before: a two-story surrounded by large trees, perfect for hiding his identity. Jack noticed it would be very easy to climb the tree and be eye level with the second floor to see inside. At first, it was daylight, and he wasn't able to see anything other than the blowing curtain. The window was open, as it was a warm summer day, but he couldn't see anyone or anything inside. He returned once it turned dark. On his second trip, he could see that it was a bedroom. A blond young woman wearing shorts and a tank top danced around her room, which immediately drew him in. He fantasized about her fate and became aroused when thinking of hurting her. He wasn't sure of her age, but she appeared older than him. She eventually lay on her bed, reading, only a lamp illuminating the small room. The curtain was still hanging, and a light breeze kept it blowing every so often.

Jack stayed in the tree until the girl eventually shut off the light next to her and he couldn't see inside any longer. He kept returning, and the thrill of watching her soon became an obsession for him. When she walked by the window naked one day, his efforts paid off. It was very brief, and had he looked away for a moment, he would have missed it. It was the first time he saw a naked female in real life rather than seeing them in nudie magazines that he found at Louie's place. This only fueled Jack to continue coming to the tree. Although he never saw her naked again, the possibility of seeing her in the nude became an addiction that he could no longer live without. At sixteen, Jack was officially a budding criminal.

Louie eventually asked Jack if he had a girlfriend because he was spending a lot more time away. That really infuriated him, because he hated girls and could only imagine harming them. He'd never had a girlfriend, was still a virgin, and rarely spoke to his female classmates. Jack eventually confided in Louie about his extracurricular activity of peeping, and Louie gave him pointers on how to avoid the police. The bond between Jack and Louie continued to strengthen because there was never any judgment between the two—only support.

CHAPTER 6
2018

True crime buffs can become desensitized by all the violence and sadness they see, which was certainly true of Gemma. The more she learned about Margot, the more she wanted to know every detail of how Margot found her aunt, and why she ran from Cape Ivy. Gemma's waking thoughts were focused on Margot. She chewed at her lip planning out her next move. Gemma liked to think she was a bit of a crime solver, much like many online detectives who thought they could crack most cases. With every new true crime documentary she watched, she logged on to *Death Toll* to discuss it with other online true crime fanatics. Online, she was the person she could create of herself, not the trauma-ridden one that others didn't fully see.

After the library trip, Gemma fell into her favorite spot on the couch to continue watching the crime series about the Crimson Spree Shooter. "It happened innocently enough. Bryan was taking his daughter out for a drive when she blurted out, 'Is Mommy going to kiss Uncle Sean again?' It was enough to stop his truck and heart. The intoxicating madness that consumed him propelled him to turn around and head back to his home. Just as his daughter indicated, he found Aimee and Sean naked in bed, but he heard the laughter first, which would dominate his thoughts during his spree. Like most men in New Berlin, he had an arsenal of weapons to choose from. Hunting was a rite of passage that any man enjoyed in their small town. Deer heads on the walls were more of a masculinity gauge than penis size. Bryan snapped when he saw the two traitors and within seconds, rage fully possessed him."

Gemma often thought about her childhood memories and those of her grandparents were the most painful. She'd often shake her head to release her brain of their memory. She had a picture of her grandparents, who she only knew to be sweet and caring. They always supplied Neapolitan ice cream or little snacks that she couldn't find in her own home. Gemma cried the most at the loss of their relationships when they died, as she always felt secure and most loved when she was at their home. As an adult, she stayed isolated from others, as she didn't think they would understand her story.

"'The couple pleaded with Bryan to put the gun down. Unable to focus on the gun barrel, her daughter, or the enraged face of the man she'd made a life commitment to, Aimee lunged for the gun. After the first bullet, she groaned in pain, with more verbal pleading. But Bryan had already gone this far, so he had to finish. They found her body riddled with bullets. 'He emptied the chamber,' the coroner would report. Sean would receive similar treatment, however the coroner's report stated, 'The number of wounds present would indicate torture.'"

Gemma kept pausing the documentary to write notes for a later discussion online. Her hand cramped from writing down all the points made. Her thoughts about meeting with Margot were instant. *I hope I can get close to Margot. She needs a friend, and I want to be there for her.* Gemma pulled the thin blanket up to her neck as the documentary continued.

"The story could have ended there. Maybe Bryan would have had mercy from a jury of his peers. Cheating was taboo, and the jurors could understand how a man could just snap. However, the shootings unleashed the mental list of people he hated and it was now or never. The worst part of all of this is that he took his daughter along for the rest of the murder spree after she witnessed the brutality of his killing of Aimee and Sean. She was his good conscience who watched his deeds but was too young to stop anything."

A text message flashed across Gemma's phone: confirmation that the Crime Three would get a front-row seat at Dr. Williams' seminar. *Good job, Carter.* Gemma's face beamed and glowed from the screen. Dr. Williams was like royalty to her. She understood the mind of a killer and had ended the rampage of one of Cape Ivy's notorious murderers when she matched up his crime scenes and saw a clear pattern. *I hope I get to talk to her. Maybe Carter can arrange that, too.* Gemma smiled at the thought of meeting one of her idols.

"Bryan's young daughter was a passenger on his murder spree, watching the desire for revenge her father kept hidden, now fully displayed in the grossest way. She'd recognize the next house: her grandparents' home. She'd remember her grandma saying, 'Oh, what a delightful surprise, my sweet granddaughter is here' with a big grin. However, before her grandmother could utter any other words, her forehead exploded. Her grandpa turned the corner and blood flew from every direction."

Gemma stopped the episode to run a hot bath with Epsom salts. *Maybe this will soothe my nerves.* She had mapped out and planned how she'd eventually meet Margot. Of course, she had no way of knowing when she would return, but she'd prepared for that day. She'd practiced mock conversations so she would appear truthful. Now that day had actually come, and Gemma had a chance to put her plans in motion. *My trauma needs a friend like your trauma.* Gemma rubbed her eyes and thought about what she'd gain by getting close to Margot. She melted as she stepped into the steaming bath water, the scent of lavender wafting through the air. Her body was temporarily pleased with the warm reprieve. *I have to prepare myself for the reality that someday my identity will be revealed.* She closed her eyes and leaned back so the water reached her chin, blanketing her.

CHAPTER 7

2010

Jack celebrated his eighteenth year as any logical man does: by making the leap from peeping into houses to breaking and entering. He wanted to "step up his game" and see how things looked up close. Inside the homes, Jack could touch the things he could only spy from the trees, swiping at what he wanted. He believed it would be real easy since he'd spent long hours watching people's daily and nightly routines, learning their rituals, and when they'd be away from home.

Peeping became child's play, and he was ready for something more exciting. He tired of the daydreams of his plans and wanted to feel the adrenaline surge of walking through a house that wasn't his own. Sure, there might be surprises, but that presented an extra thrill should someone arrive home. Jack was confident in his skills—overly confident. Louie taught him to always have two exit strategies; that way, he'd always be in control if his first option became obstructed. Louie also introduced Jack to his best ally, Glenn, a former police partner of his. Glenn was about ten years younger than Louie, with a beer gut and receding hairline.

"Who's the kid?" Glenn had asked when they met, eyeing the stranger who appeared to be comfortable on Louie's property.

"Jack, come meet Glenn. He's a cop friend of mine. I'm teaching Jack the ropes, both good and bad," Louie said with a deep laugh.

Jack dropped the wrench he was using to tighten a bolt on a pipe, wiped his hands on his jeans, and walked over to meet this new man, eyeing him suspiciously.

"Jack. How did you ever get involved with this crazy ass man?" Glenn asked, laughing and punching Louie in the arm.

Both older men laughed and went inside for a bottle of beer, leaving Jack standing alone with stained pants as he furrowed his brow and went back to work.

Glenn was also a crooked cop, but he was a lot better at not getting caught. He had great connections within the community and remained protected, both in and out of the police force. Glenn was untouchable because of what he knew, as he saw many crimes committed by both police officers and laymen. As long as they protected Glenn's secrets, they were safe with him. He was well-versed in the bribery and extortion game—he took from you and then you gave him even more.

Glenn would pull over drug dealers and let them go after they gave him rolls of cash. He'd allow local businesses to get away with not being up to code as long as they gave him a little dough under the table to make violations go away. He never had to pay for drinks at Patsy's Tavern, or lunch at Winnie's Cafe, or even show his wallet at most places around town. If Glenn arrived at a scene, his word was the gold standard—if he determined you were at fault for an accident, then that was that. Jack had met Glenn several months back but never fully trusted him; at least, not like he did with Louie. Jack mainly preferred hanging around Louie, but lately Glenn and his partner, Officer Corey, were always in tow. He had no feelings toward cops growing up, but as an adult man, he loved a crooked one. Glenn was more outgoing than Louie was, as Louie was cranky and rough around the edges, more of a crotchety older man that wouldn't take your shit —prison likely did that to him. Glenn wouldn't take your shit, either, but he'd tell you with a smile on his face.

On his birthday, Jack arrived at the Smiths' household before 7 a.m. He snuck through the woods and climbed the nearly dead oak tree that stood about a yard from their house, just waiting and watching for the family to complete the routines he'd observed so many times before. Jack sat high in the tree, his jacket zipped up to his chin with only a puff of frigid air escaping his mouth. Chris Smiths usually left around 7:30 a.m., with his wife and two kids leaving shortly after. The family rarely returned until nearly 4 p.m. each day, which left Jack plenty of time to explore. After the last of them left, Jack climbed down the tree and made his way into the house.

He walked confidently toward the garage and found the side door unlocked—he was grateful that the low crime rates in the area bolstered people's sense of security. Jack unzipped his jacket as sweat pooled in his pits. He looked for the many guns he'd seen Chris sport during several of his peeping missions. He found an antique, upright gun safe in the garage with a glass front and an etched design and began fumbling with the locks. He felt along the sides and along the top of the case until—success. Jack was rewarded with a shiny pair of keys, which promptly unlocked a case full of rifles he had been eyeing from afar. Jack couldn't believe his luck. Never having handled this caliber of gun before, he felt powerful just holding the cool metal, which was perfectly enveloped in his large hands; he immediately sensed their capacity for influence and death. He made a mental note to take as many as he could carry on his way out, but first he wanted to explore the house.

As he entered through the interior garage door, he walked through the kitchen and saw the large avocado stove and matching refrigerator, and a bar area with wooden spindles and off-white Formica counter-tops. The house was likely built in the 1960s and appeared to have the original decor and design of the time.

Jack's shoes squished and squeaked across the linoleum floor, and he soon realized he'd stepped in a sticky substance that had spilled. "Oh, shit," he said, as he didn't want to deal with cleaning up a mess. Half-eaten bowls of cereal, cups with remnants of Kool-Aid, and a pack of cigarettes littered the countertop. He surveyed the area and remarked, "Filthy pigs," under his breath. The mess, which was now stuck to the bottom of his shoes, annoyed Jack. The sticky noise from Jack's soles disrupted the quiet of the house as he carried out his illicit invasion. He moved through the living room, which showcased a large elk's head over the fireplace and a plaid sectional, one you'd find with a For Free sign on the side of the road. The couch had patches sewn on to hide whatever prior damage it had suffered.

Back in the primary bedroom, Jack found the bed unmade and lots of clothes thrown all over the floor, with several pairs of women's shoes leading out from the closet. The kids' bedrooms weren't much better, with both clothes and toys tossed everywhere. Jack maneuvered into the cluttered house, stepping on a Lego and dodging a doll. He was making his way back toward the kitchen when he heard tires on the gravel.

"Fuck!" Jack yelled, rushing to hide behind the closest door, which turned out to be the pantry.

He had forgotten to make a note of a second exit, a crucial rule he'd learned from Louie. When he heard the tires, he got spooked, forgetting to look for a real exit—his mind blanked. Jack considered running toward the garage to escape through the side door, but he figured that would make him run right into the visitor. He knew he'd left the gun safe open and exposed, and felt even more vulnerable without one of the weapons for protection. Jack heard the garage door open and his heart pounded as he waited for a gunshot to enter through the pantry door. He waited seconds, minutes, hours—he lost track, but no bullet entered.

"Come out with your hands up, you fucker."

Jack knew—they'd caught him. Maybe he could talk his way out of it or say he got confused. Fuck, he didn't know.

He opened the pantry door and saw Glenn, who busted out laughing. "Look at your face. You see a fuckin' ghost, dude? Come on, man. Let's get these guns in the car and get the fuck out of here."

Glenn wore gloves and asked why Jack wasn't wearing any. "Can't be that dumb, kid." He told him to grab a towel from the kitchen and start wiping down everything he touched. "Better make sure you don't leave any shoe prints, either."

Jack spent a good amount of time wiping down door handles and the floor, making a note that this was a valuable lesson to always remember.

"Louie fucked up not telling you about those prints, man. You gotta keep those finger and shoe prints covered up. They're your ticket to getting locked up for life."

Jack fumed inside. He knew what Louie had told him. He was angry at himself for not being more careful, and now pissed at Glenn for correcting him.

The pair grabbed all the guns and ammo in the safe, threw them in the back seat of the squad car, and booked it to Louie's place. Glenn just laughed at how scared Jack's face looked. Jack knew he needed to toughen up; he couldn't be this afraid of getting caught. He needed to be much smarter in the future. No more leaving things to chance.

"It's all right, kid, you gotta learn. Some people would have shit their damn pants if they got caught like this. Make this a learning lesson. Things won't always go as planned, and someone won't always be there to bail your ass out." Glenn checked out his appearance in the rearview mirror.

"Hey, how did you know I was there? Were you following me, or were you planning to loot the place?"

"Nah, I got a call from Officer Corey. He was on duty and saw you sneaking around the woods. He figured you were up to no good, and he knew you were under my 'watch.' So I came out to see what was going on."

God damn it. I fucked up. This left him in a very foul mood, knowing he was sloppy and not as skilled as he'd convinced himself he was. Jack clenched his jaw so hard he thought he heard a crack. He thought he was an expert lurker, but hearing this, he knew he had a lot more work to do. He sank down in the squad car, rage pulsating through his veins. His celebratory mood was long gone.

Back at Louie's, the three lawmen were full of joy playing with their new toys of war. They went out to the concrete wall along the diversion channel and fired up the machines, leaving gaping holes everywhere.

"Holy shit, these are badass!" Corey kept saying over and over, smiling behind his aviator sunglasses.

Sure, the men had fired guns before, but nothing of this caliber.

"This makes a boy into a man. Congratulations, son. Your nuts just dropped," Louie laughed with a cigarette dangling from his lower lip.

"We're all men now. Welcome to the White Boys' Club." Glenn smirked as he lit up another round into the countryside.

Jack watched as they clinked their beers, chanting in unison, "WBC! WBC! WBC!"

As the night turned dark, an inebriated Jack became angrier while the other three men laughed and fell over each other. Their howls were the loudest when the call came over the police radio of stolen property at the Smiths' household. Jack sat on the dirty lawn chair and glared as the three rolled around, roaring deep belly laughs about the missing guns. Those laughs reminded him of his mom laughing and taunting him as a kid when Paul beat him. His hands flinched at the urge to pick up one of those guns and fire a hundred holes into their brains. He clenched his jaw and slowly rocked, throwing his beer bottle into the nearby fire pit, which alerted Louie to stop laughing. Louie knew Jack's anger the best as he'd seen it twice in the past, and he'd shared with Jack his concern that his anger could land him in prison one day. Once Louie could sense the situation taking a different turn, he ended the festivities and stopped the party, with boos from Glenn and Corey.

"Hell no! It's only 9 p.m. Let's go to Patsy's Tavern and see if there are any chicks there tonight. Besides, it's our boy's eighteenth birthday. We gotta celebrate that with some babes and beer," Glenn said, throwing back the rest of his drink.

"Fuck that!" Jack wasn't interested in the women who hung at Patsy's. Most were a lot older than him and listened to some deep twang-ass country music he couldn't stand. He'd rather go to a metal bar and listen to music about anger, not sappy love songs. But, of course, they outnumbered him. He knew if he wanted to go to a bar, he had to go with these guys because he was underage and he wouldn't be able to get drinks on his own.

Jack was in no mood for fun, and someone would regret seeing him tonight.

CHAPTER 8

2018

The Crime Three walked into the rounded auditorium that had hosted many distinguished speakers, but for this crew, Dr. Williams was their rockstar.

"I put in a request to be her teaching assistant. Naturally there's a waitlist, and it's a longshot, but I had to give it a try," Carter shrugged.

"If you become her TA, you better become best friends with her so she can join our little group sessions." Margot laughed.

"You got it. I'll do my best schmoozing. I'm just excited to learn from her," Carter looked around the expansive room.

Dr. Williams took a teaching position at Ivy University "to be rooted to an area." The university website had crashed after her hire at the school, with people from all over wanting to attend one of her courses. Of the three, only Carter knew her "personally," although that was a stretch. Other than being in her Crime Scene Anatomy course, he had no other link to her.

Carter found their reserved seats and motioned the ladies over. "I feel like we're waiting for a celebrity, which she kind of is," Gemma said, her eyes darting back and forth around the auditorium. As the three sat waiting for the presentation to start, Gemma beamed and told them of her excitement. "This may be the best night of my life! I just wish I could take her college courses too, but the waitlist is ridiculous." Gemma frowned.

As the lights flickered a warning, Margot heard her stomach growl in anticipation.

There she is, Margot thought as Dr. Williams walked across the stage and stood in front of the roaring crowd. She held a microphone in her well-manicured hand, her gold bangles clinking as she moved. Her loose raven-colored braids fell just below her middle-aged shoulders. She wore purple framed glasses when she read, and Margot could see a diamond on her ring finger that sparkled as it caught the stage lights.

Dr. Williams took her seat on the flowered chair provided for her. "Hello, I'm Dr. Simone Williams. Thank you for joining me," she said as she peered over her frames. She cleared her throat, which vibrated through the microphone. "Now, let me go over how I became involved in the Bandana Rapist case. I was working as a criminologist in Illinois when I learned of a woman murdered in her apartment. Since I was involved with another case at the same local police department, they asked me to give it a look." As she spoke, her eyes slowly canvased the crowd.

"He was sloppy and left DNA. It appeared to be a panicked and rushed scene. He escaped through her top floor bedroom window, leaving the deceased on the floor." She took in a deep breath, which was richly full as everyone in the audience was holding their own.

Margot hung on each word and felt her palms tingle as she rubbed them on her jeans. Chills moved their way from her arms to shoulders as her teeth rattled. The cold auditorium air conditioner made Margot shiver as she envisioned her aunt's crime scene. Margot's mind wandered back to the pitch-black room, the smell that had hit her as she opened the door, and the lifeless body of the person she loved most. Margot couldn't escape those images as she listened to Dr. Williams discuss the killer's brutality. *I can do this. I have to do this.*

Margot considered leaving for fresh air, but took slow breaths and made Carter give her his jacket to warm up. She didn't want to miss the speech; she hoped she might get Dr. Williams' opinion on her aunt's case. However, she thought it was likely a stretch considering how in demand she was. She hoped maybe Carter could be her in, but she wasn't losing sleep over that. She could only imagine the obstacles Dr. Williams faced as the first Black woman hired as a tenure-track professor at Ivy University.

As the auditorium remained quiet, Dr. Williams continued, "I will discuss graphic details of the murder in case anyone would like to leave now." She looked around at the crowd and proceeded. "Since no one has left, don't blame me for what you hear." Dr. Williams crossed her arms and stared at her prey. "I cannot presume to know any of your tolerance for death."

Margot stole a quick glance at Gemma, who sat to her left. Gemma was listening with a fixed gaze and didn't show any signs of shivering. She had a slight smile that was full of awe. Margot wished she could find that same sense of peace.

"Knives, guns, sledgehammers, ropes, and bare hands are just a few tools of murder that a serial killer chooses from. There are cases where he might switch up his method of killing because of convenience or testing out a new MO. A killer can be any gender, although men are proportionately more likely to become serial killers, while women are their top prey." Dr. Williams turned to look behind her at the image displayed on the projector: a bloody crime scene of a woman shot to death in her bed.

Margot hadn't seen any blood when she found her aunt. However, the mask over Nadine's head confused her at first, and she thought maybe her aunt could still be alive. She even thought it might be a joke —a horrible prank. She'd since submerged herself in learning about killers, from those who haunted Cape Ivy to those on the national stage. When Margot last spoke with her mom, she told her about her recent studies on killers, which was met with skepticism. "The police haven't done anything!" Margot shouted at Stella. Detective Conway was in charge of the investigation and he'd made it clear to the family that it was likely a rogue lover.

"I see this all the time. The woman doesn't want to continue the relationship and the lover snaps. Although we haven't found the suspect, I feel in my bones that this is the right direction," Conway had told the three Mays family members. The local media had been doing their own research by reaching out to Nadine's lovers and stripping her of her privacy. There were interviews with her neighbors and coworkers, and many unanswered calls to her family.

After a brief break, Dr. Williams took the mic and got back to work. "My work on the Bandana Rapist revealed he killed nine women that we're aware of. Originally, his motivations were of a sexual nature before he began killing."

Thankfully, the killer didn't rape my aunt. If there was any relief in her death, it was that, Margot thought.

"During the day, he was unassuming—dressed as an EMT, his uniform was as welcoming as a police officer's. Yet he stalked his victims, making his move at night, and as a sexual predator, he raped, tortured, and eventually killed them for his pleasure." Dr. Williams paced the stage as she stared out into the vast auditorium, the slides changing on the overhead screen behind her.

I wonder if this is how Nadine's killer got inside? Maybe he wore a uniform that she trusted.

"Skilled at manipulation, he convinced psychiatrists and a parole board to release him early from prison after being sentenced as a sexual offender. He had been in prison for raping his underage neighbor. Psychiatrists at Menard Correctional Center recommended the killer's release in January 1981, just fifteen months after his incarceration, saying in a psychiatric evaluation that they couldn't prove he'd offend again as long as he remained incarcerated. However, once they released him, his killing spree resumed."

I can't imagine what the family of that young girl went through, knowing that they had him in prison and let him go.

"His signature was to stalk his victims, and once he became comfortable with their routine, he would break into their home and wait for their return or attack in the middle of the night. They found most of his victims bound in their beds after being tortured, raped, and eventually shot in the head, although sometimes he strangled them. His victims ranged from their twenties to their sixties. He even murdered a mother and daughter together. Out of the nine murders, five of them were in Cape Ivy."

Dr. Williams continued to pace with her flowing olive linen dress swishing behind her. When one slide stopped moving, she called for help. A college-aged guy jumped into action and the seminar continued. *Carter probably wants that gig.* Margot laughed to herself.

"Thanks to DNA advancements, they caught the killer, as the technology connected him to one of his victims. The lead detective, along with me and the other specialists, put the puzzle pieces together and believed that he may also be responsible for other heartland murders." Margot's thoughts drifted to her aunt's case and how there weren't any leads. Murder was hard enough, but without the final sentence of closure, the pain lingered.

Margot rubbed her arms as goosebumps formed while Dr. Williams discussed how the killer eventually confessed to nine murders in exchange for life imprisonment. "Although he apologized to the victims' families, he later stated he felt no remorse. However, he was grateful for receiving a life sentence, stating, 'I don't know if I could have been so generous if I were in the same situation.'"

Between the chilling testimony and the freezing room, Margot twitched with the occasional jolt. She wrapped herself tighter into Carter's jacket as Dr. Williams told them that the families could finally put a face to the monster they'd been imagining for all these years. They now knew the man who their loved one last saw and who caused so much pain. While having him rot in a prison cell brought the killer's terror to a close, the families still had to cope with the agonizing echoes of the destruction he left behind. *I can't wait until it's my turn to unmask the killer.*

Margot hoped his arrest brought the families some semblance of rest. However, she knew the town of Cape Ivy was on high alert as the horror of a new killer had emerged.

Margot shook her foot to get some heat into her system, but Dr. Williams' next words chilled her the most. As the image of the killer came into view, she saw him standing amongst other men wearing white in preparation for a wedding. Margot saw the callousness of the serial killer as he stood with his arms crossed behind his back, giving a toothy grin that didn't betray his secret. They couldn't know the depravity that lurked behind that smile or that he had just murdered a mother and daughter a mere twelve hours earlier. His smile and demeanor later shocked his coworkers, who all thought he was such a nice and understated guy.

Margot's stomach joined the dance and growled. Gemma glanced over and whispered, "Are you OK?"

Margot mouthed back, "I'm freezing in here." Gemma squeezed Margot's hand, which was the pinch of warmth she needed.

"He did not have a good childhood, calling his mother 'cold and unaffectionate' and expressing much hatred toward her. He was reportedly very shy in his adolescence and known to fondle women in public. Deemed a sexually dangerous person, he was a threat to women that the legal system did not protect us from."

After Dr. Williams finished her presentation to feverish applause, Margot glanced around for anyone who looked like they were in the media. *The last thing I need is for someone like Loni Smart to find me here.* Cape Ivy's top news reporter had been hounding the family for an interview since a month after Nadine's death. Margot needed time to process her newfound fame before she talked.

Margot's moment to get near Dr. Williams was approaching, as the Crime Three received a backstage meet and greet with their true crime hero. She walked up the stairs on the side of the stage and felt slightly dizzy. The air up on stage and the elevated height made Margot's knees buckle. She much preferred the comfort of being a spectator over the woozy tension of standing on the platform. Dr. Williams stood with her back to Margot, but spun around when she heard her approach. As they reached to shake each other's hands, Dr. Williams spoke first. "Margot, I've been wanting to talk to you."

Margot finally flushed with heat. *Dr. Williams knows who I am.*

CHAPTER 9
2010

The sound of banjos and the shrieks of wasted yahoos bounced off the walls of Patsy's Tavern. Jack hated the twisted faces of drunks—their howling at jokes and the messy way they flirted. He especially hated the women who came to these places, who wanted to fight like men once they got a little whiskey in them. The owner, Patsy, was this type of woman, but after one too many fights, she'd laid off the drinks and stayed on her side of the bar. She was very proud of her name and had shrines to Patsy Cline all over the tavern. Bar patrons often heard her singing "Back in Baby's Arms," yet every time she and her ex got back together, it ended in a sloppy quarrel. He'd recently been convicted for attempted murder after one of their fights went sour. Patsy was a woman in her mid-fifties with curly brown hair, who loved a dark lip and a scarf in her hair. Patsy's son, Patrick, worked at the bar, and like Jack, his dad had taken off before he was born. Jack marveled at the men in this city—they weren't too keen on staying and raising their offspring around here.

"What are you having, guys?" Patsy asked, showing off the scorpion tattoo on her left breast as she leaned toward them.

"A bucket of beer, for now, on the house," Glenn gave Patsy a look.

As dirty cops, they never had to pay for anything—they were like royalty around here. People were full of both awe and fear of these guys. They could revamp or destroy your life, depending on the day and condition of your relationship with them. Today was a good day for the group because of the loot they'd "found" and the enjoyment they'd had with it, so everyone could be at ease and party. People were line dancing and singing, there were pool players and, naturally, people making out in corners. Jack just sat sipping on his beer, with little to say as he watched everyone enjoy themselves. As the evening edged closer to midnight, a group of women came in, laughing and already hammered, judging by how they walked and slurred. None of them were Jack's taste, but he decided tonight was the night he needed to get laid.

It embarrassed him it had taken so long, but he was admittedly shy around women. When he was close to them, he only felt a deepening rage inside. As Jack got older, his urge to hurt women became even stronger—his desire for dominance became his focus. However, he'd suppressed these desires with his fantasies and kept busy with Louie. When Glenn found out that Jack was a virgin at eighteen, he'd teased him mercilessly, incredulous about the discovery.

"I thought most boys fucked by the age of twelve these days," Glenn had said in disbelief.

Jack fumed every time Glenn mentioned his lack of sexual prowess. He wanted to bash his face in, but he knew he couldn't. Glenn was much too powerful; he had to just take it. Glenn noticed Jack watching the women, and he called over a patron named Cora, a regular who Jack had seen other nights. She was roughly forty, with feathered bleached hair and acne scars on both of her sunburned cheeks, wearing a plaid shirt and jeans with a pack of cigarettes hanging from her front pocket. She blew out a stream of smoke as she arrived at the table. Glenn whispered into her ear and she grinned widely, exposing yellowed teeth and a gold-capped one right up front.

Cora approached Jack and rubbed his shoulders, which made him immediately flinch and tense up. He attempted to move away from her.

"Come on baby, let's go outside. I got something for you." She ran her tongue across her stained teeth.

"Um, no thanks. I'm good." Jack stared at a whiskey sign across the barroom.

"Go on, Jack. It'll be good for you. Pop your cherry so you won't be so damn tense," Louie urged. He pushed Jack a shot of vodka before nudging him one last time. "Come on, kid."

Jack slammed the shot and said, "Fuck it," then got up and followed Cora outside.

It was a chilly Missouri night, roughly thirty degrees. Jack shivered a bit as his nerves kicked in. He had masturbated with nudie magazines and seen the naked woman in the window when he was spying from the tree, but he had never touched a naked woman before. Cora was drunk, as evidenced by her slurred words, and she smelled foul from the cigarettes, badly needing mouthwash. It turned Jack off, but he also wanted to experience sex. He no longer wanted to be a virgin and wanted to get this over with, even though Cora wasn't appealing to him. In the back seat of her car, she unbuttoned his pants and sucked his dick, which slowly got hard, but not as firm as he needed it to be.

"What's the matter, dude, you gay?" She pouted her lips.

Jack punched her hard in the face. "Don't fucking talk to me like that, bitch." He would not let her talk down to his manhood that way.

"I'm sorry, sweetie. I'll be good to you. Let's just go inside now," Cora said as she raised her hands defensively to her face, moving toward the other side of the car.

Jack was immediately turned on by this power. He loved how she cowered, as he'd expected her to fight back. He immediately became rock hard and pushed her down as she attempted to sit up.

"Please, let's just go inside. I don't want any trouble with you," she pleaded.

Jack grabbed her neck. As small gasps left her lips, he pulled her pants down. Cora tried to push him off, but he was too strong for her and she suddenly stopped when he said, "You know I could kill you right now?" Cora became completely still. Jack's eyes were dark and piercing and only an inch away from hers. He could feel her rapidly breathing through her nose and her heartbeat coming through his hands, still wrapped firmly around her neck. He fucked her hard, intoxicated by his power over her. All of his pent-up anger was being released, and she was the unlucky recipient. After he climaxed, he got off Cora and told her to go clean up and to tell no one what happened out here except that she "loved every fucking minute of it."

When she didn't respond positively right away, he lunged toward her, making her scream, "Oh yes, this was the best lay of my life. I swear to God. I'll never tell a soul."

Jack walked back toward Patsy's with a little swagger. No longer a virgin, he finally felt like a man. He had a newfound sense of power that he never wanted to forget.

"How was it?" Louie asked with a grin.

"She's a dog, but she's no longer in heat," Jack said, and they all laughed big hysterical belly laughs and ordered a round of whiskey shots.

Cora never came back inside that night or for several nights after, but she eventually showed her face at Patsy's again and acted as if everything was normal. Life went on like it always had before.

She knew her role, and she played it.

CHAPTER 10

2018

There were many days Margot dreaded, and today was no exception. After locating her estranged parents, she scheduled to meet them at their new home. She dressed in black jeans and a cream pullover sweater and headed to see the two people who should understand her grief, although Margot knew they'd already buried Nadine in life and in memory.

When she'd finally connected with her mom a week after returning to Cape Ivy, Margot never received an apology for not being informed about their move. Although, she had also ghosted her parents, so maybe it ran in the family. She didn't know what to expect, but when her mom answered, she plainly said, "Hi, Margot. I've been waiting for your call."

"The phone works both ways, Mom. By the way, thanks for the heads up and making me look like an idiot showing up at a stranger's house." Margot had rolled her eyes as she looked at a dust bunny on her apartment floor.

"Well, you know how it is. Life gets busy and moving is a lot of work. But I am grateful you're back home. Come and visit us soon?"

As Margot pulled up to her parents' house on the west side of Cape Ivy, she found it looked much like all the other houses on the block.

They had traded in their 1920s Victorian for a 2018 cookie cutter box house. She checked her appearance in the rearview and walked to their perfectly manicured lawn, complete with a non-native Bradford pear tree standing prominently in their front yard. She could hear the doorbell chiming and soft footsteps approach. Her mom answered.

"Hello, Margot," Stella said as she slowly stepped aside to allow Margot in. The 55-year-old graying brunette sported a red sweater and straight-legged jeans.

"Hi, Mom. It's nice to finally see the new place." Margot looked around and didn't recognize any of the furniture. "I guess everything got an upgrade with the move?" Margot's eyes darted around the foreign space.

Charles, Margot's dad, peeked around the hallway corner and saluted Margo, then disappeared into a back room.

"It was time for a fresh start. Out with the old, in with the new. They had a big sale down at Hutson's and we kind of went overboard," Stella said with a hand on the back of the oversized reclining sofa that took up most of the living room.

Margot looked up to find painted beams, and two large brass pendant lights hanging from the vaulted ceiling. "I showed up at our old place and met a friend, so I guess it worked out."

"Please be careful, Margot. You know how dangerous the city can be." Stella crossed her arms.

"I absolutely know this. Why do you think I moved away?" Margot's chest reddened, and she considered leaving. The two women rarely saw eye to eye as Margot grew up, and now that she was an adult, she didn't have the energy for an overbearing mom. "Have you heard anything about Nadine's investigation? Are there any new leads?"

"I haven't heard a word. Honestly, I'm just moving forward at this point. It's too painful for me to go back and think about. I will always miss my sister, but I needed to push through my grief and proceed with my life," Stella moved to the couch.

"It must be nice to move on. But you weren't the one to discover her." Margot stood with her hands digging into the back of the couch.

"Margot. She was my sister, and it's not like I don't care about her. I certainly want justice, but I'm not going around searching for the killer or discussing it on a website!" She took a sip from her knock off china tea cup. A poodle came trotting into the room.

"Who is that? When did you get a dog?" Margot wondered how well she really knew her parents.

"This is Coco. She's my emotional walking companion." Stella laughed a bit too much at that.

Margot closed her mouth and debated petting her. "I can't just sit and do nothing. I need to keep Nadine's name out there or nothing will get done." Margot crossed her arms, eyeing Coco, who she really wanted to snuggle, but she refused to give her mom any form of satisfaction.

"I like to believe that it will all work itself out. I loved Nadine—and you, by the way—but it's better for me to move on," Stella said, giving Coco kisses.

"I actually came to let you know that I saw Dr. Simone Williams speak at the university auditorium. I think she might be able to help us." Margot looked down.

"I heard her on the news, but I want nothing to do with it. I don't need a forum to discuss the past." Stella threw a ball for Coco to fetch. "Margot, please try to move on and live a normal life." Her mother shook her head in pity.

"I'll move on when they catch the killer." Margot ended the visit with plans to see them over the next holiday, but her teeth stayed clenched the entire way home.

CHAPTER 11
2015

As Cape Ivy grew faster than it could handle, the company Elite Living swept in from St. Louis to take advantage of the bustling economy, with the goal of becoming the premiere apartment community in the region. When the founders had settled in Cape Ivy back in 1812, it was a trading port and eventually they built a railroad along the Mississippi River to carry goods up and down the coastline. Beyond the river, Cape Ivy had beautiful Victorian and Gothic homes built for the wealthy, and outside of that existed a healthy farming community. The original settlers couldn't have foreseen that Cape Ivy would become the bustling, overcrowded, diverse city it was today. There were young professionals and active adults who wanted the easier lifestyle that apartment living provided—no yards to mow or filters to change. Elite Living took on the massive project of converting existing buildings and constructing new state-of-the-art complexes, which brought in a lot of jobs. And Jack needed one.

After Jack completed his final year of high school and earned his diploma, he was decidedly not the college type and definitely wouldn't go into the military, as he wasn't keen on following orders. His skills lay in what he'd learned from Uncle Louie. He'd become a pretty skilled technician for odd jobs like fixing leaky faucets, unclogging drains, landscaping, or using basic equipment like a forklift or lawnmower, and he spent a few years floating from job to job. Jack had a few gigs working for cash on the side, but had never worked an actual nine-to-five, and he figured it was time to find "real" employment since he was now twenty-four years old and ready to earn steady cash. Sleeping on different couches was getting old, and at six foot one, Jack needed a bigger bed, as well as his own place with his own rules.

The interview with Elite Living couldn't have gone any better for Jack. After he met with Craig, who would become his immediate supervisor, he learned that one perk of the job was a discounted rate on one of the rental units. The company wanted their maintenance crew to live close so that they'd be on-site for emergency calls. Jack also enjoyed that he'd work fairly solo, which was right up his alley. Craig showed Jack around the grounds, including some empty units, some of which still required renovation.

"You'd paint walls and steam the carpets, or if the units have hardwood, you'd have to refinish them. We also need you to be versed in plumbing and repair work. Is that something you can do?" Craig asked.

Jack nodded. "Absolutely. That's a piece of cake. I do this kind of stuff all the time," he said smugly, giving a thin smile.

After he returned to the main office, Jack completed the rest of his employment application, embellishing the section about his work experience. Before the interview ended, he met Jameka, the thirty-year-old office manager, who arrived at the end. She quickly came through the front door, smiling, which revealed a sprinkle of freckles on her cheeks. She removed the headscarf that was protecting her from the falling rain, revealing her curly black hair.

"Sorry I'm late. I had to deal with an emergency. A tenant locked herself out of the apartment and we had to make arrangements to get her spare keys," Jameka said as she hung up her jacket. "Hi, I'm Jameka, the office manager." She sat down at her desk. "I don't know if Craig explained my role, but I'll be the one who will send the emergency and routine maintenance calls to you. So we'll get to know each other pretty well!" She beamed, looking at Jack.

Jack stared back, unsure of what to say. He had rarely spoken to women since he left high school, much less a Black woman, so this was foreign territory for him. He glanced back at Craig and waited for someone else to speak.

"Jack, I missed your work experience. Can you reiterate that for me?" Jameka asked.

"My uncle has a business out of his house repairing appliances, cars, you name it, and I've been his apprentice since I was twelve. I've basically been his flunky, and I've learned things hands on. We get hired to go into houses and do odd jobs like painting or repairing water leaks. There's nothing I can't do when it comes to fixing up one of these units. I have no doubt about it," Jack said, barely making any eye contact with her.

"I'm very impressed by your life experience. There's something to be said about that versus learning in a school setting. Many times, we learn better by hands-on living than we do by sitting in a classroom. I like what I'm hearing, Jack. We'll definitely be in touch." Jameka smiled and shook Jack's hand as the interview ended. Jack noticed Jameka pulled her hand away a bit too quickly, reaching for her cardigan and rubbing the sides of her arms, her smile slowly fading.

It took until the next week to hear from Craig, but eventually Jack received the news that they wanted to hire him as a maintenance man with Elite Living. He immediately chose one of the smallest units, a studio, since he owned little in this world, but it would be plenty big enough for his needs. He knew he had to put on his "mask" for coworkers so they wouldn't see his true self; they'd fire him if they knew he had thoughts of murder. Jack decided the best way for him to get along with everyone was to be extremely quiet, punctual, and productive.

"The best way to stay under the radar is to do the job without setting off any alarm bells," Louie always said. "Stay on the straight and narrow and never let a fucker see you sweat." It was another of Louie's life lessons, and that's what Jack intended to do.

Finally, Jack had his own place. It felt like having his own shed again—his own little oasis away from others. He never had to ask anyone for a favor again.

But though he didn't know it yet, he would need one more in the coming weeks—a huge one.

CHAPTER 12
2018

The headache came on quickly, a piercing throb on the right side that traveled toward the top of her skull with no precision. Gemma was accustomed to life with a pounding head; the pain seeped into her sleep and shifted her thoughts. While she supplied her bloodstream with caffeine and painkillers, nothing seemed to help with the overwhelming stress that she kept bottled inside. She pushed play on the final episode of the Crimson Spree Shooter documentary, propelled by curiosity to see how they wrapped it up. Gemma hated to be out of the loop and needed to know every detail of a story, especially since this documentary had the *Death Toll* chat buzzing.

"The next stop was Bryan's job. He was convinced that co-workers knew about the affair, but were protecting Sean. 'I know you knew,' a survivor would recall Bryan shouting. He added five more victims to his body count, blood loss overtaking them. That's when the police became involved. There were nine dead bodies in total by the time the police chased the red Chevy truck through corn pastures and eventually surrounded the stalled truck as Bryan ran out of gas." A picture of Bryan's truck appeared on the screen after a fleeting montage featuring photos of coworkers who didn't survive the rampage.

Gemma paused the TV on the image of a smiling Bryan, who stood next to the infamous red truck. Her face fell flat, overcome with questions about how a person could do this. *What was going through his mind? Did he even care about how this would affect his daughter, or did he intend to kill her, too?*

"Perhaps the worst part of all of this was that Bryan used his daughter as a shield. He held a gun to her braided five-year-old head amid shouts of 'Let me go or I'll shoot her next.' After a six-hour standoff in which daylight faded to the blazing lights and mics of local media, Bryan fired one more bullet into his own head. His last gift to his daughter was a stream of his blood running down her somber face. 'She's in shock,' a local doctor would report. That trauma would age with Bryan and Aimee's daughter, who has since remained off the grid —she has given no interviews, nor has any trace of her been found on social media. Bryan and Aimee's daughter is a survivor, and this case will be filed with all the other solved cases… until next time."

They got most of it right. My "shock" is now called PTSD, Gemma thought as she clicked off the TV and lay down for a rest. Her eyes searched the ceiling as she kept her dad's last words inside. Though she'd never told a soul, his last words were seared into her brain. She never forgot the dried smear of blood on her dad's cheek or the faint acrid smell of the last cigarette he'd inhaled as he told her those words: "Save yourself by trusting no one."

Those words made little sense to her as a five-year-old, but now, as an adult, she fully understood them. There seemed to be a space between his words and the gunshot, but memories were wicked and could turn on you just as quickly as a family member.

After his final words, he was gone. Blood and brains littered the truck bed, Gemma's face, and the windows. She was free, but not free. She never wanted to tell anyone this story. There were things multiple media outlets had gotten right, but so much was wrong. She remembered her mom as a loving figure, not the cheating, sex-obsessed object they'd portrayed her to be. Gemma still saw her dad as loving, too, and her fondest memories were of the times he'd taken her to breakfast on the weekends. She remembered swinging from tree ropes at Capaha Park, her dimples shining through her wide grin.

Gemma had considered her own fate and, in some ways, she couldn't say she was happy to be alive. She'd grown up trying to deal with the PTSD from her past and the chronic stress that her memories triggered. Now that her story was out there on a national platform, she hoped getting exposed wouldn't be as bad for her as it was for Margot.

CHAPTER 13

2016

Uncle Louie was a resident of the Missouri State Penitentiary for fifteen years before he moved back to Cape Ivy and went "off the grid." Uncle Louie had told Jack about his crimes related to his former job as a police officer. He'd started out on the police force back in the '70s, when he still had aspirations of making it to chief, but he quickly learned that he didn't have what it took for "the politics of the job," which included a lot of asses to kiss. He told Jack he wasn't the ass kissing type, so he learned to cut corners and make a few extra bucks by faking the system. It inspired Jack, and he put Louie on a higher pedestal.

"Of course, I never thought I'd get caught. There are a lot of motherfuckers doing a lot more serious shit than planting drugs and milking attendance cards," Louie said. "What I did was child's play compared to some of the shit that goes on in precincts around here. I just didn't play the games they wanted me to."

Louie told Jack that prison life wasn't terrible, even though he was a cop, which can be a death sentence. The Aryan Brotherhood looked up to him because of the wealth of information he provided as a former cop. Although Louie was a cranky older man, his counterparts respected him and his authority. He had an air about him—when he spoke, you listened. Jack knew how knowledgeable Louie was about police procedures and how he would be an asset to other inmates as well as himself.

"Do as I say, not as I do," Louie would often tell Jack.

Jack didn't know if prison life hardened Louie, but he came out mean, angry, and distrusting. Louie had retreated to the countryside in rural Cape Ivy, where he remained a single man. Louie didn't have his own children, and Jack hoped he filled that void. Jack enjoyed being Louie's apprentice and was always seeking Louie's approval, always asking, "Is this done right?" But Jack showed his temper to Louie a few times. When Jack was thirteen, they had their first big fight.

"No, it looks like shit," Louie had growled when Jack asked for his approval.

"Then you fucking do it!" Jack balled up his fists as his face turned red.

"What did you say to me, kid?" Louie spun toward Jack.

Jack stood in silence, taking in this shift in their relationship.

"I tell you what, you can just go home and get your ass beat right now. I don't need you here. Go on," Louie spit out a piece of tobacco.

Jack finally moved, grabbing a crowbar, and smashed it through one of the old junk car windows.

"How about that! Was that done right?" Jack smirked.

Louie struggled to his feet. "You better run, cause if I catch you, kid, I'm going to beat you worse than those bitches over yonder do."

Jack took off toward his house, seething the entire way.

It took a couple of months for the two to reconcile, but they exchanged no apologies. Eventually, they just went about their business like old times, but as Jack grew, he showed a darker side, which grew more menacing each year.

Jack later confided in Louie about his peeping behavior and fantasies of harm, but stopped short of confessing his desire to murder women. Jack never felt judged by Louie and always took his tips on how to avoid being detected as Louie's way of showing his love.

A month after Jack got the job with Elite Living, he received a call from Louie asking him to come over for some news, without Glenn or Officer Corey present.

Once Jack walked through the front door of the rundown trailer, Louie gulped down the last of his drink. "Kid, got some news to tell ya. Ain't got much more time to live. Found out I got cancer of the liver and it's got me real bad. Doctor put me on morphine and told me it could be weeks or a year or maybe two, not too sure how long," Louie said as he rocked in his recliner.

Jack's heart swelled, catching his breath as he couldn't believe what he'd just heard. He thought for a second it might be a joke—although Louie wasn't the joking kind. "We gotta get you to a better doctor. You can't die. It's too soon." Jack eyed Louie up and down. "You're in your sixties; you have more life to live. I need you around longer."

"Nah, kid. I'm ready to go. I lived all I was ready to live, and I don't want to live like this anymore. These pills got me so backed up, I haven't shit for days. I don't like doctors, and when you get the big C, you gotta keep going to see them," Louie said, lightly pounding his right fist on the armchair. "It's better that I just leave this earth, but I want to go celebrate one last time. Let's go to Patsy's and get wasted."

"But you said you might have a couple of years. Why are you saying one last time? Maybe they'll figure out some new drug or therapy within the next year. You can't give up. I need you!" Jack's voice cracked.

Jack paced the trailer and ran his hands through his hair.

"It's OK, kid. We all have to leave this earth somehow, and this is the way I'm going out. At least I get to say my goodbyes." Louie cracked open a new can of beer.

"You're my only family, or at least the closest thing I have. The only person I care about. You can't leave me," Jack said, feeling both angry that Louie wasn't doing more to fight and gutted that he was losing him.

At Louie's insistence, they went out to the bar, where they started with vodka shots that turned into multiple buckets of Budweiser. Eventually Glenn and Corey arrived, and Jack suspected they had already heard the news, as they weren't too shocked when Jack mentioned cancer. They raised their beers in unison as if Louie was already dead, which only angered Jack more. As other patrons caught word that this was Louie's celebratory outing, many free drinks kept showing up, from whiskey sours to Fireballs to vodka shots. Many options to become drunk so Louie could try anything he wanted for his "special night out." Jack drank his fair share, too.

Although Louie became a gregarious drunk, Jack was the total opposite—a vulgar one. Within an hour of their arrival, Jack slurred his words and made rude comments to the female bartender. She initially shrugged it off, but as the night proceeded, he became more and more tasteless. "Suck my dick or I'll fuck you up," Jack kept telling her. She gave him a warning and Louie told him to watch his mouth or he'd get kicked out. Jack sat fuming on a bar stool, glaring at any patron who dared to sit near him.

A few patrons played pool and a couple of dudes got into a fist-fight, which Jack cheered on. That's when Jack saw, in the far back corner, a man in a blue flannel shirt sitting half-awake with a beer bottle resting on his lap. Jack approached and noticed a small stream of drool had escaped the man's mouth. He recognized this face from his youth, and said in his deepest and loudest voice, "Beat your ass." Paul bolted awake, spilling the rest of his drink. It took Paul a second to focus his eyes, but he finally recognized Jack, the boy he used to know from dating Kathy. He stood up to shake his hand and gave him a wide grin, clearly forgetting how he'd tormented the kid. Jack just glared at him and said, "Meet me outside. I got something for ya." Paul was still drunk and unsteady on his feet, but followed Jack outside.

"How's Kathy? I haven't seen her since we broke up a couple of years ago. I miss that broad."

"How the fuck would I know? I don't miss that bitch. She can rot in hell for all I care," Jack said as he closed the gap between them, pushing Paul toward the dumpster.

Paul's grin slowly faded, his eyes widened, and he looked around the empty back lot. That was when Jack released the first blow to Paul's jaw. Paul fell stiffly to the ground and Jack threw a second punch, followed by several kicks to his gut. Jack lost count after that, and Paul fell into the deepest sleep of his life.

Jack was insatiable. He was a wild tiger in a kill, except his fists and kicks were his weapons. He later thought of how he felt no pain as he mashed Paul's teeth and bones and watched blood spew out of Paul's nose, eyes, and mouth. Each time Jack slowed his beating, he thought about his childhood torment, which made his rage throttle back up as he hit Paul even harder.

After every blow and kick, Jack hissed "Motherfucker" and "Piece of shit" through gritted teeth.

Paul never made a sound after the second blow to the head, as the force had likely knocked him out. Jack suddenly heard a gasp from behind, and he turned to see the female bartender he'd been harassing all night. She hurried back inside. Eventually, Louie, Glenn, and Corey arrived and stared at the bloody heap before them.

Corey checked to see if Paul was alive and declared him dead. The group debated dumping the body into the nearby dumpster, but the warm weather and delayed trash pickup would cause too much attention. They devised a plan to dump him into the Mississippi River. First, they chopped off his fingertips to delay any identification. Jack's blows had already knocked many of Paul's teeth out, so they didn't have to worry about dental records as an identifier.

"We'll blame Patrick for this death if they ever recover the body. I'll work my magic to frame him. Got it?" Glenn looked at the group for confirmation, and they all nodded in agreement.

Jack had cashed in his favor, and it was worth it. Watching Paul's lifeless body float down the river was pure poetry to him. His hand throbbed from the beating, but it was a beautiful reminder of the revenge he had waited years for.

He finally understood how ethereal death really was and why artists described it so eloquently.

CHAPTER 14

2018

Margot arrived at the KFCI-13 news headquarters dressed in the nicest outfit in her closet: a black blazer with a white cotton T-shirt and skinny jeans. She opened the glass doors into a vast waiting area crowded with plants, from bamboo palm to bird of paradise. The large windows provided a view of downtown Cape Ivy as busy pedestrians walked by. Margot sat on a green velvet barrel chair until Loni Smart came down in the elevator to escort her to the conference room. Dressed in a red pantsuit that hugged her fit frame, Loni walked over to greet Margot, the scent of her expensive perfume beckoning Margot to follow her. She was the type of woman everyone wanted in their corner—she had an intimidating presence, like a firecracker that doesn't detonate right away.

Loni sat across from Margot and made small talk about a restaurant that would open soon, but once the cameraman completed his countdown, the questions flew in.

"Margot, why did you go into hiding?" Loni leaned in toward Margot.

OK, we're starting like this. Margot braced herself.

"I left Cape Ivy to escape my sadness. At least, I tried; I thought that maybe if I was away, it wouldn't feel as real. I thought it would spare me from revisiting places that Nadine and I frequented," Margot said, biting her bottom lip. She now regularly passed by many of those places, like the bookstore on the Plaza and the walking trail along the Mississippi River.

"How did you learn that someone had uncovered your identity?" Loni asked, her gaze serious.

"I started getting knocks at my door, and I noticed people had started staring at me. That's when I found out that someone on a website I used occasionally had posted my image and address to the world." Margot took a deep breath and looked into the camera.

The website that kept Margot updated on all things true crime, including Nadine's murder, had turned against her when she was exposed. It had been a place she could hide out in the open and be an anonymous crime sleuth alongside other armchair detectives. She'd taken part in several threads regarding the most prolific killers in society, although she'd joined *Death Toll* to learn more about the one who haunted her waking thoughts.

Margot enjoyed connecting with other crime junkies on the website, but now she feared it had led to her own identity being exposed. She'd made many attempts to contact the website owner about removing her image, but no one had responded.

"Do you have any leads or ideas about who killed your aunt?"

"I wish I did. But I've thought of anyone that my aunt ever came into contact with. I stalk their social media pages to see if there's any clue or crumb I can follow. So far, nothing." Margot fidgeted in her chair.

"Now that you're back in Cape Ivy, where do you go from here?"

Margot paused before answering. "I want to take back my image. I don't want to be pitied or viewed as the girl in hiding. Nadine's case has gone stale, and I need to speak up for her." Margot stared straight into the camera. "I hope I keep Nadine's story out there so that I can aid in finding her fucking killer."

Loni's eyes dashed to her cameraman and producer, who cut away to a commercial.

After the interview, Margot was numb. She found herself back inside her car with no idea how she got there. The last words she remembered were Loni's apology once they returned from commercial break. Loni was Cape Ivy's top-tier journalist, and Margot's profanity may have cost her some sponsorships.

Margot sent a text to the Crime Three. "Oooops," was all she wrote, followed by a few shrug emojis. *Thankfully, I have supportive friends.* Once back at her apartment, Margot breathed a sigh of relief. She was grateful for her privacy living above a failing drug store. Months had passed, and she rarely heard anything out of the Old Town Pharmacy. They'd slowly become less busy as more customers switched to bigger pharmacy chains. Margot hoped her landlord wouldn't sell the building to a larger company, as she preferred the quiet reprieve her apartment gave her.

After she attended Dr. Williams' presentation, the eeriness of the Bandana Rapist's style of murder stuck with her. *Was my aunt stalked too? Is this a copycat killer?*

Margot had opened a P.O. Box for security, which allowed her a daily walk to the local post office three blocks away. The day after her interview, she put on sweatpants and a shirt, complete with an over-sized St. Louis Cardinals cap, and walked to get her mail. The overcast sky didn't call for sunglasses, but Margot wore them anyway. *I must look like a cross between a bank robber and a college student who just rolled out of bed.*

During her walk, she admired the unseasonably warm day, noticing the leaves were a mix of green, yellow, and red. When she opened her mailbox, she found an official invitation asking her to join Dr. Simone Wiliams at her next speech. "We would love your atten-dance as we dissect local murders and hear how these crimes have affected family members."

Margot was still in shock as she clung to her invite, rereading it many times just to make sure it was real. *I'll be sharing a stage with Dr. Williams!*

CHAPTER 15

2018

"Gemma Norris is the Daughter of the Crimson Spree Shooter."

Gemma awoke to a flood of notifications on her cell phone. Most were from TV stations who wanted to interview her, but there were also some from randos online wanting to "meet up." Also, her Crime Three group texting her "OMG" with lots of exclamation marks at the end of their messages. Gemma debated logging online for the livestream chat regarding the recent Crimson Spree Shooter documentary. TrollGod had plastered her picture all over *Death Toll*, and now she could feel the square footage of her small apartment shrinking by the minute. Stress squeezed at her neck muscles, making it difficult to turn her head. Gemma knew this would happen. The minute she saw Margot at the cemetery and approached her, she knew her own identity would soon be revealed. Gemma hated having her name out there; she dreaded the incoming media attention. The small world she had created for herself was no longer just for her. She would now have to face the same scrutiny as Margot had.

As Gemma logged in to the chat room, some users bombarded her with questions about why she didn't trust them with the information, while others shared well-wishes. For the next week, her newfound victim status gave Margot a reprieve, and she became *Death Toll's* latest true crime darling. She hoped it wouldn't last, as she knew attention spans were fleeting.

When she finally met up with Margot and Carter a week later, she feared they would be upset she hadn't confided in them. As she dressed for their meeting, she debated canceling. *I'll just tell them I don't feel well.* However, she went through the motions of getting ready, mentally preparing herself to see them. She drove around the block a few times just in case Loni Smart was stalking her, ready to pounce for an exclusive. As she parked, she craned her neck in all directions, looking for the sniper full of questions. When it seemed like the coast was clear, she took a deep breath and went inside.

"Are you OK?" Margot asked as she reached around Gemma for a hug.

Goosebumps shot up over Gemma's arms as she looked down, giving a shaky nod.

"I completely understand. It's so unfair to be exposed in that way," Margot said.

In the university study lounge, Gemma felt a bit more hidden. She thought the students would be too busy to recognize her, and thankfully, the lounge was mostly empty. One thing she'd learned in life was that most people don't pay much attention to their surroundings, and she hoped that included her newfound fame. Gemma sat and sipped on a soy latte she'd bought at the cafeteria when she saw Carter walking toward them, his face focused with no emotion. The group had chosen this location because Carter only had a brief break between classes.

"Gemma. I can't believe you kept us in the dark. I can't imagine what you're going through, but I want to be here for both you and Margot," Carter said as he looked back and forth between them.

"Thank you. I guess I was naïve to think that I could stay hidden from my reality, especially with the documentary streaming at number one. I'm trying to come to grips with being discovered, but I appreciate your support." Gemma rubbed the sides of her arms.

"Well, I'm here for you if you ever need to vent," Carter said, pulling out a chair.

"Yes, whatever you need. I'll drop everything," Margot said.

Carter leaned his elbows on the table and put his head into his hands. "I feel like I haven't protected either of you."

"What could you do? Someone online exposed us. There's a troll out there making survivors into victims. Also, we're not your responsibility." Margot grabbed her coffee cup and downed the rest of it.

"I know you didn't ask for me to protect you. I'm just saying I'm in graduate school researching criminals and should have seen something like this coming." He ran his hand through his hair.

"This isn't about you, Carter. Thank you for caring, though," Gemma said.

Somehow, seeing Carter and Margot's reaction to her news made Gemma relieved. Just knowing that they accepted her silence about her past meant the world to her. She hoped this would spur an even closer bond with Margot.

Gemma broke the silence. "So now you know; my dad murdered my entire family and left me to tell you about it."

Margot shook her head. "I'm so sorry. That isn't fair to leave you with this kind of burden. Welcome to the club nobody wants to join: the murder club."

"Both of you have so much strength. I'm lucky to know you." Carter gave a thin smile. "I mean, what are the odds of two of my friends being connected to two infamous killers?" Carter's eyes darted between Gemma and Margot.

"Unfortunately, the odds keep growing every year as murder rates keep climbing," Gemma said.

Gemma's therapist had diagnosed her with PTSD. She felt guilty for not crying more about how her life began, but she had learned to cope by distancing herself from the feelings associated with trauma. Stress was just as predictable of pain as the weather—both left their brutal marks as soon as they arrived and could linger for days.

"I do have something to share with you both," Margot said, gritting her teeth. "Dr. Williams has officially invited me to be interviewed at her next seminar. I'm in shock!" Margot showed them the invite she'd received in the mail.

"Oh. My. God. I am totally fangirling right now. Please tell me you'll reserve a ticket for me? Just don't ask me to speak," Gemma said with praying hands.

"You got it. Carter, want in?"

"Yes, please. I still haven't heard about the teaching assistant position with her, so this might be my lucky opportunity."

"Oh, sure," Margot said, rolling her eyes. "You have my full permission to tug on Dr. Williams' emotional sleeve to score you a favor as you pimp us both out." Margot winked.

"You read my mind." Carter laughed.

———

Back at home, Gemma laid in bed, thinking about how her life was now open to the public. While reading and watching true crime was her favorite pastime, being a poster child for it wasn't for her. She had neither the energy nor the desire to be interviewed or give a speech for others to hang on to each word. The mere thought of it made her cringe. No, Gemma much preferred the anonymity behind the screen, which made her even more grateful for Margot, who was willing to take the space in front of it.

Gemma knew that her own popularity would die down and the true crime community would find someone else, hopefully someone who wanted to talk. In the meantime, Gemma would do what she did best: fade into the background.

CHAPTER 16

2016

A ringing phone at 6 a.m. on a Sunday could only mean horrible things—emergencies rarely waited for normal hours. Jack had been working at Elite Living for over a year now and enjoyed his routine. He'd met a few coworkers whom he tolerated, but the urge to kill women was still present. He suppressed it successfully, at least for now. Elite Living had made quick progress in getting both old and new units ready for tenants, and nearly all the units were now occupied.

Jack fumbled for the phone in the still darkness of the morning. He found the ringing pest and groggily answered, "Hello?" with only a faint whisper of a question at the end.

"Jack, it's Glenn. Hey buddy, hate to wake you like this, but Louie's gone. He finally bit the dust. Found him in his favorite recliner. Probably went in his sleep is how it looked to me. End of an era, man. He was one of a kind."

Jack was still half-asleep, but Glenn's words sobered him. Yet he couldn't understand what they meant. He assumed Glenn meant Louie was dead, but he'd never actually said those words, and Jack needed to be sure.

"He's dead?" Jack finally asked, wanting that confirmation.

"Yeah, man. He's dead. I already called the cops and the coroner, but we already know what his last wishes were and I'm looking at the will he drafted." Glenn spouted off everything that Louie had gifted each of them. Jack tuned it out. He wasn't sure if he was struggling to process all of this because he wasn't fully awake, or because his brain refused to believe his uncle was gone.

"Jack, are you with me? Are you coming out here?"

Jack agreed to go out to Louie's house to see for himself. He was still in shock. Though he'd known Louie was sick, it wasn't processing that he was actually dead. Jack had made the trip to Louie's many times since moving into his apartment, but he didn't know how he got there this time. He drove in a haze and couldn't remember seeing anyone else on the way there.

As he pulled up to the trailer, he immediately noticed a Cape Ivy Police cruiser and the van from the medical examiner's office. He arrived just in time to see them wheel Louie out on a gurney toward the back of the examiner's vehicle. Jack stood and felt a small shiver, then a pang of sorrow met him somewhere behind his sinus cavity. He couldn't move forward, staring at what he assumed was Louie's body underneath the sheet. No one said a word to Jack. They just kept moving around him like he was invisible. Jack wasn't an actual nephew, after all—Louie probably had real blood relatives to handle his affairs. Jack was only a borrowed family member. Once again, Jack was alone in this world. The one man that had provided him with any kind of foundation was gone.

The first thing Jack saw when he walked into the trailer was Glenn. Jack resented him. He should have been the one to find Louie. Glenn was only a friend—he didn't have the close bond with Louie that he and Jack shared. Though it always ate at Jack that Louie didn't call him "son" instead of nephew. He supposed it was just a minor oversight, but he had always wanted to go back in time to that first meeting, wishing that Louie had told Jack to call him dad instead of uncle. Glenn had gathered items that were listed in Louie's will as his: some rare coins that Louie stole from a client he worked for were amongst the stash. Jack stood and watched Glenn collect Louie's belongings as the rage stormed through his veins.

"What the hell are you doing?" Jack yelled.

Glenn immediately turned, shock and anger on his face. No one spoke to him that way. "I told you, I'm collecting the stuff Louie left me in this will. Now don't ever fucking yell at me like that again. I'll let you off this time because you might be grieving, but consider this a warning."

Jack wasn't afraid of Glenn, and he no longer wanted anything of Louie's. He felt more anger than anguish, so he left, telling Glenn that he'd deal with his shit later. As he stomped out, he slammed the door in frustration and headed to his car. He wondered what would happen to all this crap on Louie's property—the rusted-out cars and appliances, the trailer that was falling apart, and the land it all sat on. Jack hated being back near his childhood home. He had too many memories of being too young to do anything about the abuse. He could only handle being here in the dark and when he drank. During the day, it all became too depressing. As he stood by his car surveying Louie's property, he heard a car coming down the gravel road. He didn't recognize the car, but why would he? Jack hadn't lived around here in years. He turned away to avoid contact, as he was in no mood for conversation should the driver recognize him, but he heard the car slow and eventually stop.

"Well, look what the ol' cat drug in." Jack knew that shrill voice from his childhood. It ripped through him like a thousand hot knives. He clenched his teeth, his jaw pulsating as he debated charging the car and pounding his fists into her vile mouth.

"Ain't you gonna come hug your Aunt Kathy? My, it's been years since I saw you, but I knew you right away cause you are just like your daddy—tall and hunched over. You still come to visit your friends, but not your actual family?" she said, shaking her head in disapproval, which made her hoop earrings hit her cheeks.

Jack turned around and glared at her. He wanted to pull her through her window by her hair, smash each of her teeth in, and bash her face until she was unrecognizable.

"Why don't you visit your mom? It's important for sons to take care of their mothers, and you haven't kept up your duties. Boys are supposed to treat their moms like a queen, and from what I can tell, you barely treat her like she's a pauper. I know I cared for my daddy until the day he died. It's our duty as children to serve our parents. Don't forget that, Jack. We raised you better than that." Kathy wagged a finger out the car window.

Jack continued to stare in disbelief. She was lecturing him in front of Louie's house, on the day of his death, on how to be an obedient son. The fury he felt inside was too much. He grabbed the closest thing he could find, which, in Louie's yard, included a lot of options. He found an old tire iron and walked up to Kathy's window.

"You have ten seconds to move on or I will bash your face in," he snarled. "Either way, I'll gladly see you in Hell."

She laughed at first until she saw the seriousness in his eyes. Finally, she sped off.

Jack's rage did not subside when Kathy left. He considered going to his mom's house and bashing her brains in, but he knew Kathy would lead the police right to him. Glenn walked out to see Jack wielding the tire iron and tried to calm him, to no avail. Jack hopped in his car and peeled out, spitting a torrent of gravel rocks into the air behind him. Eventually, he parked at Capaha Park and lit a cigarette, wishing he had something stronger to smoke. He'd decided it was time to make a plan to address the thoughts he'd suppressed in his head for so long.

He knew the power and euphoria of killing. Paul's murder was the best feeling he had ever felt, and he'd never had that rush since. He wanted—no, *needed* that back in his life. Jack needed to experience that thrill and release; the inner purpose of murder. He'd first had urges of murder when he was twelve, when he had the desire to kill Paul and his mom and aunt, but he'd suppressed it because he didn't know how he could get away with it. He hadn't had a gun, and he didn't think he could stab all of them without being overpowered. Plus, it was around the time he met Uncle Louie, who had instilled in him the importance of never getting caught. Besides, things got a little better once Kathy moved out with Paul, because she rarely came around after that. His mom was more verbally abusive, so he could deal with her a little better.

Still, Jack often had thoughts of attacking women in public, whether it was at a bar or a grocery store. He wondered how it would feel and sound to snap a neck. And now that Louie was dead, nothing was holding him back. Louie was his confidante—the one person he could entrust with his deepest thoughts. Now he only had himself, and Jack's desire to kill grew stronger all the time. Louie's death had unleashed Jack. He was ready to move on to his next plan. He believed he could easily sneak up on women as a maintenance man. *I have a right to be in a woman's apartment. My fingerprints would be all over the place because of my job, so they wouldn't raise any red flags.*

Jack thought out various ways he wanted to carry out his murders, and he realized if he was going to kill women in their apartments, he needed to make sure they wouldn't be able to make noise or call for help. He relished the quiet scream, so he decided he needed a mask. A mask that would prevent them from speaking or breathing—*a choke mask.* Jack's murderous thoughts had him in a trance. He immediately planned what he needed for the mask. Although he couldn't sew, he knew how to tie knots thanks to Louie, and he knew enough about raw materials like vinyl and fishing lines and metal brackets that he could create exactly what he needed. After he purchased all the needed materials, he began constructing his garment of death.

Monday morning came too quickly for Jack, who got almost no sleep. He thought little of Louie's death and focused only on the assembly of his choke mask. He stayed up all night making the mask out of vinyl, which would be easy to maneuver over the victim's head. Jack then constructed a rudimentary knot down the back to form a round shape to fit over the squirming skull, which held the mask together. He fastened two snaps: The first would provide a limited breathing space for the first few minutes. He would then secure the second, creating a tight fit over the victim's mouth and leaving little to no breathing room. Finally, he placed a metal piece over the nose that he would bash, fracturing the nose and sending blood seeping down their throat as they died gasping for air.

Jack couldn't believe the masterpiece he'd created. The mask was a work of art to him, and he wished he had someone to test it out on before his first kill. While he tried it on his own head to make sure it fit, he wanted to see how quickly he could get it on a struggling victim. This prompted his decision to wait for the victim to be asleep. That way, he could ambush them and they would be less likely to fight back. He also loved imagining the sheer terror that would go through their minds as they wondered if they'd live or die, unable to speak, the mask constricting every precious breath. Jack made several masks before he settled on a final version, which he believed was perfect and ready for his first victim.

He sat back and held the mask, feeling the smooth vinyl front with no holes for breathing or seeing. Admiring his craftsmanship, his knot work, and the level of horror he could inflict on his victims, he felt like nothing short of a genius. He wanted to make hundreds of these masks so that his reign of terror would never end.

It's ready.

Jack no longer wanted the quiet screams of butterflies. He wanted the muffled cries of women.

When he started his next shift, Jack leafed through the maintenance tickets that had come in over the weekend. Most of the requests were for typical things like a clogged drain or leaky faucet, but one request caught his eye. One of the older units was having an air conditioner issue. It would sporadically blow out lukewarm air, and it was company policy that maintenance try to fix it before calling in an outside repairman. Jack didn't have much experience working with these units, but this was a bigger job that would keep him away from the main office for an extended period. It would allow him to see how he could eventually make this his first victim and, best of all, she appeared to be a single woman living alone. Bingo.

Jack signed out on the maintenance log that he'd be at this unit for the entire day, working on the cooling system—Hanover unit/Tenant: Nadine Chastain.

Nadine lived in the older part of Cape Ivy, which was dotted with Victorian homes and buildings that were converted into apartments and quaint shops. Nadine's unit was a three-story walkup, a penthouse apartment that overlooked the Mississippi River in an updated old brick building. Her place had newer appliances, and a renovated bathroom, with the original hardwood floors, crown molding, and ornate fireplace mantel. Jack immediately believed that whoever lived here had money, or at least spent a lot of it. The place was full of antiques and what he thought of as "rich lady shit."

He'd never seen a place this fancy, with vases and ornate rugs. He already hated the bitch that lived like this, as he'd always wished he had the money to escape the poverty he grew up in. That made killing her all the better in his book. The best part of apartments is that most people don't check where their hot water heater is located, usually in a hallway closet. Elite Living had kept them locked to prevent kids from going in and to keep people from using them as storage. Jack decided this would be a perfect place to hide in order to pounce on his victim late into the night; he was almost giddy when he thought about it. He knew it would be a long wait, but the outcome would be completely worth it.

There was plenty of room inside for him to sit, and the doors had wooden slats so he could see out, just enough to see his victim's last steps. The next thing to do was to stalk Nadine to make out her routine. He figured he'd give it a couple of months, and if her routine didn't change, he'd feel fairly comfortable with it. That she was a single occupant was a plus—he needed to be sure there wasn't a boyfriend to worry about. In due time, he'd find out if she would be his first victim to christen the choke mask.

Jack snooped around more in Nadine's bedroom and saw pictures on the dresser of a woman in her forties and a younger female, likely a teenager. They were laughing at a restaurant in one picture and smiling on a beach in another. There was no sign of a man in any of the pictures, which Jack took as a fortuitous sign. He hoped a teenager wasn't living here, although there didn't appear to be any evidence of one—there weren't any boy band posters or overflowing clothes or even an extra bedroom. The couch definitely wasn't being used for a bed, at least not currently. Everything was neat and put together.

Jack was confident in the stalking skills he'd honed in his youth; he just needed to survey the outside to find the best vantage point. Without knowledge of Nadine's work schedule, he'd park down the street at first to see if he could recognize the woman in the picture and determine what car she drove. Then he'd at least know when she was home. Since he saw a bike in the hallway outside of her apartment, he assumed she might go on rides. That would be a perfect time for him to sneak back in once he knew her schedule. With his plan in place, Jack turned his attention to the maintenance request that had brought him there. Looking at the air conditioner, he immediately saw the issue, and it was simple—the air filter was completely clogged and wouldn't allow positive airflow. A new filter did the trick, although he was going to report a much larger issue to the office so he could spend more time plotting out how to trap his prey. As he drove home that night, Jack decided he would wake up before dawn and drive to Nadine's, hoping to see her walk to her car.

When Jack saw the attractive brunette descend the front steps the next morning, oblivious to his dark car, he felt gratified and rewarded. Now he was certain that the woman in the pictures was in fact Nadine. Her apartment was currently pitch black, which he hoped meant she lived alone. Jack began following behind her, his eyes locked on her every move like a predator hunting its prey, until a cop car pulled up next to them at a stoplight, snapping him back to reality.

As Nadine got in her car, Jack slowly drove by, blew out a puff of cigarette smoke, and said, "See you soon!"

CHAPTER 17

2016

Cool air immediately greeted Nadine as she walked into her apartment.

Thank goodness maintenance fixed the air conditioner. In this late summer heat, she needed it.

She had her doubts about the new management company, but they'd impressed her with how quickly they fixed the cooling issue when she'd submitted her request a few months back. She had lived in this apartment for roughly five years and had considered buying a house, which she could certainly afford, but she was just too busy. Nadine liked the convenience of not having to do the maintenance and upkeep herself.

As vice president of the largest communications company in the Midwest, she was always conducting meetings or traveling to smaller offices, so she could be gone for a week at a time. Nadine had climbed the ranks shortly after graduating from business college, with her sights set on getting a corner office in a field still dominated by men— her beauty turned heads, but her intelligence unlocked doors. Her family had moved to Cape Ivy from California when she was fifteen years old, as her father had taken a position at the local university. To say it was a bit of a culture shock would be an understatement. The foggy river community of Cape Ivy was a complete shift from the beautiful and bustling coastal city of San Diego.

Much like the two opposing communities, she and Stella, the only siblings of the family, were night and day as well. While the older Stella was introverted—although quite opinionated once she opened up—the younger Nadine was amiable and outgoing. Both were attractive, but Nadine knew how to fix her hair and makeup in the current fashion, while Stella preferred a natural look. Nadine could meet friends anywhere, and it only took her the first week of high school to fit in with a new clique, while Stella always ate lunch alone on a bench under a redbud tree. Often bickering and rarely seeing eye to eye, they continued their strained relationship throughout adulthood, with differing opinions on relationships, politics, and religion.

Things changed once Stella gave birth to Margot, though only slightly. Nadine took an active role in caring for Margot and found great joy in having her in her life. While she never wanted children of her own, Margot was a love she didn't know she needed. She often volunteered to take her for weekends and anytime Stella and Charles wanted to go out on a date, which wasn't often, as they tended to be homebodies. Thankfully, Stella accepted Nadine's bond with Margot, as she worked long hours as a nurse and her own nurturing skills were lackluster. She provided as a mother, but she didn't show her love openly.

Nadine tilted her head and rubbed her finger over a framed picture of her niece on her dressing table. She had never wanted children of her own, but she thought of Margot as a daughter. Their relationship was strong, and at age five, Margot had asked Nadine, "Why can't you be my mom?" That was when Nadine understood that perhaps her role was interfering with Stella and Margot's bond.

"Your mom loves you very much. She just shows it differently than I do. I'm allowed to have a lot more fun with you," Nadine had said. "Besides, if you lived with me, you'd be asking me why Stella wasn't your mom."

"I kinda doubt that," Margot had mumbled. But they'd agreed to not bring it up again. Nadine made a point never to say anything negative about Stella for fear that they would blame her for causing a wedge in their relationship. Still, she knew how her sister was. She didn't think Stella showed Margot the love and affection that a child needed.

Nadine punched the numbers into the microwave to heat her frozen Lean Cuisine dinner, shuffling through her mail until her meal was ready. It was nothing but car insurance junk mail and a home loan approval letter from her bank urging her to ACT NOW. Both went into the trash as the alarm went off on the microwave. She ate her subpar dinner standing over her kitchen bar; cooking wasn't her forte. Although Nadine was confident, she was forty-two now, and getting older made her worry about the future. Youth gives you a power that fades as you age. The confidence she'd once had in herself as a powerful go-getter slowly subsided as she kept fighting for her position in the boardroom.

There were moments at work when she feared they'd replace her if she made a single mistake. *No one wants to see an aging woman conducting business.* At least, that was the fear she kept replaying in her mind, as equal rights were slow in the business world. She was a single woman by choice and had plenty of male suitors, but she never wanted to be tied down. Rather, she preferred having multiple lovers. Nadine enjoyed a night of wine, cigarettes, and good sex—no strings attached. She didn't want or need a man influencing—or worse, controlling—what she did. She made her own money and spent it as she pleased.

Nadine changed into shorts and a T-shirt for her bike ride down to the river, an almost daily routine. She thought she wouldn't stay out too late, as she had a very busy day ahead of her tomorrow. Some executives would be in town early next week to hear her give a presentation, and she wanted to get a good night's sleep to work on it. She bounced the bike down the stairs, then ascended the seat and headed east toward the river. The evening couldn't have been more perfect— the sky was rich with pink, orange, and red, and the air was warm yet crisp as a breeze signaled the early stages of fall. It was magical weather. Summer and fall were meeting and falling in love as excitement and optimism filled the air. There was something fresh about the changing of the seasons, and it was palpable tonight. She enjoyed her rides the most on nights like these, and she felt at peace as she watched shoppers pick up last-minute items at the local shops downtown.

Nadine slammed on her brakes to wait for Phil at the Broadway Antiques store to assist a customer with a desk out to their car. With a quick grin, she accepted his apologies and went on her way. The best part was gliding down Broadway toward the river, as it was a small decline down the hill, so she didn't have to pedal—she could enjoy the magnificent sky in all her beauty. She was glad she had her camera to take snaps of the beauty before her; the way the sky bounced off the water mesmerized her. She breathed in the comforting air. The night was truly enchanting, and she didn't want to take her eyes away. The sky, the air, the entire vibe of the city embraced her like the warmest hug, giving her goosebumps. She was so warm and relaxed she could almost melt.

Once she realized how late it was getting, Nadine pedaled back with the stars shining down on her, which added to the fairy-tale aura of the night. She felt such solace that she didn't even mind the pedal back up the hill. The night reminded her of a visit back to San Diego when they'd watched the sunset on the beach. The night air had been much like it was tonight: soft, glowing, and full of love. It was the last time she'd spent a vacation with her mom before she died, and it was one of her favorite memories. She lingered with this reflection until she was the last person on the sidewalk, smiling as a small tear of remembrance of happier days formed in her eye.

Back home, she hopped in the shower and applied her favorite lavender body wash. Her muscles relaxed under the heat and water pressure. As she dressed for bed, she fell into such a trance that she was sure she would have the best sleep she'd had in a long time. It didn't take long to drift off to a comfortable slumber after the long workday and amazing evening along the riverfront.

———

Nadine gasped, suddenly awakened by what felt like a thick bag being thrown violently over her head. She didn't know how long she had been asleep, but she hadn't heard anyone enter her apartment—it was eerily quiet except for the immense pounding of her heartbeat. All she knew was that she struggled to breathe, almost as if she was breathing through just a straw. All of her muscles were fighting for air, craving more than the tiny amount the thick fabric over her face allowed. Someone heavy pinned her down and forced her onto her chest, forcefully pressing something into her back. They tied her arms behind her, binding her hands together like handcuffs. She was unable to speak, though she tried.

Millions of thoughts raced through her mind. *Who are you? I'll give you all of my money. Please don't hurt me.* They applied more force when she attempted to fight back. Whoever this was, they were very strong. *Perhaps not resisting will make them go away,* she thought, but panic and lack of air muddled her mind. Nadine hoped they would not rape her, and she made one last effort to release herself. She mustered all her strength and swung her legs, successfully freeing one from the attacker's grip, but their power proved to be too much. They tied both of her legs together so tight Nadine could feel liquid rolling down her ankles.

The next thing she heard was a voice whispering, "Let me hear you scream, bitch." It was a man's voice, but she didn't recognize it. She tried to imagine who it could be—a former lover or a coworker? Someone she saw on one of her bike rides? Her mind raced as she attempted to yell out, but whatever was over her head wouldn't allow it. Trying to talk made breathing even more difficult, and she felt like she was running out of options and time. Tears filled her eyes, as they had no place to fall. She thought about Margot, hoping she would live to see her again. The attacker tightened the bag even more. With Margot's face in her mind, Nadine gagged and writhed around, trying to search for any bit of precious oxygen when the attacker made a final blow to her nose. It was like he'd set fire to her skull—a sharp, piercing voltage of pain that kept increasing in intensity. The torment made her thrash, her lungs no longer finding oxygen outside of her body and instead searching from inside, drowning itself. She then tasted the blood, choking on it as it began pouring down her throat.

Nadine eventually died two minutes later, struggling against a monster she could not see. Her last racing thoughts were those of her precious niece, Margot.

CHAPTER 18
2016

Early morning phone calls usually meant murder. Conway groggily answered his bedside phone.

"Conway speaking."

"Detective, we've got a cold one."

After he received the address, Conway took a fast shower, made his usual black coffee, and grabbed whatever he could find for breakfast. Since his wife, Betty, had left him several months back, he was living the bachelor life again. Ashtrays full of cigarette butts and empty liquor bottles lined the kitchen countertop, with cheap bread and bologna his food of choice most days. He grew accustomed to this way of living and enjoyed his newfound single life in his brick ranch home with parquet floors.

Crime scenes never got old for Conway. In fact, he relished them. He'd wanted to work for the FBI, but his knees wouldn't allow him to pass the physical, so he settled for the ranks of the police academy in Cape Ivy and eventually worked his way up to lead homicide detective. Homicides were a growing market here in the city. As the population increased, so did people's blood pressure and hatred toward each other. It was good business for him and kept him busy. Domestic violence was the most common precursor to a woman's murder, and he could usually wrap up the cases within a day or two—at least, that's what history had taught him.

As he drove up to the crime scene, he saw a distraught young lady being escorted to a car by a man who he presumed could be her father. One reason Betty had left him was because he hated dealing with emotions. He had always promised her he'd retire early so they could move to Florida to live close to her sister, but those were lies. He loved his job more than her. She was his second marriage, and he never fully loved her. Honestly, he wasn't sure what it really meant to love a person. All he knew was that his job gave him the satisfaction he needed, and the only thing he missed about Betty was having a clean house and a home-cooked meal. However, he knew when he dealt with grieving families he needed to be comforting and not the callous man those closest to him knew he was. Conway wore a mask anytime he dealt with the public so they could trust he knew what he was doing. He was the best Cape Ivy had to offer, and crime scenes were his passion.

"Hello, I'm Detective Dan Conway. I'll be the lead detective working this case. You must be the family?" Conway leaned toward the sobbing girl and the man who comforted her.

The man nodded and gave a rundown of what had occurred that morning. "I'm Charles Mays, Nadine's brother-in-law, and I'm the one who called the police," he said as he glanced down at his daughter, who he introduced as Margot.

Conway took notes and nodded, telling Charles, "I need all three family members to come down to the station to give a full statement about what happened this morning." He gave his deepest condolences and walked towards the apartment.

At that moment, the body was being removed. "God damn it, they shouldn't have tampered with this body until I arrived and had a chance to view the scene. These motherfuckin' rookie cops don't know what the fuck they're doing around here," Conway hissed at the cop stationed by Nadine's entryway, not caring if the officers heard him.

I'm in no mood for this bullshit. The FBI doesn't have this level of incompetence, I'm sure of it.

As he stood in the doorway, his face reddened as Conway could see they had compromised the crime scene, as none of the officers were wearing protective clothing. They didn't have shoe covers, so who knew what fibers were being transferred in and out of the place? After he fastened on his own covers, he walked to the bedroom and surveyed the area where the body had been.

"Tell me everything you saw and did. Please tell me you at least took pictures and video?" Conway snarled.

An officer nervously explained that they did in fact take video, but they'd had to redo it because they didn't realize the lens cover was on. They made sure to get it right the second time. Conway stared in disbelief. This was who he had to work with on a major crime scene investigation. He wanted to say so many things, but he just huffed.

"Submit all the evidence to my office immediately. I want this entire place covered in crime tape. Do not allow anyone but me to enter this apartment from here on out, unless I give permission. God knows what kind of evidence you've lost! Was she shot, stabbed? What was her cause of death?"

The rookie officer stumbled over his words and admitted he wasn't sure. "She had a mask over her head, sir. Her hands and feet were bound, but there weren't any other obvious wounds to the body. The medical examiner didn't speak to me. He quietly removed the body and left."

Conway was half annoyed and half amused. He knew ME Thompson was just as much of an asshole as he was; he didn't have the patience to deal with half-wits like these rookie cops. But Thompson also knew enough protocol that he shouldn't have removed the body until Conway gave the signal. "I want you to stand guard at this front door until I send someone to release you," Conway ordered. "I don't give a shit if that means you don't get a lunch or a piss break —I need this door guarded. Can you handle that?" With a nod, the rookie agreed to his assignment, absently saluting Conway with his hand.

Conway descended the three flights of stairs and lit his cigarette, mumbling, "This is going to be some work. I have a bunch of mindless hamsters running backwards on a wheel working this case with me. I should have had some whiskey with my coffee this morning."

After the ten-minute drive to the medical examiner's building, Conway walked directly to Thompson's office to chew him out.

"Don't give me that tone, Conway. You know those cops don't know shit. I made sure they had the pictures and videos first. I can't stay in a room with such incompetence for that long," Thompson said. "If you want me to work with your guys, talk to your chief about hiring officers with more than half a brain cell." He threw down a file full of documents he had just signed.

"Look, Thompson, next time you wait until I arrive. Otherwise, I'll have your ass written up. This could cost me days of investigation. I had nothing to tell the goddamned family that was still standing outside when I arrived! You don't have to give them answers like I do. Now, what's the COD? I don't even know that!" Conway said, raising his arms in the air.

"Oh, asphyxiation by a mask," Thompson said.

"Oh, well, thanks, asshole. I should have known that AT THE CRIME SCENE! Never put me in that position again. I don't want to look like an ass in front of the family or the cops on the case. I don't give a fuck about your feelings or what you think of their experience. Understand?" Conway slammed his fist down on the desk.

Thompson stared, but eventually snorted and agreed. The two were very similar—they were both old, grouchy, and new bachelors in their ripe age. The biggest difference was that Thompson searched for companionship at strip clubs and bars, while Conway was married to his job—he had neither the time nor the desire to mess with love. Rumor had it Thompson had been supplying a local stripper named Angel with over a month's salary down her G-string, which she was shooting straight up her arm. Thompson might get lucky after all if she was ever wheeled into his office. He'd have her all to himself—a cold slab for him to dissect.

On the drive back to headquarters, the sky opened up and pockets of rain blanketed his car, causing moments of poor visibility. Conway wished he could just go back to sleep, as he knew he had a family waiting for answers and that he had none to give. He hated this time of year when the seasons changed, never knowing what the weather would be like or whether he needed to wear long or short sleeves. He usually opted for short sleeves and a jacket. Conway had been happy to ditch a police uniform years ago, much preferring his classic look of khakis and a polo shirt. The standard police-issue attire was what first attracted Betty to him when she'd seen him on a call at her office. "I'm just a sucker for a man in a uniform," she had told him; one of the oldest lines in the book. He'd asked her out, and they dated for a few years before they got married, a second marriage for both of them. His first ended in divorce, while hers ended in death (a heart attack, to be exact). Betty was the romantic type. She would leave love notes in the morning by his coffee mug, always had evening meals prepared when he got home, and had visions of their future retired life in Florida.

He chose marriage to keep Betty for the convenience it brought: sex, food, and clean clothes. His dream was to become a famous detective by capturing his very own serial killer. As he neared the end of his career, the odds of another serial killer were getting slimmer. When the Bandana Rapist was stalking the women of Cape Ivy and the surrounding communities, Conway wasn't a homicide detective. He could only watch from afar and dream of being in the position to catch his own murderer one day. It took Conway several years to work up to his current rank, therefore he had no plans to leave his post, regardless of the words he'd said to Betty. He didn't love her enough to abandon his career for humidity and gators. They didn't have any children together, so their split was pretty amicable, at least on his part. One day, he woke up with Betty, and the next she was gone. Just like that, he was a single man again and life went on like it always did, minus the fleeting sex life, the smells of food emanating from the stove, and the always freshly washed towels.

Back at his desk, which was piled with papers and files from various cases that were both solved and open, he glanced at the hanging poster above his desk. "Not my circus, not my monkeys," was a poster left by a former officer which remained in place on the wall and was fraying at the edges from years of being attached to the cold concrete. Conway reached into the side drawer and found a tiny bottle of gin. After using it to wash down a couple of aspirin, he grabbed a notebook and found an open interview room. He brought the Mays family in together to get their story of the events of the crime. He knew the station wasn't a warm place for families as they didn't build it for them. They built it for the criminals, the lowlifes of society, so Conway felt a rare stab of empathy anytime he had to bring a grieving family here.

Conway escorted the family of three back into the nicer conference room, where they kept the cushioned chairs, but the air was still stiff with their grief. He liked to throw the old adage of not judging a book by its cover out the window. As a cop, he had to make quick judgments as he scanned the faces of each family member and assessed their ability to become a murderer.

Margot is too young and weak to cause such damage. Stella could have had a motive for money or sibling rivalry. Perhaps Charles was having an affair with Nadine that she was about to expose. Maybe Stella found out. Conway had several rapid-fire thoughts as he began his interview.

"Again, I'm sorry for your loss. Please walk me through the last time you spoke with Nadine and the events that took place this morning. I understand it will be very difficult for you, but the more information I know, the faster I'm able to solve this case."

Margot attempted to speak, but the words were strained. Conway could see she was in agony. Instead, Charles spoke first. He said he had received a call from Margot, who had gone over to Nadine's, but had found her dead. After he received the frantic call, he and his wife, Stella, rushed over to Nadine's apartment, where they found her body on the bed with the mask covering her head.

"We tried to find a pulse, but it was too late. Her pulse was gone and the mask wouldn't come off, no matter how hard Stella yanked. We contacted the police and now here we sit," Charles recounted, staring down at Conway's notepad.

"Do you remember seeing anything out of the ordinary? Anything missing? Has Nadine's behavior been different? Was she dating someone?" Conway asked. "I need to know those kinds of specific details."

Stella spoke up. "Nadine didn't have a boyfriend, per se, but she certainly had lovers. I couldn't say who they were, but no one she was serious about. She enjoyed her single life and didn't want to be tied down." She folded her arms.

Conway nodded in agreement. He wondered where he could find a lady like this. *Was Charles one of those loose lovers?* Conway eyed Charles to see if there was any change in his demeanor.

"We'll need to track down who these lovers were. It's possible one of them wanted more than she did and things went horribly wrong." Conway jotted a note to have Nadine's phone records subpoenaed.

Stella stated otherwise, insisting that Nadine was very busy with her job and nothing seemed out of the ordinary. According to Stella, she was very career focused and had plans for a vacation next summer. She was always careful about locking her door. Nadine was fit and took nightly bike rides, which Stella reported warning her about. "I'm not sure if she ever listened to me?" Stella wondered. "I told her that nothing good happens being out after dark." Stella sighed and looked at the ground.

Margot gulped back sobs. "Nadine meant the world to me, and I just want her back." Tears choked her, and she couldn't stop their flow. She said she had nothing to tell Conway right now, but that she didn't know who could do this to her aunt. She asked again if he was sure it was Nadine. "Did you see her face?"

Conway said he would arrange for Stella to identify Nadine's body with the medical examiner's office, but right now, they had no reason to believe otherwise.

As the family rose to leave, Margot said, "I remember one thing. Nadine told me that a car was following her last week when she was riding her bike. She rode her bike down to the river most nights and she noticed a car, but she didn't give me a description."

"That's good. Now, if you remember anything else like that, big or small, I need to know. Even if you think it's mundane. Here's another card." Conway reached into his shirt pocket and grabbed one of his business cards, handing it to Margot. He watched as the family walked out. It could be a jilted lover. He had seen it before—a beautiful, professional woman who didn't want the advances of a man that would later succumb to his impulse for vengeance. Conway immediately requested a subpoena of Nadine's bank account and phone records. He wanted to see if there was any activity that would raise suspicion. *Paperwork is the shittiest part of police work,* Conway bitched to himself.

Next, Conway looked up the owner of Nadine's building to make them aware that a murder had occurred on their property. A St. Louis company, Elite Living, which was apparently buying up quite a few properties in Cape Ivy, had recently taken over the building. It did not impress Conway when outsiders came into town and tried to take over. They would probably tear down some of the older historic units. He hated new buildings; they were eyesores made with cheap materials. *Crappy ass mouse houses all over our city.*

"Thank you for calling Elite Living. This is Jameka. How may I assist you?"

"Hello, this is Detective Dan Conway with the Cape Ivy Police Department. I need to speak with someone about one of your residents at 755 Hanover Street, Apt. 3."

"Yes, sir. Let me look that up. Nadine Chastain lives there. I am the manager at Elite Living properties. Is there a problem I can help you with?"

"She's been the victim of a homicide. Her apartment is a crime scene, and it's now off-limits. Are you aware of any recent activity in her apartment?"

"Oh, my God. That's horrible. Does her family know?" Conway heard Jameka typing on her computer, probably to open the maintenance records. "I see she had a request a few months ago, in fact. Her air conditioner wasn't working, so we sent out Jack Moore, one of our maintenance workers, and he repaired it that same day," Jameka said.

"Can you have Jack contact me? I'll need to have him come down to my office to give a statement. We're ruling out anyone who's had contact with her in the recent past. I'd like to know if he saw anything while he was there, since it was just a few months ago."

"Absolutely. I'll call him now and give him the afternoon off to go down for an interview. In my ten years as an apartment manager, I've never experienced a murder."

Jameka immediately paged Jack to come to the office for an important message. She paced the office until he arrived, fidgeting with the rings on her fingers. Approximately thirty minutes later, Jack walked through the front door. The office frequently paged Jack and the other maintenance workers to handle emergencies. Maintenance requests never took time off. "Jack, I just received a call from Detective Conway. He's the lead homicide detective working on the murder of our tenant at 755 Hanover Street, Nadine Chastain. Do you remember fixing her air conditioner?" Jameka asked, not making eye contact.

Jack didn't hesitate to answer. "Of course I remember. Routine job. Nothing to it. Damn, homicide? That lady is dead?" He shifted his stance.

She stared at Jack and nodded. "Yes, she's dead. The detective needs you to go down to the station and give him an interview. He says he's interviewing anyone that was in her apartment within the last few months, just to see if you saw anything out of the ordinary."

"No shit. Hell, I have nothing to tell him. I went there and did my job and left. I ain't got nothing to say to a detective." Jack's voice raised a bit.

"I've given you the afternoon off so you can go down there." Jameka gave Jack Conway's phone number and told him she wanted to see him the next morning for an update. They'd need a plan to work with Nadine's family to clear out the apartment once the investigation was complete.

After he left the office, Jack checked his appearance in his visor. He had to calm down—his pupils showed his fury at his sloppiness. His features had filled out over the years; his Adam's apple was now more prominent, and his nose had grown so it protruded from his firm face. He kept his light hair cut short, nearly buzzed, and his blue eyes almost always looked dilated. Along the way to the station, he smoked four cigarettes and blasted his favorite rock channel. "Just tell them about the maintenance repair. That's all they need to know," he repeated to himself, advice he'd learned from Louie.

As he sat across from Conway, Jack's knee bounced up and down, while Conway shuffled a stack of papers.

"So Mr. Moore, I understand you're the maintenance worker who was called out to Nadine's apartment to fix an air conditioner. Is that correct?" Conway asked without glancing up from his notes.

"Yes," Jack said with a blank face.

"Can you tell me if you saw anything unusual during your visit?" Conway glanced up.

"No. It was routine," Jack said, fixing his eyes on Conway's second forehead wrinkle.

"Was the victim home during the time you were there?" Conway glanced at the clock on the wall.

"No."

"Have you ever met Nadine?"

"No."

"How long did it take to repair the cooling issue?" Conway asked, looking Jack in the eyes.

Jack took a little longer to answer this question. "All day."

"Was it a difficult job?" Conway still stared at Jack.

"Average. It's an older building, so it took longer," Jack said, relaxing his face.

Jack left the police station feeling confident that he hadn't given too much information away, but he knew he needed to be more careful in the future and delay his next kill. As Jack drove off, he saw Conway in his rearview mirror. The detective looked right back at him as he lit up a cigarette.

Fuck.

CHAPTER 19

2016

The night Nadine died was one of the best nights of Jack's life —a dream realized. He had been craving murder, and the opportunity had presented itself. In some ways, murder made him feel like he'd accomplished something he set his mind to; finally, his confidence and ability were in sync. He had a plan and followed it through, and it worked beautifully. He stared at the confined walls of his studio apartment and thought about his night with Nadine and how seamless it all went.

Jack had followed Nadine for a few months until he decided he knew her routine well enough. He tracked Nadine's bike riding route, down to the river and back, which usually took between thirty and sixty minutes. Then he'd watch her lights go out roughly an hour later, and he assumed she was asleep soon after. The only thing he wished was that he could see into her apartment like in the old days of his youth, peeping in to watch her movements, glimpsing her final days inside her home. But since Nadine was in the top-floor apartment, he could only use his imagination to picture what she was doing. On the night of her death, he waited until she went on her bike ride. Once she took off around the corner, he made his move.

The late summer air made for a majestic night for Jack as he scaled the stairs to Nadine's unit with his bag of destruction, packed with his specially constructed kill mask. Before he left the office, he'd grabbed Nadine's apartment key from the rack so he wouldn't need to break in. He wore gloves and protective foot gear as he entered her apartment and headed straight to the utility closet, which he had already scoped out. It was plenty big enough for him to sit down inside, and the door had slats so he could see out, but he wore a black mask, just in case she could see his face. Once he was comfortable inside the closet, he grew hungry for what was to come. It reminded him so much of the old shed of his childhood—it wasn't much bigger and was just as cramped, but it was his. He much preferred these smaller spaces to large open rooms and crowds. In tight quarters, he had more control.

Almost time. I'll be a legend after this; everyone will know about my mask.

Jack took slow, steady breaths. His heart was ready, racing so fast it was at maximum speed.

Jack remembered a valuable lesson from Louie: "Trust nothing with two legs. They can fire a gun between your eyes just as quickly as they tell you a lie or write you a love song." Louie had a lot of sayings, but now that the one person Jack trusted the most in this world was gone, he concealed his true self again. Besides, it was always better to have a few secrets just for yourself—like his taste for murdering women. That way, he never had to second guess who he could trust. There was also something sacred about having the knowledge of murder all to himself —the mask provided another level of the invisibility he relished.

Light bumps sounded outside on the stairwell, then a turn of the front door lock. Footsteps creaked closer. Jack was no longer alone, and he needed to remain as still as possible. The noise of water rushed along the wall to his back, which he recognized as the bathroom. She was taking a shower. He could breathe—his presence had gone unnoticed. The closet felt a little warmer. Maybe it was from the water heater, maybe it was from his adrenaline; he wasn't sure. He checked his watch too many times, as it felt like she stayed in the shower for an eternity.

Finally, the water shut off, and he waited to hear more sounds. He could hear hums and footsteps in the kitchen, a glass that touched the counter a little too hard, some liquid being poured, then footsteps heading toward the bedroom. He was glad this apartment had hardwood floors, so he could hear things like footsteps. Witnessing his victim's last moments gave him an extra jolt of pleasure. Jack could see the glow of a light that remained on, but it was in the far room in the corner, her bedroom, so he assumed she might be reading in bed. It wouldn't be much longer until he could strike.

Jack replayed his plan over and over in his head, imagining how he would approach the victim, how he would move. He planned to crawl out of the closet, keeping low to the ground so that no outside light would reveal him. He kept his weapon of choice, the choke mask, tucked in the front of his pants, readily available to slip out when he needed it. The trickiest part would be to raise up over the bed and aggressively slide the mask over her head. Jack knew it had to be done so quickly that the victim wouldn't have time to fight back or scream. He was at an advantage knowing she'd be in a deep sleep, as he'd wait to hear her make some sleeping noises. He'd turn her over onto her chest and pin his knee to her back, taking her breath away, ramming the mask over her head and fastening it tight around her skull. Jack had practiced on his own head. Of course, it wasn't the same at all, so this was an exciting and anxious trial. But he'd rehearsed it so many times in his mind that he felt so confident it had to work.

The bedroom light went out. It was 10 p.m., according to his watch. He wouldn't even consider making a move until well after 11. *I have to time this just right.* Jack decided if she woke up and caught him, he'd have to knock her unconscious and then kill her. He hoped it didn't come to that, because the thrill was in the slow death while she was awake, but he knew he needed to be prepared with a Plan B.

Eleven o'clock came, and he still felt that maybe it wasn't time yet. Plus, he couldn't hear any audible sleeping sounds, and he hoped for a sign. He didn't hear her toss, so he waited until midnight to be sure. His nerves were on fire, but not from fear—from the desire to experience his first mask kill. When he'd killed Paul, it was euphoric, but being drunk and having others present tainted the experience. This kill and the planning that had gone into it would be all his own to savor, and he just knew he'd get away with it.

When the time came, Jack was prepared. The moment felt absolutely perfect, his plans lining up like the luck of finding a rare Miami blue butterfly. Jack had been in the darkness for so long that when he left the closet, the moonlight was enough for him to see by. However, darkness and fear would blind his victim. He slithered his way toward Nadine's room. He heard no sounds except those from the street outside: distant tires on pavement, rustling leaves in trees, and the late-night honking of Canada geese flying overhead.

Crouching next to the bed, Jack could hear soft breathing as Nadine lay on her left side, which exposed her back to him. *This is perfect positioning,* Jack thought, as he slowly rose, mask in hand, and pounced on Nadine's back with such force he thought he might have heard a crack. He loved how her head violently slammed into the pillow and wished he could hear her neck crack, too. Jack marveled at the speed of his skill, at how smoothly the mask went over her head. He loved the sound of her whimpers from behind the mask and the feeling of her body squirming and fighting back.

Jack whipped her around and tightened the mask even more, fastening the second snap. He could hear her struggle to breathe and feel her wriggle as she tried to search her body for any bit of oxygen. He smiled at his work, marveling at his artistry. It was pure bliss holding her down, and he stared at what he had done. It had been a long time coming, fulfilling this dream he'd been pushing off for years.

For the last phase of his kill, he made use of the metal piece that he'd installed within the nose cavity. He bashed the metal section, breaking Nadine's nose, which allowed blood to flow down her nasal passage into her throat, choking her to death. Jack stood in awe over her as she struggled and watched the torture that he'd caused. He felt almost rapturous, perhaps finally understanding what the revivalists from his old church were talking about. He waited for Nadine's body to stop moving, turning limp and cold, while Jack's body was full of warmth and vitality.

After he checked Nadine's pulse, making sure she was dead, he grabbed his belongings and locked up the utility closet and the front door, careful not to leave any signs that he'd been there. He slowly inched out of her front door and checked that no one else was outside, but given the hour, he was alone. Safely in his car, he drove away from the scene and turned on his favorite rock music, banging his hands against the steering wheel to the beat. As he cruised down Broadway in a state of jubilation, propelled home by adrenaline and euphoria, Jack couldn't stop staring at himself in his side mirror.

You did it. You're a fucking killer. And your mask will be infamous.

CHAPTER 20
2019

Margot opened the door to both Gemma and Carter, who'd arrived simultaneously. Gemma brought some snacks as they found seats in Margot's quaint living room. "Sorry I don't have more furniture, but I wasn't sure how long I'd stay living here. Just grab a box and have a seat." Margot swung her arm toward her living room.

"I like it. It's very minimalist and good for keeping you on track with your goal." Carter looked over at Margot, who rolled her eyes at him.

"So, where do we begin? I want to go at your pace, Margot." Gemma's gaze was full of sympathy.

"I have to treat this like any other research subject. Don't worry about me. I'm prepared for this to get tough," Margot said, taking a deep breath.

The group was meeting ahead of Margot's speech with Dr. Williams. Although Margot's TV interview had gone fairly well, this would be in front of a live audience of strangers, which was a foreign experience for her. Those eyes staring back at her was an uncomfortable familiarity she'd learned to live with.

"OK, let us know if we need a break. First, we need to discuss your aunt. We need to know all the details of her murder and anything that the police have found," Gemma said as she wrote some notes.

"You found her, Margot? Do you feel up to telling us how that went down?" Carter asked, taking a sip of water.

"Um, yes. I'm ready. Let's just dive in," Margot said as a slow trickle of tears began falling faster. "I feel so guilty." Margot bawled, pushing her head into her hands.

"Margot, why would you feel guilty? This wasn't your fault." Gemma creased her brows.

Margot just shook her head as her lips trembled at the image of Nadine's lifeless body. The tears felt hot against her cold skin, but they provided no warmth to Margot's mood.

"I went over there like usual and used the key she gave me. I was immediately hit with the most awful smell I've ever smelled in my life as I walked through the front door I've crossed so many times before. Decayed death is the best way to describe it. Somehow I just knew it was death, even though I'd never experienced it before. It sticks to the inside of your nose and days later you get a whiff when you least expect it," Margot said, rubbing her arms.

Gemma nodded and took a deep breath.

"Margot, I can't imagine," Carter slowly shook his head.

"The living room was pitch-black. It was a cloudy day. No sunlight was coming through the closed blinds, so it was impossible to see anything once the front door shut. I couldn't find anything to prop it open, so I tried to find my way in the dark. My reflexes were jumpy, like someone was in there with me—I was unsure if they were behind or in front of me. I lost track of where I was in the room and quickly ran toward where I thought a wall was, feeling all around for the light switch."

Margot had heard her own voice yell out, "Nadine?" but she heard no return response—just an eerie silence where life used to happen. She'd fumbled for a light switch that she struggled to locate. Once she hit the switch, it finally illuminated a still room. Nothing was out of place in the Parisian-themed apartment that Nadine had loved so much, carefully decorated with antiques picked up on her travels.

"Once I turned the light on, I spun around and saw the living room furniture I've seen so many times before. Nothing looked moved or messed with."

"What was going through your mind?" Gemma asked.

"I was terrified, but I had to know if Nadine was inside. I moved closer to the bedroom, first through the kitchen, and with each step, the smell got stronger."

Margot had coughed sharply as the stench permeated deeper with each step. She reached the kitchen bar and found the two barstools that she knew well. She and Nadine would often sit there and eat pizza and cookies and anything else they'd cook, chatting about boys and life. Margot never laughed or cried more in her life than at that bar, like the time she talked about her first heartbreak, when her first love dumped her for her "best friend." Or when they laughed hysterically about childhood stories of her mom, Stella, and her yearbook pictures with braces and frizzy hair.

As she stood at the closed bedroom door, Margot could taste the beating heartbeat that made its way up her throat. She was nervous to find what was on the other side but hopeful the smell wasn't from her aunt but something her brain couldn't quite process at the moment. A wave of stomach flutters overcame Margot when she opened the door and the foul smell became even stronger. She instinctively covered her mouth and nose. She struggled to find the light switch to the eerily dark room, feeling all over the wall. Finally, light illuminated the room, revealing the horrific reason for the appalling smell.

Gemma massaged her temples, reached into her purse, and removed a small white pill she popped into her mouth, followed by water.

"I saw my aunt on the bed with a mask covering her head. I lost my breath—I couldn't speak and could barely breathe. It felt like I was inside a wind tunnel with my brain both telling me to run and get help, but also to run toward her and check on her. Fight or flight was tugging me in both directions, and fight won at first. I ran to Nadine. It scared me to touch her, but when I did, she was cold. There was no life left in her. When I saw the mask up close, that's when flight won and I took off running outside, unsure if whoever did this to her was still inside. I thought I could be next." Margot stared off to the side before continuing. "After I called my house, my mom and dad arrived shortly afterwards. As we walked back through the apartment, I felt like I would be sick. The adrenaline helped with the smell the first time, but now it made my stomach turn. I kept breathing quick breaths. I needed to make sure it was Nadine, but I already knew it was her. My mom attempted to remove the mask, but it wouldn't budge. She yanked so hard it made Nadine's entire head move up and down. I yelled at her, 'Stop, you're hurting her!'" Margot covered her eyes briefly to shield the image in her memory. Gemma and Carter moved closer to Margot with a similar expression of pity.

"But my mom looked at me and said, 'She's already gone, Margot.' My dad grabbed me and tried to take me outside, away from Nadine, but I broke free and lunged toward her. But my dad was faster than me and tackled me to the ground, eventually carrying me outside to the car, where I wailed. I cried huge sobs from the bottom of my stomach. I was gutted. All I could do was watch the police eventually show up and wheel Nadine's body away under a sheet on a gurney. I don't wish that fate on anyone," Margot said, gulping back painful tears.

Gemma reached for some tissues and handed them over to Margot.

Margot had been having nightmares of Nadine's lifeless body, with a mask covering her face. Only, in her nightmares, she could remove the mask and see Nadine's face all battered and bloodied. Sometimes Nadine was alive and gasping for air, her face revealing a distorted and bruised image. The nightmares weren't nightly, but strong enough to make Margot fear going to sleep. But even as the nightmares had since subsided, the grief was still present. Margot often choked on suppressed tears, but she was grateful to have friends and an audience to share Nadine's story. She found comfort in their presence, especially Gemma, who could understand the profound sadness that came with murder. When she lived away from Cape Ivy, she found it easier to separate herself from those raw emotions.

Cape Ivy had a way of bringing bottled-up feelings to the riverfront surface.

Patience wasn't Jack's best quality, but murder required it. He was itching for his next kill, and he already had someone in mind: Jameka. When Jack thought back to speaking with her the day he'd met with Conway, he was a mixture of nerves and rage. He wasn't happy with how Jameka had spoken to him, and he'd had the urge to kill her right there in the office—she deserved a hammer to her head. However, he knew it wouldn't be the right place, with too many people coming and going. It was best to stick with his plan, as he quite enjoyed the slow kill the mask provided. But if Jameka continued to give him orders, he'd gladly give her the mask treatment—no woman would dominate him. *The way she glares and talks down to me needs to stop.* Jack thought about how his interview with Conway had gone, and he debated just pleading the Fifth next time, but he knew that would be stupid. He wasn't an official suspect, and that would make him look suspicious and guilty. He knew he needed to answer the questions without looking flustered.

Jack felt confident in his skills of elusion, but he didn't enjoy talking to cops on this side of the table. He told himself to toughen up. *I'm a murderer, for fuck's sake.* It embarrassed him he wasn't calmer and his nervousness came with shame. But Jack hadn't prepared to be in front of a cop answering questions so soon. He was much more accustomed to speaking with his "other" cop friends, who discussed how to avoid legal matters. Jack noticed Conway seemed preoccupied, which put him at ease and, based on his questioning, he got the impression he wasn't being considered a suspect. Jack thought of Louie's words. "If a cop ever pulls you over or interviews you, you have the upper hand on him. He wants info out of you. Keep silent or, if you gotta talk, only tell a little. The more you give, the less power you have." That was precisely what Jack had done, and Conway hadn't seemed the least bit interested in him. Success.

After meeting with Detective Conway, Jack realized he needed to select his next victim differently. With Nadine, he'd chosen her because of her maintenance request, at random. But he couldn't risk being the same maintenance person for each murder. He believed this time he'd eluded the detective, but if his name kept coming up, it would become a real problem. He would still find victims through the apartment setting, as he had access to all of their keys. Keys just waiting for a killer to take and find his way inside the comfort of his victims' homes.

Naturally, Nadine's murder erupted the terror that had been buried since the last killer. Gloom covered Cape Ivy as murder returned. Jack had to be satisfied with Nadine's murder as it would be months if not years before he could claim a new victim. Jack had it all planned out and felt like he'd already outsmarted Conway, though he couldn't escape all the lawmen that would litter Elite Living for the foreseeable future, as a murdered white woman was their top priority. Murderous desire filled Jack's thoughts with the memory of his last kill, which had to suffice for quite some time. Cape Ivy was still suffering from another murderer's spree, so the foundation wasn't firm enough for a new killer—the filled cracks opened wide, showing grief and despair.

Once he believed he was in the clear with Nadine's murder, he felt comfortable returning to his stalker ways to locate his next victim the old-fashioned way—by hunting them down. He rather liked this idea better, as it reminded him of his old peeping days, where he could pursue his victim based on how easy a prey they would make. As soon as he killed a second woman in an apartment setting, it would create a pattern. But he felt very confident that avoiding taking maintenance requests in any of the units would help him avoid being considered a suspect. The longer Jack had to wait, his appetite to kill grew hungrier each day.

CHAPTER 22

2019

True crime took its toll on Margot mentally and physically, but there was nothing else in this world she'd have rather been doing. Margot stood up to stretch and get a drink. Her study session with Gemma and Carter was rough, but she slept better that night than she had in ages. Next month, she would have her presentation with Dr. Williams, which still seemed surreal. *A pioneer in the true crime world wants to hear me speak,* Margot thought on loop. Margot's excitement over having Dr. Williams learn more about Nadine was consuming. *Maybe she'll hear the details and give me pointers on what type of man could do this.* At least then Margot would know what direction to look in.

A strong wind knocked a twig into the window of her living room. Startled, Margot nearly dropped her glass. She turned on the television to get her mind off of murder for a bit, although even there she couldn't escape the numerous crime-related TV shows. That's when she saw the image of Loni Smart, who stood outside the news station on Broadway Boulevard. She wore a black blazer with a navy satin camisole underneath, and the wind blew her brown hair, styled in a long pixie cut, in all directions. Margot could immediately tell that something serious was happening by Loni's intense face. Then she saw the breaking news scroll flash. Loni stated, "Police say they found Becky Conrad in her apartment, deceased, with a mask covering her head. Authorities report it appears Cape Ivy has a repeat offender, who is now being called the Choke Mask Killer." The Choke Mask Killer Strikes Again kept scrolling at the bottom of the screen.

This time, Margot's glass fell to the floor, tiny shards flying in every direction. In the back of her mind, she'd thought the killer might have died or moved. Now she knew he breathed the same hot air as her.

CHAPTER 23
2019

Uniforms and badges littered the Elite Living properties for the first few months after Nadine's death and slowly faded to a handful after the first year. They thoroughly vetted the staff, including Jack, and he was keenly aware of the eyes of the enemy staring at him as he worked. As much as he loved the power of murder, he hated the collapse of control.

They're always fucking watching me. I should give them a show.

Jack hated the prying eyes of the law—of anyone, for that matter. It reminded him of being watched by Sandy and Kathy, or being at church. He no longer wanted to be corrected, especially by a woman.

The cops found no leads after Nadine's murder, but Cape Ivy police remained on site to canvas the area and perform routine patrols. However, their investigation stayed open with no suspects. Initially, Elite Living hired off-duty police to patrol the units, but without a suspect, their investigation grew stale. Management asked the maintenance department to complete regular security checks as life went back to normal.

"We will have every on-call maintenance worker patrol the Elite Living community when they aren't working at an apartment. That way, we'll always have someone on watch. But let's hope that this murder is solved quickly and Cape Ivy women are safe again," Jameka announced during a staff meeting.

Perfect. Now I'll have a reason to be out at night. It will give me more time to stalk my next victim.

Several days later, on a routine plumbing call, Jack spotted her. The woman, who he later learned was named Becky, captured his attention because she looked very much like his mom. It stopped him in his tracks. She had the same body shape, shoulder-length dark hair parted down the middle, and a prominent jawline as Sandy. If anyone saw him, they'd think he was smitten with her because he stared at her like she was the most beautiful woman he'd ever seen. But through Jack's eyes, it meant she was an impeccable target. He observed Becky leaving her car wearing hospital scrubs, walking to a second-story apartment and carrying a grocery bag. Jack flexed his fists as his building rage made him want to kill her with his bare hands. His right eye twitched and his teeth gnawed as he walked back toward his car, turned up his rock music, and lit a cigarette. His heart raced a little less as he smoked a second cigarette, waiting until he was calm enough to return to his job. She had to be his next victim; she just looked so much like his mom. He wanted to go up to her apartment and choke her out now, but the wait and eventual killing would be worth it. Just imagining she was his mom would be a bit of sweet revenge.

Jack found stalking Becky pretty easy, as she lived in the same complex as he did, but on the farthest end from him. He couldn't see her unit from his, but if he sat in his car at night, no one would question it, since he was a resident there as well. Jack often sat in his car at night, smoking cigarettes. He watched the clueless tenants walk by. He was a figure in a dark night with only the glow of his cigarette butt giving away his presence if anyone dared to look close enough.

Once he figured out Becky's work schedule, which was a typical nine-to-five, he snuck her key from the board at the main office. Management kept all the residents' keys hanging on a hook inside Jameka's office, so all Jack had to do was snatch Becky's when no one was looking. He planned to play dumb if he ever got caught and say he accidentally grabbed the wrong one, which was easy to do since the keys didn't list the tenant's name, just the corresponding number of the tenant's unit. Other workers had done it, arriving at a site only to find they'd grabbed the wrong key.

Jack checked his surroundings as he walked into Becky's apartment. He found it to be unkempt. It was walkable, but the countertops and tables were full of trash, mostly discarded fast food boxes and bags and papers strewn all over. Wrinkled scrubs littered the living room, open boxes full of dishes and books she'd never unpacked lined the kitchen, and stacks of magazines sat by her bed. From the looks of it, she probably hadn't cleaned or organized since she moved in last year. There was no sign of a man or family, with no pictures or evidence of friends. It appeared she went to work, then came home—a true loner, which Jack could relate to. Her apartment had a slight odor, likely from her trash not being thrown out routinely, which Jack thought would make for a rough night waiting in the utility closet. He checked out the closet space and found it to be plenty big for him to wait in on the big night. He made plans to murder her after a few more weeks of stalking.

Planning for this kill excited him in a different way—it felt almost personal. He knew another murder would create hysteria in Cape Ivy, which could make this his favorite murder yet.

CHAPTER 24

2019

Becky was used to a solitary lifestyle. As she made the thirty-minute drive home from the hospital, she listened to country music and replayed the day's events, doubting some of her decisions. Becky had always second-guessed herself, ever since she was little. The lifelong inner voice that told her she was never good enough only got louder as she aged, heightening her fear of making a life-or-death mistake while working in the medical field. She never considered her own health or well-being and always put others before herself, which was one reason she ran to food as a comfort. She didn't feel confident in her own skin, and she believed patients questioned her abilities. *Who would listen to a nurse's advice about health when my own is at risk?*

Once home, she climbed the flight of stairs to her apartment. When she signed the lease, she'd made a conscious choice to pick the second story. She thought it would help her tone up by forcing her to get some exercise anytime she walked up those stairs to get to her place. Within a month of moving in, she already regretted the decision and planned to move once her lease was up. Unfortunately, there were very few housing options closer to work, so she had to make a longer commute than she preferred.

She threw down her bags of groceries and plopped into her kitchen chair before rummaging through the bags for a snack. Chips were her favorite—any flavor would do—and she munched on a few before putting the rest of the food away. She looked around at her messy place, vowing to clean it one day. *I really need to straighten this mess up before I become a full-fledged hoarder,* she thought to herself. But today wasn't that day; she didn't have the energy after being on her feet for most of it as a nurse. She had always been exceptional at science in school, and she loved her profession. Her patients often remarked on her pleasant bedside manner, and it always brightened her day. Yet she still assumed that her patients would doubt her authority as soon as she left the room. She watched as their eyes moved from her face down to the rest of her body. Some looks were more subtle than others, which she could appreciate, but all of them hurt. Her body's added barrier of protection had the complete opposite effect. She wasn't able to camouflage her figure amid other colleagues who were fit and thin.

She unwrapped the large frozen supreme pizza and placed it in the hot oven, setting the timer for twenty minutes and hurrying to get in the shower before the buzzer went off. As she rushed back with just a towel wrapped around her hair, she ignored the "healthy eating" reminder held on the refrigerator by sunshine and rainbow magnets and grabbed the pizza out of the oven to let it cool off while she put on her pajamas.

Becky's nightly routine was just that: routine. After arriving home, she made dinner, showered, ate, watched TV, read, and then went to bed. Her life was borderline boring to most people, but she didn't have any social outlets. She had been fodder for bullies all the way through high school, considered a loner throughout. She'd contemplated killing herself or quitting school in favor of her GED, but her mom wouldn't allow her to drop out, so she continued her education and ate her emotions. Things improved somewhat after school once she saw a therapist and started college. She still didn't trust anyone enough to form friendships, but she engaged in school activities with classmates she would call "acquaintances." Although she enjoyed the camaraderie of working with her classmates on assignments, she never spoke to any of them again after the activities were over. Becky had one "real" boyfriend after college, but he forced himself on her one night and all the progress she had made began to backslide, her food addiction picking up in full force. The assault brought up experiences from her past that she had tried to move past, but she realized she had just suppressed them.

Startled by a ringing phone, Becky reluctantly answered. It was her sister Kelly, calling with some family updates. "Hey, Kelly. What's going on?"

"Well, I'm getting divorced and Mom is going into a nursing home. I guess you don't really care about those things, but it's my duty to let you know, I suppose."

"Wait, you're getting divorced? I assumed Mom was heading toward a nursing home. It's really hard to care for patients who've had a stroke in their own home. They require 24/7 support and a nursing home can give her the oversight she requires—" Kelly cut Becky off before she could finish.

"Yeah, we figured that out. Mom fell again, so we decided that was the final straw. She's at River Manor Care, if you ever wanted to visit her."

Becky stared at the ceiling. "I'll think about it. Mom and I haven't spoken in years and I don't have a relationship with her or care to resolve our differences right now."

"Well, I hope you don't regret that, Becky." Kelly always added an extra emphasis on the last syllable of Becky's name, so it sounded like *Beck-eeee*.

"Why are you getting divorced?" Becky asked, staring at the muted television as contestants struggled to solve an easy crossword puzzle.

"Oh, Brock cheated on me. Apparently he likes brunettes now. I'm moving on. I'm seeing my boss. My next husband will be for money. Screw love."

"Oh, yeah? Good for you. I hope that works out for you. Anyway, I need to get ready for bed."

"It's 6 p.m., Becky. Just say you don't want to talk next time." Click.

Becky decided she might just let Kelly's future phone calls go straight to voicemail to avoid the negativity that always came with them. Her family caused most, if not all, of her trauma. Her sister had always been the favored one—skinny and pretty.

When Becky was five, the molestation by her maternal uncle began. At first it was just tickling. She thought they were playing, and she enjoyed the extra attention he gave her. The family all loved Uncle Michael, but eventually he would call her into her closet and tell her he had a secret, whispering, "You're my favorite niece. Now close the door. I have a gift for you." That's when his penis became the gift she never wanted. Of course, his whispers turned into threats if she ever told, which terrified and humiliated her.

Becky's mom invited Uncle Michael over often for every family event, Christmas, and birthday, so she could never escape him. Becky ate to forget her pain and believed it would make her less attractive to him. It didn't work, but food tasted so good and gave her a sense of control over what went into her mouth. She found the courage to tell her mom at fifteen, but her mom ridiculed her and called her a liar and a whore. "No brother of mine would ever do that to a child, especially his own niece." She took his side and never once considered that Becky was telling the truth.

Ever since that day, there'd been a wedge between them, but realistically, she was always the black sheep because she was so obese as a child. She wasn't naturally pretty or petite, like her sister, who always denied being molested. Becky wondered why Uncle Michael picked her over her sister, not that she'd want her sister to suffer that fate. But she'd never fit in with her family, and maybe a predator could sense the weak link or the oddball in the group—the one who never belonged with the others, who they deemed the "disposable" one. Kelly relished her role as the golden daughter after Becky's "big lie," as it became known. She went along with the teasing both at home and at school and never once took Becky's side, which Becky could never forgive and certainly never forget. Kelly often told her to "apologize for making it up," but Becky would much rather disown her entire family and consider herself an orphan.

Per usual after a family call or visit, Becky sensed the negative haze working its way into her system. She reached for her nearest therapy, which meant ice cream today. Instant but fleeting gratification was calling her name. It briefly quieted that looming tear. Becky unmuted the TV, which helped to temporarily free her mind from the pain caused by her sister's words. She had no desire to visit her mom or her sister. Becky wanted to move on from the pain, but the trauma that her family put her through was too much for her to accept. She'd change her name, run away, and take on a new identity if she could, but she didn't have the courage for that. *Maybe I'll just change my phone number.*

Next year, once her lease was up, she planned to move without giving anyone her new address. Her family didn't need to contact her for anything. If her mom died, they'd handle it. They wouldn't need her input, and she wanted nothing from her mom's estate. As she went to bed that night, she felt more at peace with a clearer goal for the future. The idea of cutting ties with her family empowered her. After they all turned their backs on her, she would give them the middle finger, letting them know she didn't need them anymore. She fell asleep feeling much more in control, with less worry and more hope for the future—until a few hours later, when something took away all of her control. Becky found herself trapped in a mask, unable to breathe, unable to fight, panicked for her last breath, wishing for someone—anyone—to save her. But just like with her Uncle Michael, no one came to save her, and she died gasping for air, choking on blood, not in her closet, but in her own bed.

CHAPTER 25
2019

Margot rushed into the library and found Gemma, who immediately stood when she approached. "Margot! How are you doing? I wasn't sure if you'd come today with all the breaking news."

"I'm numb, but this just solidifies that whoever killed my aunt is back at it." Margot narrowed her eyes.

"True. Unless it's a copycat." Gemma twisted her lips.

Margot raised her eyebrows. "Either way, we have a killer who needs to be stopped. Are you in?"

"Can I help?" Carter asked as he dropped his backpack onto the table.

"Did you hear the news? The killer has struck again! The news is calling him the Choke Mask Killer," Gemma said, twisting the ring on her finger.

"What the fuck? No, I haven't heard that. Who, where, what?"

"They haven't released all the details, but the news reported that they found a woman dead in her apartment with a mask over her head. That totally fits my aunt's murder."

"It's all over *Death Toll*. How have you not seen the coverage?" Gemma scowled at Carter.

"I've been…busy. I've been preparing for the TA position interview and haven't had time for much else. My gut says I'm out of the running." Carter sulked. "But I'm here to help now. Operation Arrest the Bastard? Are you ready, ladies?"

Margot glared. "OK, I'll give you that title."

Carter saluted Margot and winked at Gemma.

"You're lame," Gemma muttered.

The group compiled an outline of what they knew so far. Since Becky's murder had just happened, they didn't know much about her personal life—only what they'd heard on the news.

"Two women, living alone, found dead in their beds with a mask," Gemma said.

Margot shuddered. "Yes, that's right." Her mind drifted to the side of Nadine's bed.

"It says here that Becky didn't have a boyfriend, and she was basically estranged from her family," Carter read aloud from KFCI-13's website.

"How sad. Hopefully, they can find a connection and a name that associates him with Nadine, too." Margot stared off, thinking of her own estrangement with her parents.

"What if the victims willingly allowed their killer into their home? I was just reading about a killer dubbed the Cable Guy who was a former cop from Florida and later became a TV installer. What if it's someone like that? Someone that people invite inside because they're providing some type of service?" Gemma said.

"That could be possible. Neither apartment had signs of a break-in, which means they were either let in or the killer had keys," Carter chimed in.

Margot paused as a couple of students walked by, lowering her voice. "These ideas are better than what we have now: a wronged lover gone rogue." Margot sighed. She wasn't feeling hopeful about the jilted lover theory.

Once the group disbanded, Margot floated all the possibilities they had come up with. She closed her eyes before she opened her car door, breathing in the wafting fumes of Dino's Pizza near the Ivy University campus. Margot's thoughts snapped back to the present moment at the sound of loud applause as the Redhawks scored a touchdown.

CHAPTER 26
2019

Murder had gone smoothly for Jack. After his latest victim, he felt he had perfected his kill. He wondered if all killers found committing their crimes this easy, or if they struggled—personally, his confidence was growing each time. With Paul, it was sweet revenge. His death had fulfilled a childhood fantasy that Louie wasn't able to help him with, but Jack relished beating Paul all on his own.

After Louie's death, Jack felt an emptiness without his confidante. He no longer spoke with Officer Glenn or Corey, as he never considered them to be part of his own inner circle. *It's better to be alone and keep my savage desires inside.*

Occasionally, he'd hear about the Choke Mask Killer on the news or at work, as management was in a frenzy with phone calls from frantic tenants wanting to flee their dwellings and yet never leave the safety of home. He absolutely loved his killer moniker and knew the next murder would only solidify the tension and fear that had settled in Cape Ivy. Jack learned to stay chill and keep to himself without giving rise to any of the chatter about the threat to their serenity. Jack always had an apathetic stare—some might say he was brooding—and his face gave no indication that he knew anything about the deaths. He was a man of few words and rarely listened to any reports about the murders, as he just didn't give a fuck what people had to say about him. Early on, he'd learned to keep to himself and follow his own lead.

Becky's murder heightened Jack's euphoria because she looked like Sandy, which made him more ravenous. Jack had savored his kill differently this time. He knew what to expect, so he could relax and take his time.

After killing Becky, he'd imagined for a moment that it was his mom, Sandy. *I must be fucking hallucinating. This bitch looks like my mom and I just want to laugh in her dead face.* Jack stood over Becky's body longer than he'd intended, but this kill felt personal. *I want to scream, but I'd wake the entire fucking neighborhood.* He entered her apartment before she arrived home from work, making sure that any potential prying eyes were diverted. As he sat in the cramped utility closet, he listened as she set the timer on the oven for her frozen pizza and could hear her watching a game show before receiving a phone call. He heard her crying after the call ended, but she uttered no words. Just like with Nadine, he made his move once she fell asleep, and now the kill lived in his sweet memories.

In the weeks that followed Becky's murder, the cops and press were all over the apartments. Conway didn't interview Jack this time, but he knew he needed to lie low for a while. He did his best to avoid the microphones of the various news stations that flooded the complex and just kept his head down and focused on his job.

But he always kept one eye open for his next victim.

CHAPTER 27

2019

Margot needed some caffeine, so she spent her afternoon at the Soy Nook, which had a mix of pastries, mini sandwiches, and fancy coffees, plus a variety of books. There was an intimate patio seating area out back where she took her almond hazelnut latte and the empty journal she'd brought to write some notes for her upcoming panel with Dr. Williams next week. Though she already had her talking points outlined, she wanted to be prepared for any questions or last-minute thoughts. It was a perfect day, with a light breeze, chirping sparrows nibbling for sandwich droppings, and sunshine peeking through the willow trees.

"Margot?" a deep male voice asked.

Margot looked up from her journal to see a guy who immediately mesmerized her, handsome with chocolate eyes, olive skin, and dark brown hair that lightly swept down onto his forehead. Maybe the coffee was strong here, but she found herself entranced by this man. She noticed his muscular hands as he reached out to shake hers. "Hi, I'm Lucas. I recognized you and just had to meet you. I'm so sorry about your aunt, but I admire what you're doing to keep her name alive."

"Oh, thanks. Yeah, I hope my efforts pay off." Margot turned back to her journal.

"I'm so sorry to bother you. I'm a current student of Dr. Williams, so I know you have a big speech soon, but when I saw you here, I wanted to introduce myself. As her new teaching assistant, I hope I'll get to learn more about the case," he said, grinning as his gaze darted around her face, landing on her eyes.

His voice was the perfect amount of deep, yet soft and sensuous at the same time. She wondered if she was floating, but when she tapped her feet, they were still on the ground.

"Thank you. And congratulations on the new job," Margot said, clearing her throat, which suddenly felt dry. *Should I break the news to Carter or just play dumb?*

The sound of a chair dragging over the concrete patio interrupted the quiet.

"It's serendipitous that I ran into you. You could say I'm in the business of true crime and caught your interview on KFCI-13." Lucas smiled, and Margot immediately felt her cheeks flush. Maybe the sun was getting to her. "Having your identity exposed on *Death Toll* had to be difficult."

"Oh, my manners. You can sit down." She pointed to the empty chair. "I figured since someone exposed me, I might as well make use of my new fame. But I'd definitely have preferred to stay hidden for longer," Margot said, fiddling with her empty coffee cup.

"Margot, you're doing amazing," Lucas said, staring into her eyes as if he was trying to hypnotize her.

Margot tried to avert her eyes from his. "Thanks. I guess if they catch this killer, I can finally rest." Margot looked down at her fingernails, which she had meant to trim.

Silence fell between them, with Margot's eyes darting between Lucas and the words in her journal.

"Do you have a minute? After watching you, I think it's time I reveal my past. I admire your courage to be so open, and I'd like to express that same spirit," he said with a pained expression.

Oh God, please don't be a murderer. Margot glanced toward the French doors to freedom.

"I'm all ears if you want to share." She immediately felt stupid for using the expression, which sounded like something a dad would say.

"Well, I went into criminal justice because of what happened to my older sister. Someone kidnapped and murdered her before I was born, and it's haunted the walls of my house for years. You could say I felt pulled to go into this line of work so that I can do my part in protecting families. Which is why I really support all that you're doing," Lucas said with furrowed brows.

Margot immediately gasped. "I'm so sorry," was all she could muster.

"Thank you." Lucas put his hand over his chest. "We have some things in common because my sister's case remains unsolved to this day." He cleared his throat.

Margot knew the pain of the long wait for justice. A wave of sympathy overcame her. "Oh, no. I'm sure the grief never left your parents." Margot frowned.

"No. They had her picture framed everywhere, but we weren't supposed to talk about it. It was an unspoken rule. But I guess I think it's more important to be vocal about what's happened to us. There are various ways to deal with grief, and I like how you're not hiding from it."

"Don't forget I stayed hidden for a couple of years! The grief is miserable, but the not knowing is just as bad. The agony of learning another woman likely died at the same hands as my aunt is over-whelming. Can I ask what led up to your sister's disappearance?" Margot creased her brows.

"My sister, Sierra, was four years old when someone kidnapped and murdered her. Crystal, our neighborhood babysitter, invited her boyfriend over and when he left, my sister was gone."

"How awful," Margot slowly shook her head.

"I sometimes feel bad that I don't hold the same level of grief. It would be different if I grew up with her, but I only knew her from the pictures on the wall." Lucas shrugged. "My life has always been as the child that was born to heal his parents from their agony."

"Again, I'm so sorry. Your parents' grief has filled your life, and you couldn't escape that." Margot leaned in, putting her hand on the table near Lucas's.

"Yeah. It was pretty dark sometimes. I had to watch what I said, or at least I thought I should. I never wanted to make my parents upset. The ghost of my sister sat at the corners of our house as a reminder to my parents of what they lost."

"Ugh. That is so sad." Margot paused and Nadine's image, alive and vibrant, flashed through her mind.

Lucas nodded and ran his hand through his wavy hair. "When Crystal went to check on Sierra, she was gone—no sign of her anywhere. When my parents arrived home, Crystal was in a panic. They all searched every inch of the house, every closet and under the beds, the shower, everywhere, but, again, there was no sign. They went outside and yelled, waking up several neighbors, who eventually joined in the search."

"Such a devastating and desperate feeling," Margot said.

"News media got involved, and it became a big event for our area —the town of Hickory, Tennessee was now on the map." Lucas took a deep breath. "Search crews convened on the anniversary of her disappearance and two years later, they found her remains in an abandoned barn two miles outside of town."

Margot shook her head in sympathy, unsure of what to say. She was used to the awkwardness of people trying to comfort her with words. Being on the other side was a novelty to her.

"The town gossip was that Sierra woke up while Crystal was with Ethan and wandered outside, where a neighbor or passerby abducted her. Ethan was a prime suspect from the start, but the police couldn't connect him to the crime," Lucas concluded, rocking back in his chair.

Margot was stunned. She had never heard of this case, not that she would have. Thousands of cases just like this occurred every year in America.

"I can't believe that happened to you. What an awful way to grow up with that death keeping your household in perpetual mourning."

"Thank you, Margot. Honestly, that's why I love your story. You returned to Cape Ivy and are doing what you need to find your aunt's killer," Lucas said, lightly pounding his fist on the table.

Margot knew from her own experience that a murder in the family completely shifted everyone's life. It could take years to regain the strength to walk on the newly paved path. She realized the last drops of her coffee had long since gone cold and the breakfast menu had turned into lunch. It was time to head back home.

"Please, allow me to walk you out," Lucas insisted.

OK, I think I can trust him, Margot thought, letting her guard down.

As they walked toward her car, Margot admired a church with Gothic architecture, complete with gargoyles looking out at her and statues of saints blessing them on their way. It had to be a sign that they, too, thought Lucas was impressive. At the end of the street corner, Margot awkwardly parted with Lucas by waving goodbye as he moved closer to give her a hug. With her hand wedged in between their chests, Margot thought, *I'm so out of practice. Why am I so awkward?*

CHAPTER 28

2019

The reprieve Cape Ivy had enjoyed was temporary, as Jack was fully invested in returning to murder.

Months after Becky's murder, the people of Cape Ivy once again believed they had eluded the killer's grasp as they resumed their mundane activities. Perhaps he had died, they probably thought, been locked up in prison, or given up his ways. But Jack had just decided on the next apartment complex he'd search for his next victim, which was on the north end of the city in an area full of shops and walking trails. There were many stores, including a grocery chain, restaurants, pet shops, and clothing boutiques. It was part of the *Make Cape Ivy Greener* project that mostly consisted of drab concrete structures, which wasn't lost on a good deal of townspeople. They designed a beautiful stone waterfall leading into the new shopping center that was often taken over by a few mallard ducks going for a quick swim. Less than a mile away from the new shopping center was Elite Living's newest contemporary apartment community, complete with laminate wood floors, stainless appliances, and state-of-the-art landscaping. It was the most modern apartment the company offered. Jack liked them because they were new and didn't have too many maintenance problems, but especially because their utility closets were the nicest, as they were roomier than the other ones.

Maintenance calls at these apartments were rare, but because the units were new, they needed paint and appliances installed before being rented, so Jack spent a lot of time working alone there, blasting his favorite local rock station on his radio. That was when he saw his next victim leaving her home—an older woman with short, salt-and-pepper hair and wire-rim glasses, who wore a badge from a local grocery store and walked alone on the trail. He liked her place because it was along the back side of the parking lot, facing the walking trail, so there would be plenty of privacy for him to enter and exit. Of course, he needed to make sure she lived alone, but he had several new units to paint and could follow her routine just like the others, making sure he saw no one else enter or leave her apartment. Satisfied with his surveillance, he planned his next attack, eager to resume his killing skills.

———

Reading glasses, a Danielle Steel book, and a bottle of hand lotion filled the nightstand. She had few pictures and fewer clothes, and her apartment looked like no one actually lived in it, except for the small antenna TV and quilt on her bed. Jack observed some mail on her dresser that let him know her name was Deborah. There were pictures of her with other smiling faces on horses. Her twin bed looked like a raft in an ocean within the primary bedroom, as there wasn't any other furniture to fill out the rest of the room. As Jack walked around, he could hear a slight echo as the tall ceilings offered better acoustics than the older units.

After he felt confident in Deborah's routine, Jack knew it was time to make his move. She was always on time except for her occasional stops to chat with dog owners on the trail that led from the grocery store where she worked right to her apartment. Jack had often observed her petting the dogs and stopping to greet them, although he was grateful she didn't have one herself.

Jack painstakingly planned the night Deborah died, just like he had with the others. He walked by her apartment windows to watch her nighttime routine, which ended earlier than the other two. He did a trial run by spending the night inside the closet and listened to reports about his case as she watched the local news. "Loni Smart reporting. The police are still searching for leads in the unsolved cases of the Choke Mask Killer. Cape Ivy Detective Dan Conway has asked the public to contact his office with any relevant information."

Soon to be a new victim.

After flawlessly executing his plan to kill Deborah, Jack left as he came in, albeit much happier and filled with a sense of accomplishment. He breathed in the fresh air from the pine trees surrounding the apartment and considered moving to this side of Cape Ivy.

I like dogs.

CHAPTER 29
2019

Margot walked on stage to applause she could have never dreamed of after that July day. It was like walking on a balance beam as she approached the gray tweed chair set out for her next to one for Dr. Williams. Fear and dedication pulled her in opposite directions as she heard her own heeled footsteps in the vast auditorium. Nerves she didn't know she had were ignited, and she was glad that her two friends were in the audience, putting her more at ease. With her anxiety stuck in her throat, she was relieved her judgmental mom had turned down the offer to attend.

"Let's welcome Margot Mays. She has graciously agreed to sit down with us and discuss her aunt, Nadine's, case," Dr. Williams said as the audience clapped.

"Thank you so much for that. I can't tell you how much that means to me. I've never spoken in a public forum except for my one-on-one interview with Loni Smart. I'm so grateful that you're giving me a platform tonight to discuss my aunt's murder and to seek help in solving the case. Two years ago I found my Aunt Nadine murdered during the summer I turned twenty-one. Someone had turned the world as I knew it upside down. You hear that expression a lot, but let me tell you, it's real." Margot paused, taking a deep breath.

You can do this.

"We know some facts about the case, but please tell us how you're doing." Dr. Williams looked up from her notes.

"When someone murders your favorite, most beloved person, it's like everything you ever cared about before ceases to exist. The world is a black pit of misery, and your mind replays seeing the dead body and hearing the words confirming it's someone you loved. It will take months, maybe years, before you catch yourself laughing again, and once you do, you question whether you should feel guilty for it. Those first couple of months, I couldn't get out of bed, barely ate anything, and fell into a deep depression. I dropped out of college as I couldn't concentrate on anything outside of what I saw inside Nadine's apartment," Margot paused, closing her eyes, which pooled with tears. "I went to grief counseling, but I found it too difficult to talk about it back then. There are still moments where I'll hear a song or I'll drive by one of our hangouts and immediately tear up."

She paused again to look out into the dark audience, hoping her words resonated. The audience was eerily quiet, no whispers or sniffles to be heard—quieter than an empty house when home alone. All Margot could see was the first row of guests. Otherwise, it was pitch-black.

"What can you tell us that hasn't already been published? What can you remember about the day you found Nadine?" Dr. Williams leaned in as her voice softened.

Margot glanced up at the stage lights, which shone too brightly in her eyes. "I haven't made this public, but I have a lot of guilt about that day." Her heart pounded so hard she hoped no one could see it through her shirt. *Why did I go off script? Just get the words out.* "I was supposed to be at my aunt's place on the night of her murder." Margot heard a few gasps from the audience. *Keep going.*

Margot looked for the red exit sign, calculating how close it was. "I was going to stay over that night with Nadine, but I wasn't feeling well, so I stayed home. I can't shake the feeling that I could have saved her," she said as she grabbed the glass of water, which had turned lukewarm. *Deep breath.*

"Margot, I am so sorry to hear that you've been holding on to this.

I'm sure you know a killer like this takes his time scoping out his victims. My guess, and it's really a hunch, is that if you were there, he'd have killed you as well, or he would have just returned on a different day after more observation," Dr. Williams put her hand on Margot's knee.

"I know he may have killed me, too." Margot closed her eyes. "But some days it's too painful to live without Nadine and I...anyway, I wished I was there to do something." Margot took a deep breath, which resonated throughout the pin-drop quiet room.

"I know this is hard for you, but you're doing great. I have found with other people that the more they discuss their grief, the easier it becomes and the pain can soften just enough to keep going."

Margot nodded in agreement. "What I've learned is that grief never fully goes away. It can fade into the back of your mind and reappear when you least expect it to. I can be happy and joking one minute, then the next I'll remember that Nadine should be enjoying happy moments with me. Nadine should be sitting across from me having dinner, or waiting up to hear how my date went, or offering the warm embrace I always expected from her. I've also learned that it's OK to grieve for as long as I need; there's never a set timeframe, regardless of what anyone else tells me." Margot paused to dab the tears from her eyes. "Life has no finite rules, and most of us are making them up as we go. Nadine couldn't have prevented the outcome, but I feel compelled to do what I can to sound the alarm for others so they won't fall prey to a killer, because the Choke Mask Killer must be stopped. And for the thousands of killers like my aunt's murderer born every day, I will warn anyone to protect themselves against these predators—that is my purpose, and justice will have the final sentence."

Even now, chills ran down Margot's arms as she mentioned the moniker given to Nadine's killer. She hoped her speech with Dr. Williams would help finally unmask the monster, as she painstakingly counted the days until he would face his retribution. Margot could never have imagined two years ago while in hiding that she could give a speech that would garner a standing ovation, but as she finished, the crowd rose to their feet. Her heart was fuller than it had been since that July day.

"Bravo, Margot. You have spoken eloquently about how a murder continues to affect the victim's family for years," Dr. Williams said, standing along with the audience.

————

Backstage, as she headed to the adjoining event space, she immediately saw Lucas. "Margot, that was fantastic!"

"Thank you. I'm just getting the feeling back in my body. Did it really sound OK? I kind of froze up in the middle." Margot took a deep breath.

"Yes. It was incredible. I didn't want to tell you this before, but Dr. Williams asked me to record this. She wants to replay it at future events." Lucas grinned widely.

"Oh, that's fine." Margot suddenly felt ill. She hoped she sounded good enough to be played on repeat.

"That was great!" Gemma said as she approached. "Carter told me to tell you that you were awesome, but he had someplace to be." Gemma shrugged.

I guess he found out about the TA position and couldn't face the winner. Margot introduced the two and waited to get Dr. Williams' attention. "Margot, I want to thank you for coming today," Dr. Williams said, grabbing Margot's hand.

Gemma edged herself nearer to Margot, getting as close to Dr. Williams as socially appropriate.

"I want you to know that I'm fully invested in working on the Choke Mask Killer case. You have my full support." Dr. Williams smiled.

Pinch me. It's happening. "I don't know what to say except thank you. I am so grateful and honored to receive any help you can provide." Margot put her free hand on top of their handshake.

"Great. I'll contact Detective Conway tomorrow and let him know that I'm starting my own investigation. I'll keep you updated on any new leads." Dr Williams bowed her head and left the backstage area.

"Oh, my God. You killed it! I mean, you now have Dr. Williams in your corner! That's huge!" Gemma shook her head in disbelief.

"Is this real?" Margot looked at the two faces staring back at her. *We're going to get this solved, Nadine.*

Lucas leaned forward. "Hey, Margot, I wanted to say how sorry I am that your parents haven't supported you through all of this," Lucas said. "And Gemma, I'm really sorry to hear that you don't have support from your extended family. But it sounds like Carter has been your rock, so that's good."

Margot and Gemma looked at each other and then back at Lucas. "Who told you this?" they said in unison.

"Oh, Carter was raving about you two in class one day and he said that he was basically your support system, since both of your families have bailed."

Margot stood in shock, her face flushing a bright red.

"That asshole." Gemma said, taking out her phone. Margot watched her type out a heated text.

Margot gulped down the pit forming in her stomach. She went from a high to a low in a matter of minutes.

CHAPTER 30

2019

Another knock at the front door. "Flowers for Margot," the delivery man announced, which made the fourth bouquet she'd received since she presented with Dr. Williams. There were no cards showing who was sending the flowers, but Margot assumed it was an admirer or fan of some sort. Margot lined it up with all the other bouquets on her kitchen counter, where they stayed until they became too dead to keep around.

Margot needed fresh air, away from the dead flowers that kept wilting in her apartment. There was nothing like a drive to the riverfront early in the day, with soft wind blowing, light sunshine beaming down, and the vibrant colors of the maple and dogwood trees lining the walking path. Margot found a secluded bench and put on her sunglasses—a barrier to any stranger that may think he could approach her.

Deep in thought with images from her brutal research floating in her mind, Margot watched various people walking along the trail. Some wore exercise clothes, while others casually strolled along in shorts and a T-shirt. Amongst the roving crowd, Margot spotted Carter. A hard lump hit the back of her throat as she debated fleeing back to her car. Ever since the panel, Carter hadn't been coming to their Crime Three meetings, and both she and Gemma had gladly ghosted him. She watched as he paced along the walking path with his cell phone to his ear.

I'm not in the mood for Carter right now.

As Margot watched, Carter raised his right arm, gesturing to punctuate his words. If he could see Margot, he'd know to dodge the many daggers she was sending his way with her eyes, but the sunshine shone like a beacon over her and he spotted her shiny auburn hair. Carter walked toward the bench and Margot played dumb, pretending she hadn't even seen him. As he approached, his tense demeanor turned into a wide grin.

"Hey, Margot!" Carter stopped when he was standing next to her.

"What's up?" Margot said, hoping to keep this short.

"Oh, nothing much. Just getting some fresh air. What are you doing out here?" Carter nodded to the spot where he'd been talking on his phone.

"Lucas told me he got the TA position," Margot said, watching Carter for any reaction. "Oh, and he told us you're basically our lifeline? Actually, he said you're our rock." Margot studied his movements, trying to interpret his body language.

"Oh, that. Yeah, I screwed up one day and my mouth got the better of me. Still pretty bummed about the TA position, though," Carter scowled, crossing his arms.

"You've betrayed our confidence," Margot said as a chill shot up her back.

"Look, I'm sorry. What can I do to make it up to you?"

Margot abruptly got up to leave. Her heart pounded as she walked to her car and she took a shortcut through the grass, unsure if Carter was following.

Once she reached her car, she scanned the riverfront but didn't see Carter. Margot fumbled for her keys, wanting to get away from the scene without running into anyone else. She let out a brief scream when she saw a shape in her backseat. *Just a grocery bag. Get it together, girl.*

On the way home, Margot's jittery hands tightened into fuming fists as she thought about how Carter had broken her trust. She stopped by Nadine's grave as she hadn't been since before her speech. She always wondered how often her mom visited, but she didn't think it would be right to ask—grief is personal. As she settled into her familiar parking spot, she noticed a gigantic bouquet of roses resting on Nadine's gravesite. Margot had been the only one to leave flowers in the past, so this was a completely foreign sight. She approached the grave and read the card attached to the bouquet.

"Nadine, your niece is breathtaking." Margot quickly dropped the card and turned to search the cemetery to see if anyone was watching.

Margot's shaky hands returned, and she felt too exposed standing out in the open, terrified of whoever had been at Nadine's grave. She scanned the cemetery, which no longer held the peace it once had, now a creepy place full of danger.

Margot's breakfast churned in her stomach, and she thought she was going to throw up. She made her way back to her car as she searched the grounds for anyone looking at her. Of course, a graveyard is a perfect place to stalk someone—there are so many headstones to hide behind. The cemetery's eerie vibe terrified her. What else was out there?

Back inside her car, Margot locked her car doors with quivering hands. She shrieked out loud as her trunk slowly rose. *I must have accidentally hit the latch, jumping in so fast. I have to stop freaking myself out!*

Margot drove straight home to gather herself, checking her rearview and side mirrors more times than she could count. She was certain that no one was following her when she entered her apartment and locked her dead bolt, checking it just to be sure. It was part of her CMK ritual, along with surveying all the rooms to make sure they were clear. Margot thought of her next steps, wondering if she had a stalker on her hands.

Who could this be? The Choke Mask Killer? A prank? Someone close to me?

Margot convinced herself to drive over to the police station to file a report. The last time she was there was the day she'd found Nadine dead, but she knew she had to walk back through those doors. As she drove to the station, she noted her surroundings and felt that no one had been following her.

As she walked inside the police station, it seemed foreign to her. The last time she was here seemed like a blur—tears could definitely do that. Margot walked to the front desk and told them she had a potential stalker and needed to file a report.

"Sending flowers or leaving them anonymously on a grave is not a crime. Unless the notes turn threatening, we just don't have enough to open a case right now. I'd advise you not to go to your aunt's grave by yourself until things settle down," Officer Rich said.

Margot was delirious with frustration, and now the cops wouldn't help. *I can't visit Nadine by myself? That's my routine!*

Margot felt hopeless. She didn't want to wait for things to turn threatening. She wanted the police to do more now! Margot left the station feeling defeated.

Maybe I'm overreacting. This could be a horrible prank.

Margot returned to her car with the sun setting on her back, wanting to both cry and scream. *I don't need this bullshit. Between this potential stalker and CMK, it's too much. I need both of these assholes locked up!*

After she took a deep breath, Margot was heading back toward her apartment when she noticed a car with its passenger side headlight flickering. The car kept making the same turns as she did, raising her suspicions. Margot started making turns in alleyways and into parking lots, and the car continued to follow her. She wasn't able to make out who was driving, but she could see the car was an older model Buick, like an older unmarked police car, which didn't look familiar. Margot drove faster, going through yellow lights and making multiple turns, eventually finding herself lost in the city of her birth. Her palms were sweating, and she knew she had to get out of this neighborhood and drive toward an area that she was familiar with.

After she made several turns, she found herself back on Pacific Street, a main roadway that she knew well. She seemed to have ditched the flickering headlight. She searched every mirror as she drove around for the next thirty minutes to make sure the suspicious car was long gone. Unfortunately, she'd made too many turns to get a clear picture of the license plate in the dark. She grappled with whether she was just spooking herself or whether someone was actually following her. With no sign of anyone behind her, she pulled into her parking lot and made a mad dash to her apartment, locking her dead bolt. With her newly purchased stun gun in hand, she checked every room and didn't find anyone else inside with her.

Margot sat down on her couch and looked at the note left on Nadine's grave. Chills went up her arms and neck as she tried to figure out who could have written it. When she felt a cool breeze on her face, she turned to her left and noticed her living room window was cracked open.

What the hell? I didn't open this. Or did I? I'm losing my mind!

After she locked the window, Margot quickly checked her apartment again for an intruder. Still finding it empty, she attempted to sleep, tossing most of the night. Suddenly, a loud knock at her door woke her. The sun was already filtering into the room and her clock indicated it was nearly lunchtime.

Fear and curiosity propelled her forward as she peered through the peephole and saw more flowers being delivered. A note attached to the red roses read, "Stay safe, sadgirlxx."

CHAPTER 31

2019

When Deb first walked around her new apartment, she soaked in the fresh smell of paint and new wood. "I've never lived in a place where no one else has lived before," she told Jameka. She nearly teared up as she signed the lease.

"Well, welcome home! I hope you love it here. If you ever need anything, just contact me. We're so glad to have you as part of the Elite Living family." Jameka beamed and left a basket of goodies on Deb's new kitchen countertop.

When Deb first moved to Cape Ivy, she'd stayed with her best friend, Judy. "A fresh haircut always makes a woman feel brand new," Judy had told Deb as they teased each other about their hometown in "the sticks" of Zionstown, Missouri. She had been trying to get Deb to move for a few years, but Deb always told her she needed to take care of her aging parents. In many ways, Deb was now learning to start over in life.

Anyone who knew Deb knew her as down to earth, hardworking, reliable, and committed to family values. Although she'd never married, she lived with her parents in her small town in rural Missouri. She never strayed from Zionstown and had only been to Cape Ivy for an occasional day trip, believing it was like visiting a sprawling metropolis like Nashville or Dallas. Deb led a sheltered life, and when her parents died, she wasn't sure where her life would end up. All her life she'd cared for others, and at fifty-five, it was time to live for herself. That was when Judy convinced Deb to move to the city for more opportunities.

Deb surprised even herself with the agreement to leave for Cape Ivy, but she had always wanted out of that small town, and now was her chance. At first she stayed in a spare room of Judy's, eventually getting a job at a local grocery store and quickly moving up to assistant manager. She enjoyed her job, as it was the only paying job she'd ever had. Eventually, she earned the money to live on her own, and moved into Elite Living's newest apartment homes close to the store. Unable to drive because she had poor vision, she loved her apartment because it was close enough to walk to work.

Deb felt warm and accepted in her new life as she stood in the middle of her new home, marveling at where she was. Finally, at this stage in her life, she had a place all to herself and never had to share it with anyone else unless she chose to. Deb was happily alone, and that was how she preferred it. Over the next month, she slowly decorated her apartment. Although it was plain, it was just as Deb envisioned it. She chuckled to herself. *It looks like Sister Catherine's room in here.* She thought of her childhood teacher's convent room, which she'd seen when she went inside one day for a bandage. A young Deb noticed the nuns lived modestly and now she did, too, minus the crucifixes on the walls. She marveled at how convenient everything was near her work and loved the benefit of having practically everything she needed—her bank, doctor, pharmacy, clothing, and, of course, food—within feet of each other. Initially, she thought she couldn't make it in a city without a car, but she now realized not having a car was more difficult in the country.

Once, when she needed a specialist appointment at Cape Ivy Hospital, she got a taxicab—taxis were such a luxury that she never had in the country. If you needed a ride, you'd ask Jasper or Roger down the road and they'd come by in their pickup truck, nothing fancy. When the taxi arrived to take her to her appointment, she giggled to herself, thinking this was what celebrities did—never in her wildest dreams did she think she'd experience this kind of treatment. She felt like a queen for the day, finally living the life she had only dreamed of.

The first time Deb walked to work was pure bliss. It had such a woodsy feel, with the trees touching and kissing above the sidewalk, perfectly shading whoever walked below while still allowing some glimpses of sunshine to break through. She didn't love walking home after dark, but there always seemed to be someone walking their dog or jogging late, so she was never truly alone. Growing up in the country, she'd always feared the "boogeyman" who seemed to lurk in the big city, but after making this trek for several months, she let her guard down and no longer thought about the spooky man with sinister intentions. As she walked home at dusk, she greeted several neighbors she had gotten to know from her routine walk. Those neighbors included several dogs who she loved and knew the names of better than some of their owners.

When Deb arrived home, she made dinner, which was a turkey sandwich and a side of chips. She wasn't much of a cook or baker, opting for quick meals so she wouldn't have to worry about messing up the kitchen. In the evenings, she much preferred reading over watching TV, but she always watched the local news. It was a nightly ritual she had with her parents, and she kept it up even as an adult on her own. "I like to see what's going on in the world," her dad always said and now so did she, if only out of habit. After her nightly shower, she put on her pajamas, grabbed the latest Danielle Steel book, and got comfortable in bed. She mostly enjoyed romance novels over any other genre, but it still didn't make her want a man in her life. She had dated a couple of guys when she was younger, but they were "duds," as she called them. The guys from up the gravel road weren't the type any woman would bring home to Mom, and certainly not Dad, as he'd likely get the shotgun out after them. The last guy Deb had dated was more interested in his alcohol than impressing her. Unfortunately, it had taken her longer than it should have to break things off with him, and it got messy one night when he came by after midnight extremely drunk. Once her dad showed him the barrel of his shotgun, that was the end of that relationship.

Deb believed the kind of love she read about in love stories only existed in books. Men like that just didn't exist for her. She never met a man who put a woman first or wrote her a love letter or opened a door for her. But she read those books to escape from the loss of love she never had. She would never say she missed it, but if a man like Mrs. Steel wrote about ever walked into her life, well, she just might think she was dreaming.

————

By the time she realized that something was over her head and something hard was pushing into her back, it was too late to fight. She had always been a heavy sleeper—she had to be, because her dad snored so loud that the house rippled. Unable to move and barely able to breathe, Deb's mind raced as she wondered what was happening to her. Deb found herself unable to fight back. Tied down, suffocating and choking on her own blood, she realized, *The city boogeyman got me.*

CHAPTER 32

2019

rollGod Allegedly Revealed as Dr. Simone Williams' Assistant, the recent thread on *Death Toll* announced.

Margot drove to meet Gemma for lunch. She needed to process the recent chat room news, and Gemma was the only person she could trust at the moment. She had cut off communication with Carter even though he'd continued to blow up her texts and left several voicemails.

Margot pulled up to her favorite Thai restaurant and immediately saw Gemma, who sat on a rustic teak bench just inside the entrance. The two walked in together and the server seated them at a corner table. The restaurant was spotless, with wooden walls, a water feature by the front door, and modern lighting that bounced red and white lights off the ceiling.

"Hey, Margot. I'm so glad to see you. We have a lot to catch up on." Gemma's mouth turned downward.

"I can't believe it. There's a new murder *and* Lucas is the one who exposed both of our identities? I'm livid that I didn't see through him. Plus, I just feel so betrayed by Carter. I feel emotionally drained from sadness, fear, and anger with everything going on right now." Margot pulled her sweater higher onto her shoulders.

"I'm so sorry. This is way too much to deal with. I'm here for you whenever you need to talk it through. If it's any consolation, I got eerie vibes from Lucas on the night of your presentation. I couldn't put my finger on it then, but now it makes sense," Gemma said.

Margot sighed. "I can't believe Lucas was able to get that close to Dr. Williams, even if he denies being TrollGod," she said, shaking her head. "I worry it may jeopardize finding Nadine's killer. Is Dr. Williams still going to help me? She may not have time for me now." Margot took a sip of the lemon water she'd ordered.

"That's a tough one. She might disengage from the drama as she's a very busy woman. It would be understandable if she needed to put her focus elsewhere." Gemma shrugged.

Margot glanced around the restaurant to check that no one was listening in. "Ugh. Plus, there's a new murder! He killed his new victim exactly like my aunt and Becky Conrad. At least that's what I heard on the news. I haven't heard anything from Detective Conway, but that's nothing new. When I heard the details on KFCI-13, I couldn't stop shaking. I hope her family didn't find her like that," Margot lowered her voice.

"I'm sorry, Margot. I can't imagine how you're dealing with all of this. It's so scary, as we're both single women living alone." Gemma paused as the waiter delivered their lunch order. "Now that you know about Lucas, do you see any red flags from your first meeting?"

Margot thought, but eventually shook her head. "I guess I believed what he told me. His position with Dr. Williams blinded me to any danger signals." Margot sighed.

"One thing I'm good at is Googling true crime. Let me see what I can find out about him," Gemma said as she punched in his information into her phone. "Was the case local?"

"No, it was near his hometown in Hickory, Tennessee," Margot said.

"Hmm, okay. What else did he say about it?" Gemma asked, twisting her lips.

"Well, her name was Sierra Mason, and he said they found her dead in an old barn months after her disappearance," Margot said, trying to peek at Gemma's search results.

"Well, nothing is coming back on my search. Maybe that story was all a ruse to get close to you." Gemma took a bite out of a steaming spring roll.

"Great. If I wasn't so preoccupied with my presentation, maybe I would have been more diligent and researched this." Margot put her head into her hands.

"It's completely understandable. I mean, I always Google anyone I meet, but I'm a lot less trusting than you. This isn't your fault, and he's an ass for using his sister's death to play on your emotions," Gemma said.

Margot sat back in her chair, shaking her head. "I know. I just feel like everything's falling apart right now."

Gemma returned her phone to her purse. "We know he is familiar with true crime, so maybe he just picked up a story from his studies. I mean, cases like this happen far too often, so it's totally believable."

"Yeah, maybe. I mean, he's working alongside the top criminologist in our area. He must hear about death all the time." Margot stared off to the side. "I would think that Dr. Williams would have done a background check." Margot sat motionless and numb. "I just want to put Lucas and his story behind me. I have a killer and a stalker to deal with. Unless Lucas was the one leaving the flowers and notes?"

Gemma's eyes widened. "Anything is possible. What would be his motivation?"

"I honestly don't know. We only met twice, so it's hard to say." Margot shrugged.

"You and I both know that people will try to get close to us, and some of their reasons are nefarious." Gemma kept eye contact with Margot. "No one understands what we've gone through, and some may say we are more likely to be distrusting of others based on our tragedies. But our reality is, we also welcome people into our lives because we lost someone. We want to fill the void of murder." Gemma sighed.

"You're right. I guess I let my guard down, but I've learned a big lesson this time. However, I need to be pickier about who I let get close to me," Margot said.

"Well, it's OK. I mean, if you didn't let your guard down, then maybe we wouldn't be close friends." Gemma smirked.

"Thank God I met you! I'd be back on the road trying to find my next hideout destination by now!" Margot said, as she lightly pounded the table and laughed.

The two finished their lunch and discussed meeting without Carter, as they still weren't sure if they could trust him again.

Back inside her car, Margot received another text from Carter.

Margot. Can we talk? I think you have the wrong idea about things.

She stared at the screen, then wrote and deleted several responses.

Let's meet at our usual spot tomorrow. M

Margot turned off her phone with a growing knot in her stomach. Deep breaths weren't coming close to quieting the gnawing in her gut.

CHAPTER 33

2019

Margot rounded the corner of the library section where they kept the criminology books when she saw a couple sitting at the Crime Three's usual spot. She found a nearby desk and watched to see if they would move, but based on the amount of open books sitting in front of them, she thought maybe they'd be there awhile. Margot wanted the comfort of familiarity that their usual spot provided.

Gemma showed up shortly after and immediately scanned the area. "Want me to pull a fire alarm?" she teased.

Five minutes past their meeting time, Carter arrived. He grinned and walked with little purpose as he stopped twice to grab a book off a shelf. As he approached the two women, he stared back at their usual spot and frowned. "Guess we're meeting here today?"

Margot, already antsy over their meeting, just said, "Looks like it."

"Brilliant observation," Gemma rolled her eyes, looking back at Margot.

"What can I do to fix this and end the silent treatment?" Carter said, louder than a whisper.

"Why did you disclose our private information in your class?" Margot narrowed her eyes at Carter.

"It got away from me. I guess my excitement took over and when I talked about you both, I got confused about what was already out in the public and what we've discussed in private." Carter looked down at his feet.

"You know how hard things are for me right now. I don't need anyone around me who isn't on my side. I can't trust you." Margot fidgeted.

"I can't say I ever really trusted you." Gemma pursed her lips.

Margot looked around the library, the new spot giving her a different perspective of the building she loved so much. From her new vantage point, she could see the front entrance. She focused on the various students who came and went, some running with large backpacks bouncing behind them. There were others who were clearly stepping foot in the building for the first time. They craned their necks to the painted ceiling and clumsily walked down aisles to find the right books for their assignments.

"I'm sorry. I know how it looks, but I promise you, I'm here for you and Gemma. It was a simple mistake. I swear I immediately stopped when I realized my error." Carter looked at both women, who stared back at him.

"We don't even really know you. Everyone knows about us, thanks to TrollGod." Margot sighed.

"Oh, me? I, um... Well, I don't have anything in my past like the two of you. What I mean is, there was no murder in my past, unless you count...never mind," Carter said.

"You can't just say that and then take it back." Margot crossed her arms.

"It's minor compared to you guys, though. I don't want you to think I'm comparing my situation to the trauma you two have had to deal with."

"Spit it out. If you want our trust, tell us!" Gemma leaned in toward Carter.

Carter cleared his throat and glanced at the studious couple at their regular spot. "Well, I can understand how being distant from your parents feels because I basically disowned mine."

"OK. Yeah, murder has a way of distancing you from people," Margot retorted.

"Right. This isn't murder, but it's about how I was raised. It was an emotionally and physically abusive household, which is why I went into criminology. I wanted to understand the minds of psychopaths." Carter looked up at the library ceiling, inhaling a deep breath.

The two women watched and waited for more.

"Let me give you an example of how my childhood was." Carter took another deep breath and began. "When I was twelve years old, I had the best dog, Molly. She'd sleep with me, follow me around the house, and wait for me when I got on and off the school bus. I'd teach her tricks and she would lick and kiss my face anytime she could—we were inseparable, except for when I went to school. One day when I returned home, she wasn't waiting for me." Carter's lips quivered as he closed his eyes to the memory. "I called all over and searched the house and the neighborhood. My dad was inside eating, shoveling a giant portion of mashed potatoes into his mouth, telling me to 'eat or go wash up.' But I needed to find Molly! When I asked my parents, my dad finally told me, 'Oh, I put that bitch down with my rifle today. She got into the trash and I warned you to keep her tied up when you went to school cause I was tired of cleaning up her mess.'"

"Oh my God, Carter. Please tell me he was lying!" Margot said in disbelief.

"Unfortunately, he wasn't. My dad wasn't a liar, but I was stunned to hear those words and I had to see for myself. It was dark outside by then, so I grabbed a flashlight from the shed and shone the light..." Carter choked up as he recounted how the flashlight illuminated the path to truth, where he could see ashes, burnt branches, and, yes, burned bones and teeth. "I screamed and fell to my knees, crying for what felt like hours. My heart was so full of pain and tears were coming from my eyes and nose. My stomach roiled with revulsion, but I had revenge on my mind. I didn't know if I wanted to march into the kitchen with a shotgun and shoot my dad or puke my guts out onto the burn pile. Eventually I walked toward the house, the flashlight illuminating the lonely path and I vowed I'd never get a dog again, because my heart can't take the pain of what humans do to them."

Gemma twisted her mouth. "Damn, that's so sad."

Margot was on the verge of tears. "That's awful, Carter. I'm so sorry."

"I thought that story would give insight into my childhood. It got worse from there and I learned to hate my parents. But I want you to see how much I relate to what you've gone through. I know my loss isn't near what you two have experienced, but I can empathize."

"Damn. I thought my parents were tough. They look superb right now," Margot said.

"My parents win as the worst." Gemma smiled, and they all started laughing.

"That's the key for us. We all have crappy parents! Maybe that's why we bonded so fast." Carter smiled.

"OK, slow it down. You're still not off the hook, but in honor of Molly, I forgive you," Margot said.

Carter did a little chair dance.

"I take it back." Margot smiled.

"You guys love me." Carter smirked.

"Meh. Love is closer to hate. You want us to like you, and the jury's still out," Gemma said.

"Yeah, we just tolerate you most days." Margot laughed.

Margot and Carter walked toward the book check-out as Gemma lingered behind them.

CHAPTER 34
2019

Gemma wasn't as keen on giving Carter the benefit of the doubt. Her own life history had shown her that people couldn't be trusted. A skeptic at birth and a realist by experience, she vowed to keep one eye on him. It wasn't an easy life, always assuming that people were up to wicked behavior. Gemma believed that most people were capable of deceit, even murder if the circumstances were just right. People snapped every day and then life went on.

Gemma only had faint memories of her life before her father's spree, but what happened afterwards was still stuck in her brain like a revolving door of images. The authorities shuffled her around to various family members' homes, which felt less like stability and more like a Russian Roulette of where she'd land next. Some of the family would bring up the events of "that day" and try to coax her to talk about the trauma. Like her maternal aunt, who often told her how she and Gemma's mom never saw eye to eye. Or her paternal cousin, who would just shake his head when he came across a picture of her dad.

Gemma attempted to suppress the images and thoughts that popped into her head from the rampage. Although, the more she tried to force it out of her mind, the deeper it sank and got comfortable. The depression and anxiety were constant companions, and she became accustomed to medical appointments, therapist waiting rooms, and pharmacies. There were no miracle words or drugs to treat the tragedy imprinted inside of her.

Back inside her car, Gemma watched Margot and Carter walk by after their library session. Margot held on to her purse strap as if someone would try to rob her of it. Carter walked too close to her as if they were lovers. Gemma could see that Carter was infatuated with Margot, but not as a love interest. He seemed more "in love" with her victim status. Gemma could recognize a killer-chaser, and Carter was one.

Eventually losing sight of them behind a new row of students hustling across campus, she sat with raging thoughts. There was a growing envy behind Gemma's glasses. She couldn't help feeling the painful pangs of jealousy and the fear of being isolated. Gemma craved a close bond, which she felt with Margot. She and Margot were trauma sisters, and she couldn't let anyone put a wedge between them, including Carter. Gemma lived with the torment that had taken so many things away from her. She envied the students who were full of excitement for learning, with plans for their future. Life had taught her that feeling close to someone didn't always last, and isolation made her cling to people in fear that they'd leave. The feelings of inadequacy rooted deep inside as she wondered if they'd still continue to be friends with the flawed woman in front of them.

She pulled out of the parking lot, her thoughts still fixated on the jealousy that was percolating between her ears when she slammed on her brakes. *Fuck.*

Her hands clutched the steering wheel and her fingernails embedded themselves in her skin. She peered through her windshield to see a furry mask with an oversized beak, much too large for its head, and glassy red pupils fixated on hers. Ivy University's mascot slammed his paws on her hood.

Fucking Rowdy.

CHAPTER 35
2020

Hair salons were full of chatter about boyfriend trouble and the latest killer lurking in Cape Ivy.

"I'm so glad I have Travis with me. I swear I'd move back in with my mom and dad with this killer on the loose," Jamie said as she snipped a long strand of hair.

"I agree. I can't stop watching the coverage about him. Have things improved with you and Travis? Has he moved in?" Jamie's client, Olivia, asked.

"Unfortunately, no. But he sleeps over often enough. It gives me some kind of comfort and hope for our future. It's just a matter of time before he settles down with me." Jamie smiled into the mirror.

At twenty-five, Jamie dreamed of marriage with her on-again, off-again boyfriend, Travis. She desperately wanted children and the white picket fence life, but she'd chosen a man who wasn't quite ready to end his player ways. Everyone in the salon, both hair stylists and clients, knew about Jamie's boyfriend struggles. She talked the ears off each of the heads in her chair, always giving them a new tidbit about the toxic relationship she cherished.

"Did I tell you I caught him cheating? I found his phone, and he was texting with another woman. I've forgiven him and hope he finishes sowing his wild oats sooner than later," Jamie said.

"Oh, Jamie. Are you sure Travis is the right man for you? I don't think I could put up with a man cheating like that," Olivia said, the lines between her eyes deepening.

"I know. I've heard it all before. But he's the love of my life." Jamie pointed to a picture of her with Travis that she'd placed in a frame decorated with astrology signs. "We got our astrological charts done and I believe we're destined to be together." Jamie beamed.

She believed their love was written in the stars. Once she had their astrological charts mapped out, she ignored the parts that showed any trouble because she knew he was just misunderstood, maybe even by the Gods. She put him on a pedestal and never thought he deserved less, even blaming herself when his eyes would stray away from hers. He never introduced her to his family, and she didn't have any long-term plans scheduled with him beyond the next late-night fling.

"He sat in this same chair over a year ago, and that's when I fell in love with him." Jamie giggled.

Jamie's bubbly personality made her a great hairstylist, but she wasn't so great at confrontation when she saw evidence of his wandering eye. Besides the flirty text on his cell phone, she'd found a long strand of hair on his car seat that wasn't hers. Then there was the devastating news from her favorite coworker, Tiffany. She admitted she'd had a one-night stand with Travis during a drunken tryst and needed to come clean for her conscience. When Jamie heard this, she was obviously upset, but not enough to dump him; he had her wrapped around his finger. She just forgave him and continued to date him like normal, hoping he would eventually appreciate her. As for Tiffany, their relationship became strained and the closeness they once had was now fractured.

Jamie had moved into the Valley View apartments last year. Although she wanted a townhouse, they were out of her price range. The apartments were in a quiet part of Cape Ivy, so she splurged a bit, but could only afford the ground floor, one-bedroom unit. During her tour of the unit with the assistant apartment manager, Tom, she asked about crime in the area, to which Tom replied, "The apartments are very safe, and the prior tenant had no complaints about neighbors or any other safety concerns." Jamie checked the window locks and clicked the dead bolt on the front door to make sure they worked. "Elite Living apartments are the safest units and provide state-of-the-art tenant satisfaction," Tom added.

"I'll take it. It's perfect for me," Jamie said, standing behind the small kitchen island. "My sister told me to get a second-story apartment, though. She had an incident with someone peeking into her windows who she called her 'creeper,' so she warned me to not make the same mistake." Jamie checked out her soon-to-be closet.

But Jamie couldn't afford her sister's advice and besides, how often did a Peeping Tom hit up the same family? She liked that her unit was at the rear of the complex, away from the constant foot traction of early risers and latecomers. She enjoyed the serenity and privacy the backside of her unit provided. Jamie would later learn that her upstairs neighbor was pretty reserved. In fact, he was gone a good deal of the time. She'd only seen him twice leaving with a suitcase, but she never really got to chat with him too much, assuming people talked little in apartment dwellings. She once arrived home at the same time as he did, but he just kept his head down and she barely heard an audible, "Hello."

She hoped that this was a temporary move, because she wished Travis would propose soon so they could move into a new house. Her dream was to buy at least a four-bedroom so they could have three kids, hoping she would have a boy first, who they could name Travis, Jr. After a long day on her feet, Jamie returned home to her vision board. As she opened her front door, she fixed her eyes on the wall behind her couch where she kept the board prominently displayed. She stopped just feet from it, repeating her mantra: "I am remarkable and deserve a loving partner." It was an instant reminder to embody the words that floated on the board: Perseverance, Gratitude, and Devotion.

Jamie believed if she could get pregnant, Travis would finally see that they would make the perfect little family. Travis actually had two other children with two different women, but it did not deter Jamie from trying for her own family unit. Jamie's family and friends didn't approve of Travis; they could see right through him, and they expressed their feelings to Jamie. She often heard "You can do so much better" and "He's just using you for sex" from multiple family and friends, but she didn't care and didn't believe others knew his true self to make those kinds of judgments. He wasn't her first boyfriend, but she was just the clingy type. She molded herself to whoever she was dating, adopted their beliefs and values, and gave up whatever dreams she held prior to their relationship. If Travis liked football, then Jamie would start wearing that team's jersey—shocking everyone at work when she arrived in a Green Bay Packers jersey—but no one dared to ask her who any players were or the score of the game. She completely lost herself when she was with a guy, having no powerful convictions of her own.

With Travis, Jamie saw herself as a stay-at-home mom, making dinner and taking care of the kids until he came home. She wanted this life more than anything, but she either couldn't see or refused to see that Travis would never provide this type of lifestyle for her, at least according to those closest to her. But she devised a plan that she hoped was going to trap him, which came to fruition one night after she stopped taking birth control. When she and Travis had sex during her ovulation period, she was so hopeful about getting pregnant. Of course, Travis refused to wear condoms, as he had claimed he was allergic to latex and that it was the girl's job to handle pregnancy prevention. He had no role in his two kids' lives, and Jamie wasn't exactly sure if he'd had his son or daughter first. He rarely spoke of them and when she brought them up on rare occasions, he would get mad and they'd end up in a fight. Even though he didn't see his other kids, she felt they had a special bond and he wouldn't do that to her and their children—things would be different for their family. In Jamie's mind, they were soulmates. *No one knows that kind of love,* she thought. *Our destiny isn't earthbound.*

Jamie had hoped it would take a week, but it took three months until she began feeling nauseous and couldn't keep her breakfast down.

"Sophia, will you watch my client? I just put conditioner on her hair and she's under the dryer. I need to run to the restroom," Jamie asked a stylist she worked with. Jamie noticed her breasts had become swollen, and she felt dizzy after standing too long at work. As soon as Jamie left for the bathroom, her coworkers rolled their eyes. They had heard of her recent scheme and weren't fans of Travis.

Jamie frantically pried open the pregnancy test box, and the tube dropped to the floor. *Take a deep breath. One step at a time.* Her hands were unsteady with sweaty palms and the nervous shakes as she peed on the stick and waited a long three minutes for an answer. Positive. She tried in vain to catch her breath, and she couldn't believe her luck that it actually worked! When she emerged from the bathroom, she couldn't control her emotions. Her hands went to her cheeks, and she proclaimed, "We're pregnant!" Everyone gave her congratulatory hugs, including Tiffany. Her hands continued to shake as she made plans for a celebration with Travis later that night.

After she left work, she went to the local party store and bought balloons and streamers to decorate her apartment, then to the grocery store to buy cake mix, then finally home to prepare for her big night. Even though Travis normally didn't come by on Wednesdays since that was his pool tournament night. He was in a men's league, and she had begged to come and watch, but he told her he needed "time with the boys." She knew Travis wouldn't respond during work hours, so she busied herself with getting her apartment decorated and baked a cake with the message, "We're pregnant!" She showered and waited for Travis to stop by. The hours went by anxiously, then painfully and finally, angrily. Attempts to call Travis went unanswered, going immediately to voicemail. Jamie finally prepared for bed, removed her makeup and contacts, and fell asleep by midnight with disappointment and tears in her eyes.

———

She heard the faintest sound and opened her eyes. *Finally*, she thought, *Travis is here.* Eyes cloudy from sleep and vision blurry without contacts, she believed the clock read 1:45, but she was unable to rub the haziness from her eyes. *Damn, Travis, I wish I knew it would be this late!* Still in a sleepy stupor, she willed herself to roll from her left side to her right in order to get out of bed. That's when she saw the figure upon her, although it was hard to make out with her poor vision. The figure wasn't crawling into bed next to her, but standing over her. It loomed over her side of the bed. Jamie tensed, as this wasn't part of her and Travis's routine. She wanted to scream but no sounds would come out, like someone had completely ripped her voice box out.

A Peeping Tom broke into my apartment came to her mind instantly. She wanted to run, but she froze. Time stood still, yet it was all so fast. *Maybe he's just here to rob me. Or is it for rape?* The first bash from the long, hard object stunned her, but the pain came seconds later. Jamie was unable to process what was happening until the second, third, and fourth blow to her head. "Don't hurt my baby," she tried to say, but it came out as only a fleeting mumble as the looming figure continued assaulting her. She'd do anything to save her baby—he could take her life, just let her baby live. Jamie wanted to run and scream, but the pain of shattered bones and a fractured skull immobilized her, a piercing affliction deep within. She couldn't comprehend who would do this to her. *Travis should be here to protect his family.* Death overcame her desire to live. Jamie and her baby left this world, and her last thoughts, like most nights, were, *Where is Travis?*

CHAPTER 36
2020

A call for a wellness check turned up a heap of cracked skull, splattered blood, and what appeared to be a surprise party, complete with an uneaten cake.

Detective Conway arrived on scene an hour later, pleased that the junior cops had put up crime scene tape and kept the apartment protected from any contamination.

"Good work, boys. What do we have here? Same as the others? Mask again?" Conway asked, noticing the faint smell of death in the air.

"No. Blunt force trauma. Massive head and upper torso injuries. Quite a bloody scene, detective," Officer Allen pointed toward the bedroom.

Conway surveyed the apartment and found a celebratory cake. "Where's the dad?" he said as they left the living room.

"We haven't located him yet. She was the only victim, and her coworker was the one who alerted us she didn't show up for work today." Officer Allen stared down at the bloody body.

"Looks like she was planning a surprise for the father-to-be, and he might not have liked his gift," Conway said, looking around for clues.

The oldest motive in the book.

Conway still believed the angle that the CMK murders were related to a romance gone wrong, and now he had a smoking gun. The media had scared Cape Ivy into believing this was a rogue killer preying upon its women. He had to admit they may be right, but he still clung to his original belief, never conceding the idea that a random serial killer haunted his own city under his watch. He wanted to speak with the victim's boyfriend immediately. It was pretty easy to find out who the boyfriend was; she had his picture in various frames, and his name was on her vision board and spelled out in refrigerator magnets. As Conway looked through her closet, he came across some men's clothes and found a shirt from a mechanic shop, Broadway Auto Parts, that matched one "Travis" was wearing in one picture Jamie had displayed.

"I want you to go to Broadway Auto Parts and see if they have a Travis working there who resembles this picture, and if so, ask him to come down to the station. I need to talk to him today," Conway told Officer Allen.

Conway sported a wide grin and hoped he had his man. If Travis found out his girlfriend was pregnant and didn't want this baby, he may have killed her to avoid becoming a father. Or, he was the real-life serial killer Conway had been searching for his entire career. *A killer and a womanizer.* Conway didn't have any leads in the Choke Mask Killer case. All leads in Nadine's case went nowhere. After reviewing all of her lovers and coworkers, each had an alibi and none had any vendetta against her. In fact, all were quite heartbroken to learn of her passing. Her past lovers had very open relationships and never reported jealousy or a possessive love. All avenues led to a dead end in her case.

The second victim, Becky, had even fewer suspects. Becky led a reclusive life, other than going to work. Conway couldn't locate any boyfriends, except one that she'd had after college, but he died in a motorcycle accident before her murder. When Conway interviewed her coworkers, they barely knew anything about her outside of work. The third victim, Deborah, was a beloved member of her work team, and they were despondent to learn of her murder. She had only been in Cape Ivy for about a year and didn't have any enemies, or at least no one that would want to kill her.

Conway was excited at the prospect of Travis as a suspect—the first genuine lead he'd had in the CMK case since it began. Even though the killer didn't use a mask, Conway knew he could be toying with the police and experimenting with other ways to kill.

———

Arriving at Broadway Auto Parts, Officer Allen showed his badge, even though he arrived in a police car and was wearing a uniform. He asked if Travis worked there.

The front desk person nodded and asked, "Which one do you want?"

Officer Allen raised his eyebrows as he felt his face momentarily flush. "Um, let me see both of them."

He had barely looked at the pictures back at the crime scene and hadn't brought one with him. A bead of sweat formed on his forehead as he stood motionless in the stuffy waiting room until he could observe the potential suspects.

When he saw two men approaching, he breathed a sigh of relief. One Travis was white and one was Black. That would be easy—the white one. After pulling the correct Travis aside, he asked, "Are you currently dating a woman by the name of Jamie?"

He shifted his stance and nodded in agreement. "I don't call it dating, exactly."

"We just discovered her body. Are you aware of her murder?" Officer Allen leaned in.

Travis widened his eyes. "Oh, shit! I hadn't heard about that. I haven't talked to Jamie in a couple of days."

"We need you to come to the station for questioning with the homicide detective, Dan Conway. He needs to see you today. Can you take off from work now?" Officer Allen looked at his watch.

Travis looked around with his hands in his jean pockets. "Can't it wait until my shift is over? I have an engine to restore."

———

Upon hearing about this exchange, Conway was quite suspicious, as he believed Travis showed no urgency in helping solve this case or genuine shock that Jamie was dead. Conway was practically giddy to dust off his interrogation skills. He had been waiting his entire career for someone like Travis.

Travis showed up thirty minutes late, which really pissed Conway off who cracked his knuckles numerous times in anticipation. Travis swore he'd told Officer Allen that he got off at six and it would take him "about 30 minutes to wrap shit up at work and drive to the station." Both Travis and Conway began the interview in the worst mood.

"How long have you and Jamie dated?" Conway asked.

"See, that's the thing. We weren't really a couple. I have a few chicks I see. She always thought we were more than we really were, and I felt sorry for her. She knew I saw other women, but she still let me come back to her bed," Travis said. "That's all I saw her as. I would never be with her or stay with her for life, but she was delusional and clingy. I can't help it if she thought we were more." Travis slouched in his chair.

"So you led her on? She has your picture framed everywhere. You got her pregnant!" Conway slammed his fist on the table.

"Pregnant? I didn't know she was pregnant. She never told me that!" Travis crossed his arms.

Conway leaned closer to Travis. "Where were you last night?"

"I really don't want to say because I could get someone in trouble. But I wasn't with Jamie, if that's what you want to know," he said, looking up at the ceiling.

"You're going to need to tell me a lot more than that, because it's not 'someone else' who'll be in trouble. It's your ass on the line." Conway pointed his finger at him.

"Me? What the fuck did I do?" Raising his voice, Travis sat up straight in his chair. "Wait a minute. If you're accusing me of killing Jamie, then I'm going to stop right here. I've watched enough cop shows to know how this shit ends. I didn't love Jamie, but I wouldn't kill her. And you think I'd kill her because I found out she's pregnant?

Come on, man. I got two kids. That wouldn't make me kill." Travis slumped back into his chair.

"Maybe you don't want more child support. Maybe two is enough. There are lots of reasons men kill their lovers." Conway leaned back, gesturing with his hands.

"This is bullshit. I'm done talking to you." Travis crossed his feet.

"I'll be getting a subpoena for your phone and work records. I'll know about every woman you've been with. Tell me, do the names Nadine, Becky, and Deborah ring a bell?" Conway glared at Travis.

Travis stared straight ahead and refused to answer any more questions. Since he wasn't under arrest, just under suspicion, he was free to go. He'd soon find that his house and work would be under surveillance. He no longer had the freedom he once enjoyed.

Travis would eventually hire a lawyer, which took every bit of savings he had planned on using to buy a vintage Corvette. Conway had laser beam eyes on him, and Travis couldn't fight the system alone, even if his ego thought he could. After Conway received Travis's phone records, he could see what a playboy he was. Travis called many women; Jamie was one of twenty that he rotated through his schedule. On the night of Jamie's murder, he was with one of those women, a married mom of two, but neither of them were his kids. Unfortunately, none of the numbers matched Nadine, Becky, or Deborah, but Conway would work on that connection. Once he solved Jamie's murder, it would be easier to determine the connection to the others. He saw Jamie texted Travis many times on the night of her murder and believed that she told him they were having a baby, which angered him and made him kill her. He already had two children he rarely saw and was often behind on child support, so a third would be an even greater financial and personal burden than he was willing to accept.

Conway wrung his hands in preparation of receiving an arrest warrant and wanted it to be big news, so he alerted a contact at the local news station, making them aware to be present at Travis's job. It pleased Conway to think of the image of Travis's "perp walk" to be blasted all over the news, and he wanted to give the interview that would seal his fate in history for catching one of Cape Ivy's biggest serial killers. Conway got his wish—Travis's arrest was everywhere.

His head hung low as he tried to avoid the cameras, both video and photographs, but when they turned him around to cuff him, he couldn't escape the lenses. The image that splashed across the front page of the local newspaper was of Travis with a slight smirk, which really paved the way for social media commenters to call him "evil, twisted, and demented."

Immediately following Travis' arrest, his lawyer conducted a press conference. He said all the right things: "Travis is innocent. We will prove he was nowhere near the crime scene. He cared for Jamie and did not know she was pregnant. Travis is being wrongfully accused by an overzealous police detective, and we will work tirelessly until they release him." When he walked away from the crowd, reporters shouted, "Why did he do it?" while curious onlookers screamed, "You should be ashamed of yourself for supporting a baby killer."

Conway watched the press conference in the police headquarters lunchroom, chuckling at the lawyer and the comments that followed. "Good luck—you'll need it," he mumbled under his breath. He held his head up high and asked a few of the officers working the case if they wanted to go for a celebratory drink. Naturally, they all agreed. They looked up to Conway, and many had aspirations of becoming a detective one day.

While Conway celebrated, he imagined Travis sitting alone on his jail bed, contemplating his next move.

CHAPTER 37

2020

A petite blonde with fresh makeup and streaks of highlights sat waiting for him.

"Excuse me, are you Tiffany Carson?" Conway cleared his throat.

"Yes!" Tiffany jumped up from her chair with her purse dangling on her forearm.

Conway escorted her to the larger conference room and introduced her to Officer Allen, who had just inhaled his last Tootsie Roll and could barely open his jaws to introduce himself.

"Thank you for coming down to the station. I need to ask you a few questions about your coworker, Jamie Holly. I understand you were the one to call in for a welfare check?" Conway unfolded his notepad.

"Yes, I did. But she was much more than a coworker. She was my best friend. At least until we had a falling out. But I'd like to forget about that part." Tiffany batted her eyelashes as a mascara-stained tear fell across her cheek.

Officer Allen rose to grab a box of tissues and handed it to Tiffany.

"Tell me everything you can remember about the last time you saw her," Conway started.

"Jamie was super excited when she found out she was pregnant.

She came out of the bathroom and was practically screaming about it." Tiffany rolled her eyes. "So she left work early to plan a surprise for Travis." Tiffany nodded with each fact.

"What can you tell me about their relationship?" Conway looked up from his notes.

"Jamie was in over her head with Travis. She could never tame him, and honestly, it became really annoying. She was borderline obsessed and everyone at work went from feeling sorry for her to feeling irritated. I mean, it was clear to everyone but Jamie that Travis didn't love her and definitely wouldn't be happy with her getting pregnant." Tiffany pursed her lips and sat back in her chair as she crossed her arms.

"So you agree that this would have been an unwanted pregnancy for Travis?" Conway questioned.

"Oh, I'm sure. Travis isn't much of the father type. At least, he hasn't found the right woman. He's what you'd call a player. Jamie tried to tame him, but he was too wild for her," Tiffany crossed her legs.

"It sounds like you know quite a bit about Travis. What's your relationship with him?" Conway raised his eyebrows.

"Ugh. Well, this is why Jamie and I stopped being besties. We both had a thing for Travis and after she started, I'd guess you call it, dating him—well, I slept with him. Just once! But honestly, it was worth it. Jamie knew my true feelings for Travis, and he just wasn't right for her. She tried to make him a white picket fence kind of guy, but he's an end-of-the-bar, get-home-late dude. You know?" Tiffany grinned.

"So, how did Jamie find out about you and Travis?" Conway asked.

"Oh, I told her. I grew up Catholic and I couldn't live with the guilt. I figured she'd be mad, but I didn't think she'd stop being my best friend. Honestly, she believed in a lot of astrology and manifestation shit, but it never stopped Travis from cheating on her. Truth be told, I thought she'd break up with him and he and I could be together, but it wasn't working out like that." Tiffany looked at a chipped nail.

"When was the last time you saw Jamie?"

"After work." Tiffany stared at the ceiling.

Conway turned back toward Tiffany after waiting for Officer

Allen's sneezing fit to stop. "After work? You saw Jamie after she left to go home and decorate?" He leaned in.

"Oh, no. I mean, after she left the building, I saw her drive off." Tiffany looked back at Conway, a smile slowly forming.

"Hmm, okay. And you became concerned the next morning?"

"Oh yes. We all were worried, because we wanted to hear how the surprise went. We all pitched in to cover Jamie's clients and our own, so we became really swamped. When I could get away, I called her number at least ten times throughout the day, but I got no response, so I thought it would be a good idea just to have someone check on her, you know?" Tiffany looked back and forth at both men.

"Since you know Travis, did you call him?"

"Oh, I didn't want to spoil the baby surprise if he didn't already know."

Conway concluded the interview and Tiffany left, but the scent of her sandalwood perfume lingered. Conway's thoughts wandered back to Travis, who remained inside a Cape Ivy jail cell.

CHAPTER 38
2020

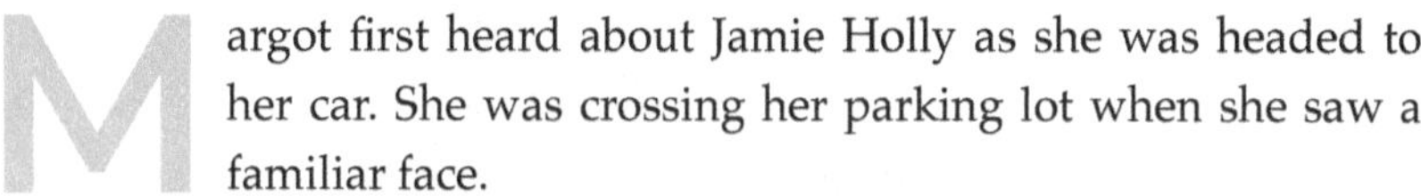

Margot first heard about Jamie Holly as she was headed to her car. She was crossing her parking lot when she saw a familiar face.

How does she know where I live and why is she here?

Loni Smart immediately shoved her way through the growing crowd of reporters to get Margot's first words. "Margot, what are your thoughts on a possible arrest in the CMK case?" Loni positioned herself front and center amongst the journalists.

"What are you talking about? What arrest?" Margot looked at all the ambitious faces, hoping for answers.

"There's been a new victim, Jamie Holly, who they found dead in her bed, bludgeoned to death. They've arrested her boyfriend, who they believe may be behind the CMK murders," Loni said, aiming the microphone toward Margot's gaping mouth. "How do you feel knowing this victim was pregnant?" Loni shouted over the other reporters.

"I need to go." Margot ran to her car, shielding her face. She needed to ditch these reporters and get somewhere safe. She spun her tires getting out of the parking lot and made sure she wasn't being followed. Her hands shook as she replayed Loni's words. Margot had distanced herself from *Death Toll* as she no longer needed that outlet, but this would have been the top breaking news all over the chat.

No mask? Bludgeoned to death? How is this connected? Pregnant? Oh. My. God. This keeps getting worse.

Her heart was in her stomach and it took her back to the day she'd discovered Nadine's body, dead on her bed. She reached for her phone when she saw the missed text from Gemma checking in on her regarding the recent murder. Margot needed to get answers. She mis-dialed twice before finally leaving a voicemail for Detective Conway.

"Yes, hello, this is Margot Mays. I was just accosted by the media in my parking lot about a potential arrest. Is it true that this new victim's boyfriend is being held for Nadine's murder, too? Is he possibly CMK? I hear she was pregnant? Please call me back immediately. I'm waiting by the phone."

———

"How does a detective not alert the family first? This is unacceptable," Margot said into her cell phone as she learned her parents were also in the dark.

"We definitely haven't heard a word, but we know how busy the police can get," Stella said.

"Well, that's their job. It doesn't take but a minute to give us a heads up. Also, I'm sick to my stomach learning that this latest victim was pregnant."

"Yes, that's very troubling. I hope her family will have peace if they can catch this man soon," Stella said.

"I don't know. It's been so long for us I can't imagine what peace would feel like. My grief has turned to anger. The cops aren't doing enough and now I've become the face of the CMK survivor." Margot gripped the steering wheel. "The scariest part is not knowing if this is the work of the same person. And if it's someone else, then we have two killers on the loose."

"Margot, are you going to be OK? I don't want you driving with all of this on your mind," Stella said.

"News flash, mom. This shit is always on my mind. But to answer your question, yes. I've taken all the necessary precautions, and I always make sure I lock my door. I'm always on alert, checking my surroundings, almost obsessively. It's terrible living like this, but I see the world differently. I'm aware of the evil that exists; I can't just wake up and ignore it," Margot pulled over in a gravel parking lot.

"You've come so far, Margot, and I think it's perfectly fine for you to take precautions, as long as it doesn't interfere with your day-to-day life. The fact that you're able to function and get out of the house speaks volumes," Stella said.

Margot hung up with her mom, which only fueled her frustration over the lack of information from the police department. As she usually did to relieve stress, she drove the path to the cemetery on this cloudy day and parked in her usual spot, but still didn't approach Nadine's grave because of the fear that she might encounter her stalker. She looked around and wondered if they buried any of CMK's other victims nearby.

"Nadine, they may have your murderer. It still doesn't feel real to me. I'm not sure how I'm supposed to feel, but I guess I thought I'd be more…gratified? I thought I would feel more relief than I do, but I have some doubts. Maybe that's the pessimist in me? I also know that until I hear all the evidence, they won't convince me, so maybe once I see the concrete proof, then I'll know for sure," Margot said out loud, looking out toward Nadine's grave.

Margot rolled down her window and breathed in the faint scent of honeysuckle as she dialed Detective Conway's number again.

"Conway speaking."

"Finally! This is Margot Mays. I've been trying to reach you about the potential break in the CMK case! Is it true?" Margot dug her nail into her thigh.

Margot could hear the distinct sound of a hand over a cell phone receiver as Conway's phone went silent.

"Margot. I am so sorry you had to find out that way, and I'm sorry they've invaded your privacy. Everything happened so fast and I haven't had a moment to line all my ducks in a row. I can't confirm that Travis, the boyfriend, is CMK, but I'm working on making a connection. I don't have any definitive answers for you today, but I promise that you and the family members will know before any media outlets do the next time," Conway said.

Margot placed her hand on her forehead in frustration. "Please keep your word on that. It's hard enough going through a murder, but learning information through the media is unfair."

"I give you my word."

Margot pulled away from the cemetery, hoping that Travis *was* CMK so they could solve the case and she could close that chapter and move on to the next one—the justice years. But she had her doubts and didn't understand the connection. *This doesn't feel like it's the right guy.*

CHAPTER 39

2020

When Jack first heard of Travis's arrest as the Choke Mask Killer, his reaction was laughter. He cracked open a beer and watched as much news coverage on the case as possible. Jack enjoyed watching the reporters attempt to tie Travis to several unsolved murders that he hadn't even heard of. Suddenly, Travis became the monster who put razors into Halloween candy and the mystery predator who spied on women trying on clothes at Kmart. He thought Travis was a moron for getting himself caught up in this case and didn't have any sympathy for the bastard.

Once a killer, it was hard to be normal, but Jack learned to assimilate with the harmless population. He'd kept a low profile since his last murder as he waited for the perfect time to return to the hunt. While they kept Travis locked up, Jack's hands felt tied, which was torturous for a killer. He needed to wait until the cops figured out their mistake, so he had to keep his head down and let them believe they had the right guy. At first, he rather enjoyed lying low and being unseen without the worry of getting caught. Jack went about his work and days just like normal, except without the killing in between. It gave him time to relish in his prior murders and develop a hunger for his next victim. But after a few months, Jack was tired of waiting for his next kill. The coverage made him irate, and he tired of hearing pundits talk about their theories of CMK's motives.

The TV talking heads speculated that the Choke Mask Killer was a deviant and must receive sexual gratification from his kills. "The killer likes to dominate women and having control over them gives him a power that satisfies his hedonistic nature," Dr. Tom Wiley, a psychiatrist with Life Tree Therapy, Inc. had stated during a recent segment on *Cape Ivy This Morning.* However, Dr. Simone Williams challenged him when she called in to say that "perhaps the killer was power focused." Dr. Williams stated, "There is some crossover with hedonism and control where the killer finds satisfaction in watching his defenseless victim slowly die." The pair agreed that the killer most likely had a troubled childhood, which enraged Jack, who crushed a can with his bare hands.

You have no fucking idea.

———

Police finally had to release Travis from jail after failing to gather enough evidence to charge him with Jamie's murder. There weren't any other suspects and they couldn't make the timeline work with his alibi after the woman he was with that night vouched for his version of events. Based on what Jack saw on the news, that didn't stop Conway from believing in Travis's guilt.

Jack watched as Travis continued to be public enemy number one. The media continued to name him as the alleged Choke Mask Killer, which reportedly got him fired from his job and made him a recluse in his parents' home. Even after his release from jail without charges, the media harassed him and his family by camping outside their house, waiting for a comment they refused to provide. Travis's attorney, who did little except hold press conferences, was probably costing him thousands of dollars. Eventually, Travis sued the media for slander because of his destroyed name and reputation. Not only did they call him a murderer, but they published names of women that he had been seeing, which also ruined their lives, as many of them were married and all were now linked to the possible killer. The public didn't have to hate him for being a killer; they could still hate him for being a womanizer. After Travis sued the local newspaper and television station, both settled out of court for an undisclosed amount, and the judge sealed the case. Shortly after, rumor had it that Travis moved out of Cape Ivy and hadn't returned.

Once they released Travis, the tension in Jack's neck subsided. He wanted his name back—the Choke Mask Killer. He also enjoyed the sense of doom that permeated the city again now that the residents knew the killer prevailed and still lurked amongst them. While Jack was always on the lookout for new victims, he wouldn't remain idle for too long. He knew he had to continue to lie low, but it wouldn't keep him from his stalking ways. A man needed to satiate his vile thoughts somehow. Jack often drove the streets of Cape Ivy to follow a woman walking or driving alone. When he'd spot a potential victim, his body hair raised as visions of her dead behind his mask came to the forefront of his mind.

He left his apartment community to investigate the central part of Cape Ivy, where professors and artists lived. A mid-century modern home piqued his interest, as it had beautiful floor-to-ceiling windows that indicated its inhabitants were more interested in letting in light and nature than keeping out voyeurs and danger.

As nightfall approached, Jack, dressed in dark clothing, stood next to a row of tall evergreen shrubs, which were perfect for concealing his tall frame. He watched a middle-aged woman who sat at a disheveled desk typing on a computer with a large shelf full of books to her back. She had slick brunette hair that fell in a lazy part toward her cheeks. She wore her glasses affixed at the bridge of her nose and mouthed along with the words she typed while her Persian cat lay sleepily on a footstool nearby.

I don't have to worry about tenants hearing her scream.

Jack was still contemplating murder and whether he should follow his impulse when a pair of headlights lit up the hems of his pant legs. He remained still as the lights continued up the driveway and drove into the garage. A minute later, he saw a man enter the office and give the woman a kiss on the lips. The two stood up and left the room.

Fuck. Maybe I'll throw the cops off by killing a dude too.

But Jack's heart wasn't in killing men. Sure, killing Paul was pure satisfaction, but he knew killing random men wouldn't satisfy him like killing women. The front porch light turned on only five feet from where Jack stood. He held his breath to prevent detection. The night was full of crickets and buzzing insects, which he would later curse for feeding on him. A woman's voice broke through the chirping.

"I'll be right out, Steve. I forgot my phone," the smoky voice said.

As Steve crossed the front door's threshold, Jack moved until he was only a couple of feet from him. The man looked down at his brightly lit phone with a soft, wicked laugh. Unable to see what he was looking at, Jack watched as Steve walked to another car parked along the curb in front of the house. A minute later, the woman he saw earlier walked through the door. As she fumbled with her keys, Jack leaned in closer. He could smell her scent and felt a slight shift in the temperature; he wanted to have death on the tip of his tongue. As she locked the front door, he breathed in her woodsy perfume, eyes fixed on her bare arms in her sundress and her pink lips that slightly parted. In an instant, she and Steve sped off, and Jack resolved to return to his apartment setting—single women were much easier to locate that way.

CHAPTER 40
2020

Margot had seen enough flowers at her doorstep for a lifetime. She contacted the flower shop and let them know she was refusing all future deliveries, as well as deliveries to Nadine's grave. She was angry that the police had advised her to avoid going to Nadine's gravesite alone because of her stalker.

How dare he take away my aunt!

Margot drove to the library and sat at the Crime Three's unassigned meeting desk in front of the picture window. She looked outside at a family of wrens perched on the large oak tree. She could almost recognize the bird families since she'd started coming here—at least, she wanted to believe that comforting thought.

"Hey, Margot. How's it going?" Carter asked as he plopped into a chair.

"I'm still pretty anxious and angry about the stalker. I miss going to visit my aunt, and I'm just so tired of waiting." Margot let out a deep sigh.

"Damn, I'm sorry. Are the police able to do anything?" Carter leaned forward.

"The police can't do a lot until they catch the stalker in the act. They said they'd do some drive-bys at the graveyard, but that's about it," Margot shook her head.

Gemma sat down across from Carter, next to Margot. "Hey guys. Margot, you've been on my mind. Are you holding up OK?"

"I'm frustrated with the lack of answers. The stalking has continued, which I assume is Lucas or CMK, or just a really horrible prank. But I can't rule out someone I know. If it is Lucas, what's keeping him from getting revenge for losing his teaching position and being outed on *Death Toll*? Maybe he sees me as an easy target." Margot twisted her lips.

"Do you feel safe being alone? If not, is there someone you can stay with until they catch the stalker? You're welcome to stay with me," Gemma said.

"I have my stun gun, which helps me feel a little safer. Honestly, my fear is turning more to anger. So I refuse to move out of my apartment." Margot lifted her chin defiantly.

Carter stared at Margot, nodding.

"I'm angry I've had to change my routine. I had learned to live my life coexisting with CMK in my world. Of course, I always knew his danger lurked, but I always kept a dead bolt on my front door and checked every room of my apartment before I went to bed. This CMK ritual became part of my life, but I didn't think I'd have to deal with a killer and a stalker at the same time." Margot wrapped herself tighter into her sweater to ward off the chilly sensation overwhelming her.

"He probably knows when you go grocery shopping or any time you leave your apartment. His one and only job is knowing everything about you," Carter said.

"I know! Trust me, I have thought about all of this."

Gemma pursed her lips. "Anything I can do, just ask."

———

As Margot drove away from the library, she instinctively drove toward Lorimier Cemetery. She knew she was becoming borderline obsessed with looking for the car that had followed her as she checked for more flowers on Nadine's grave. She drove around the perimeter of the cemetery, but there was no sign of the vehicle from the other night. Nadine's gravesite was too far from the parking lot to see if there was anything left on the grave, so she couldn't tell if more signs of a stalker were there.

Margot drove back to her apartment, taking a varied route home just in case; her heart in her stomach the entire way. She checked her surroundings like she always did, but noticed nothing out of the ordinary. Then, as she reached the top of the stairs, she noticed her welcome mat had moved. It was no longer in front of her door, having shifted about a foot to the side. Margot was fairly certain she hadn't moved it, but she tried to convince herself that maybe a delivery person or a mailman had kicked it by accident, even though there wasn't a package.

Her heart pounded as she debated running back to her car, but the logical side of her propelled her forward. She was closer to safety—her apartment with a dead bolt and her stun gun. Margot could clearly see that no one was in the hall, so she ran up the remaining two steps, swinging her purse around her shoulder, and untangled her keys to unlock the door. Her hands shook uncontrollably as she turned to look behind her, worried that someone would be there, but she was still alone in the narrow hallway. Finally able to unlock her door, she slammed it shut, locking the dead bolt.

She was checking it again when she realized someone had been inside.

CHAPTER 41
2020

Margot jumped at the sound of a glass crashing off of the table and quickly spun to make a run for the door. As soon as she opened it, she saw Gemma standing on the other side.

"Margot, hey. I came to check up on you."

Margot's body shook as she turned to look back toward her living room. "Let me gather my thoughts. Someone was in here."

"Let me look around," Gemma said, taking a quick glance around the small apartment. "I don't see anyone. What makes you think someone was here?" She walked back in from the hallway.

Margot's eyes darted toward the hallway for an elusive intruder. "I saw this note on the floor that says, 'I'll just deliver the flowers myself.'" Margot shakily handed the note to Gemma.

Margot's bare arms formed goosebumps, shattering any façade of stoicism. She tried to quiet the shivering that was making its way through her nervous system and out of her pores. Gemma pulled down a thin throw blanket that was draped over the couch and handed it to Margot. Gemma took another walk around the apartment, which seemed to settle Margot's nerves.

"Margot, you don't need to be alone right now," Gemma said.

"Thank you. I appreciate all of your support. But I can't let whoever is doing this win." Margot took a deep breath. "If I chicken out, I promise I'll call you and come stay with you for the night."

Once Gemma left, Margot mentally ran through a checklist of who could be stalking her. The most obvious people were Lucas or the faceless killer. However, Margot assumed that the killer would have already murdered her by now, unless he was toying with her. As far as Lucas, she now knew he'd lied to her, and desperation made people do drastic things. Of course, there were Gemma and Carter, but she couldn't bring herself to be suspicious of Gemma when she'd been so welcoming and understanding. *Although it was strange that she was suddenly here, right as I opened the door.* Margot had her doubts about Carter's loyalty, but after their discussion, she believed they'd moved on.

Margot pondered all the potential suspects and barely slept at all that night. She lay with her hand on her stun gun under the pillow next to her, just to be sure it was still there. When she had bought it, she told herself it was just for peace of mind and she'd never have to use it. She hadn't even fired it yet. *What if it doesn't go off when I need it?* She would soon find out, reaching for it after she heard an unfriendly creak in her floorboards. Was it just the moonlit night casting menacing figures across her wall, or was it an actual person?

CHAPTER 42
2020

On this Saturday night, Jack found himself surrounded by loud chants, the smell of draft beer and chicken wings, and torn vinyl barstools. He ordered a beer and found a secluded table at the back of the Corner Pub—a different crowd from Patsy's. This bar had college football playing on big screens and a younger frat vibe, but Jack went unnoticed at the back table along the brick wall. The town was abuzz with CMK still on the prowl and the local news devoting nightly segments to highlight the victims and various theories circulating about the killer. Jack decided he needed to give *Heartland Matters* a listen to see what everyone was talking about, especially since he'd learned one guest was Nadine's niece. *I want to know how it felt on the other side of that night.*

While Jack enjoyed the strain that the murders put on Cape Ivy, it forced him to be cautious to avoid becoming a suspect. They'd already interviewed him during Nadine's investigation, and he didn't want to give them a reason to link him to the others. It grew more difficult to find new victims to pursue because the maintenance crew were on higher alert since the latest murders. Jameka hired extra security to patrol the apartments and drive around looking for anything suspicious throughout the night, which certainly made killing a challenge. It was bad enough the cops were on patrol, but now management tasked maintenance with watching out for the elusive killer.

Jack searched for Loni Smart's show, which was uploaded to the internet, where she highlighted all the recent murders attributed to CMK. He couldn't believe how much he enjoyed reliving that night. As he listened to Margot's words through his earbuds, he savored her account of finding her aunt. A warmth overcame his body as the euphoria of being on the other side, hearing how his havoc affected others. He felt lucky and wondered if other killers enjoyed the same luxury of hearing about the aftermath of their work. Everything worked out just as he'd planned, and he'd been chasing the murder high since his first victim. As he listened to Margot describe finding Nadine's body, it was almost as satisfying as the real thing, and Jack rewound the episode to listen to her description several times. With each listen, the vicious smile on his face grew wider.

As screams of bar goers yelling for the Redhawks to score a touch-down interjected themselves between Margot's words, Jack reveled in the juxtaposition of the football game against Margot's interview.

"Let's go Redhawks. Defense!" the crowd of frat boys cheered.

"I will never forget the eerie dread that sunk into my gut. When Nadine didn't respond to my calls, I just knew something horrible happened. Our conversations were like clockwork."

Jack stared straight ahead, watching college kids clad in football jerseys down their beers.

"The smell hit me first. I instantly knew it was death, but I kept hoping. My mind played tricks on me, and I negotiated with it. Maybe it was soured trash and Nadine was just sleeping. I wanted to run straight to her bedroom, but I didn't know if I was alone or not."

Jack eagerly anticipated the next part. Though he knew what to expect, he was excited to hear Margot's interpretation.

"You dumb fuck, they should fire you," one of the frat boys yelled at a referee on the screen.

"When I saw Nadine on the bed, for a split second I wondered if it was a joke. I mean, Nadine wasn't one to pull a trick like that, but my mind couldn't comprehend what it was seeing. As I got closer, I saw the smooth leather tightly wrapped around her head, with a trickle of blood running down her neck. I don't remember how I got out of there, but in some ways, I never left."

Jack removed the EarPods from his ears, savoring those last words. As much as he enjoyed listening to her interview, it hindered his ability to kill. Now everyone was talking about the Choke Mask Killer, and not just the local news—it had made national headlines.

Margot was making it much more difficult for Jack to stalk his next victim, much less murder her.

She needs to be stopped.

CHAPTER 43
2020

The creak in the floorboard turned out to be a masked person who stood menacingly at the side of her bed. The flash of the stun gun briefly dazed Margot as the pulsating lights flashed in her eyes. She stumbled out of bed, immediately tripping over a stack of books that she'd left piled on the floor. As she regained her balance, she wondered if whoever she'd shot with the stun gun was still in shock or if he'd found his strength. *Could it possibly be CMK?* She knew she had to keep running, keep fighting to escape her apartment, or else death was likely to come. Margot rounded the corner into the hallway and banged her shoulder hard on the wall—complete darkness and fear made a person forget paths they normally knew by heart. She winced in pain, instinctively reaching up to rub her shoulder, and peeked behind her to see if she was being chased.

Although it was dark, she could have sworn she saw movement—the darkness was playing tricks on her. Her eyes still saw spots from when the stun gun went off. As she finally reached her front door, her heart pounded so loud that she feared it would give away her exact location. She struggled to find the locks she knew so well. Her CMK ritual was instinctive, but she'd never tested it with an intruder on her heels.

The footsteps were getting closer, but she couldn't see where he was as she finally unlocked the first of the two locks. She heard something crash to the floor, followed by a loud boom—he must have hit something and fell. The sound of shattering glass echoed through the room. Margot had recently added a P.E. Guerin brass end table with a glass top from Nadine's collection to spruce up her place, which was likely what had caused the sound. She could hear the intruder sliding toward her, getting closer with each second.

As her hands shook, Margot finally opened her front door and flew down the stairs into the chilly night air. Without her cell phone or car keys, she ran onto Broadway Boulevard, but there were no open stores, and the streets were empty except for parked cars and flashing street lights. Margot ran down the middle of Broadway until she saw a car, which blared its horn, but the driver didn't stop.

After she ran several blocks, the cold air burning her throat, Margot found herself on a part of the street where the streetlights were few and only the moon lit the tops of trees, casting shadows onto the pavement. The wind picked up and Margot gasped. She'd thought the stalker was standing behind her, but it was just a branch that looked like an ominous hand reaching for her. Finally, she ran into a gas station at Themis and convinced the attendant to call the police.

"Margot, I came as soon as I heard what happened," Detective Conway said after he parked his car in the gas station parking lot.

Margot sipped cheap coffee and wrapped herself in the itchy blanket the police had given her, still shaking from the night's events.

Margot told Conway what happened and begged to ride along back to her apartment. She needed to make sure that they finally arrested whoever this man was. "He's harassed me for the last time. I won't be able to rest until I watch you handcuff him!" Margot pleaded.

"Look, I'll send other units to your apartment to clear it first, and we'll stay in my cruiser. You're not getting anywhere near him," Conway said.

———

Back at Margot's apartment, she and Conway sat in his patrol car. She attempted to open the door, but he had them locked, with no way for her to get out. She stared at the outside entrance to her apartment, just waiting for movement.

Margot could hear the wailing sound of an ambulance in the distance. It kept getting closer until it eventually pulled in next to Conway. Finally, the outside door to the apartment opened and Margot saw the silhouette of the masked intruder sitting on the bottom stair with his hands on his head.

"Looks like he might have fallen chasing after you," Conway said.

"Oh, my God," Margot said, still in shock from the incident.

I need to see his face.

She watched as the EMTs checked over the intruder and eventually left. The police then handcuffed him and walked him to a squad car that was parked behind Conway's. She could overhear the officers talking.

"The victim is the niece of Nadine Chastain, one of CMK's victims. He says this is all a big misunderstanding," Officer Breyer relayed the details to the lead detective.

Margot gaped out the window, trying to catch a glimpse of the stranger who broke in. Another officer carried a bag marked Police Evidence, which she could see had the mask inside.

"Oh my God. They removed the mask. Please, Conway, let me out!" Margot begged, fogging up the backseat window of Conway's patrol car.

That's when she saw the person being escorted into Officer Breyer's police car. Margot's hands were damp with sweat and her mind raced, trying to piece the puzzle together.

"Do you know who that is?" Conway asked, looking back in his rearview mirror.

It had been a growing fear of Margot's that she may have been inviting CMK into her life all this time. She couldn't live with herself if she had welcomed Nadine's killer into her home.

As Margot got a good look at the intruder, her stomach revolted at the knowledge of who'd invaded her privacy. "I'm not sure who I know anymore." Margot slumped back into Conway's police car, which smelled of sweat and coffee.

CHAPTER 44

2020

Cape Ivy became unholy ground for anyone who dared to argue that Travis wasn't CMK. It divided the city in two and you either believed or didn't; the grays had to take a side. It had been weeks since Jack's last kill, and his frustration was maddening. He'd started following two different women, but after a few tries, neither one panned out. One woman began dating a man who moved into her apartment, and the other woman had such a varied schedule that it was too unpredictable for Jack.

The city remained on edge, and management beefed up security at all Elite Living apartments again. Jack felt like a tiger without his fangs —once so powerful, now useless. His patience grew thinner as the months went along and his desire for murder grew.

Jack's thoughts became more reckless as he considered other means of murder. He no longer cared about the meticulous planning he usually took with stalking his victims and the scoping out of the utility closet. Now he thought of quicker ways to satiate his violent impulses.

A gun would be much easier. I could just break in and shoot the bitch in the face, or bash it in with a bat and end it as she falls asleep.

Jack was no longer satisfied as a murderer as he drove around Cape Ivy looking for his next victim. He was no longer sticking to his original plan of apartments, instead driving through residential neighborhoods. He hoped to find a woman walking alone so that he could follow her home and peep on her, even though the streets in this part of the city were foreign to him.

Maybe I should go back to the country. I know the woods better, and I can conceal myself within the trees, just like I used to. Maybe return to the Smiths' house.

The idea of reliving his first break-in pressed on his mind for days until he finally caved and made plans to return to his old stomping ground. He decided if anyone were to catch him, he'd just say he was reminiscing about his Uncle Louie and lost track of the property line. It was a plausible excuse, but he also knew country folk shoot first and ask questions later, so he didn't plan on getting caught.

When the evening came for his return to the woods, Jack felt a sense of relief to set out on this adventure. All day his muscles relaxed as the plan to return to his old stomping grounds came nearer. He did not know if the Smiths family still lived in that house, but he was eager to find out. He blasted his favorite rock station and smoked several cigarettes on the way, turning down a street a few blocks from his mom's house. Jack definitely didn't want to run into her.

He found a secluded area to park his car that was shielded from the main road and hidden behind a couple of pine trees. Dusk was setting on the woods, which made the walk feel somewhat tranquil for Jack, who had been dreaming of this night for weeks.

The sounds of twigs snapping under Jack's shoes and crisp leaves falling from nearly barren limbs, with the screech of owls in the distance, broke the quiet. Jack's breath was a trail of smoke, both from his cigarette and the frigid evening air.

As he turned the corner to where the Smiths' house once stood, Jack's cigarette dangled on his bottom lip. "What the fuck?" he surveyed the area.

In disbelief, Jack stood for a minute and stared at the new surroundings where the Smiths' house had been. It was now a large garage holding tractors and farm equipment. The once tall oak he'd peeped from was also gone to make room for the massive structure.

There was nothing to observe except plows and tillers, and he did not come for that.

Jack walked back to his car, crushing his half-smoked cigarette in his hand. He gripped the steering wheel, slammed the car into reverse, and drove past Louie's old land. The rusted trailer and corroded appliances still stood in the yard, covered with a couple feet of grass. Jack wasn't sure who owned the land now, but it no longer had the magic of his youth. It was part of the country landscape he wanted to forget and seeing it in its deteriorated state ignited a fury in Jack that burned from his gut into his head. He made a turn toward his mom's street as a slow smile formed on his somber face with a new plan to indulge his urges. He could see a light on in the front room, but no movement. After he put the car in park, he sat and debated his next move.

If I kill my mom, they'll probably know it's me. But damn it, I'm so close right now. But I don't have an alibi. Maybe that's my new plan—schedule a long maintenance repair and then come down here and kill her.

Jack leered as he thought through a plan to kill his mom, with thoughts of killing his Aunt Kathy, too. But before he pulled his car away, he saw a flicker of movement inside the house. It was a younger woman holding a baby. She laughed as a man came up behind her and hugged them.

Jack peeled out of there and drove ninety down the county road back to his apartment. His agitation grew, and he doubted his abilities. He was the little boy who couldn't do anything right and "would never amount to nothin'." Jack paced his small studio, which could barely contain his explosive fury.

Maybe it's time to move to a new city. A change of scenery and pace may make finding a victim much easier.

CHAPTER 45

2020

Margot and Gemma arranged a brunch date now that their crime group had gotten smaller.

Gemma waved Margot over to a table. "I'm so glad to see you. I hope this table is OK?" The Morning Spoon had recently opened in the historic Marquette Hotel in downtown Cape Ivy. Once a major attraction for wealthier travelers, it had closed after falling on hard times. The new owners had worked to revitalize the building to its once majestic glory.

As they ordered avocado toast and a fruit bowl, Margot rehashed what had happened just a few weeks ago when Carter broke into her apartment. "I'm sorry it's taken so long for me to meet up with you, but I've had to meet with detectives and the prosecutors. I've also moved out of my apartment into a house with a lot better security." Margot looked up at the limestone wall.

"I don't blame you. Margot, I can't imagine all the stress you've been through. I've been following everything on the news, and I'm sure I only know half of what happened." Gemma shook her head.

"I wish I had been more careful that first day I met him," Margot whispered, although the new restaurant was abuzz with noise as the growing waiting list showed how packed they were. "I'm just in shock that all of this happened, but I'm doing much better now that he's been arrested. It seems Carter was a true crime addict; he intentionally sought out and rented part of my old house." Margot let out a deep breath.

Gemma listened with wide eyes as she grabbed a grape.

"Carter told the police he wasn't there to kill me, just to scare me. He thought I'd assume it was Lucas and wanted me to live in constant fear. He told them it was exciting, and he got a thrill out of this. Although, I still question whether he would have killed me if I hadn't fired my stun gun. When I first saw the shadow, I actually believed it was CMK, coming to silence me for good," Margot said.

"Oh, Margot. I can't imagine all of this. I'm so glad this is over. Honestly, I feel like I'm partially to blame since I didn't see this side of Carter either. All the time we spent at the library together and all along, he was planning ways to stalk you." Gemma looked down. "This whole time, I also assumed it was Lucas." She shook her head, frowning.

"The cops still haven't been able to confirm whether Lucas was really behind the *Death Toll* exposures, but now I wonder if it was Carter?" Margot shrugged. "We're both victims here and now we don't have to deal with either one anymore." Margot raised her glass to toast Gemma.

"You're right. At least we have each other," Gemma said. "Whoever TrollGod is did a good job of avoiding detection." Gemma twisted her lips.

"Yes. In fact, the cybercrimes detective determined that he created an account at the university library. At least, that's where the IP address came from."

Gemma's eyes darted. "Well, both of them have access to the university library."

Margot took another sip of orange juice and looked around to make sure no one was listening. "Carter is facing up to ten years for stalking and harassment, so I'll have to deal with his upcoming trial. The good news is there's two less men I have to worry about. Now I can go back to focusing on CMK."

"Do the police believe there's any connection between Carter or Lucas and the murders?" Gemma leaned in.

"As of now, no. Neither of them was in Cape Ivy for my aunt's murder per their alibis, but the police are still looking for any connections to the others."

"Imagine if we've been sitting next to a murderer this entire time!" Gemma's mouth gaped.

"I know! All this time I was running from murder and here I was, walking right to a dangerous man's door. 'Hi, are you looking for me?'" Margot put her hand to her forehead.

"This is all too much. You need a vacation," Gemma said.

"Absolutely! I could use one. My shoulders are so tense I don't think I've been able to relax in months, maybe years. I'm definitely going to plan a trip to a beach once they catch CMK! You must come with me." Margot finally flashed a smile for the first time since sitting down at the corner booth.

"Oh, I've never been to a beach. Count me in!" Gemma smiled.

"It's going to be so much fun. We deserve it," Margot said.

"I guess that's the end of *Death Toll*?" Gemma asked.

"Maybe? I don't know what will happen to it. When I last checked it, I saw a 404 message." Margot shrugged.

"I suppose I'll need to find a new hobby if *Death Toll* goes away." Gemma smirked.

"Honestly, I'm ready to be done with it for good." Margot took a bite of toast.

"Do you think Dr. Williams is innocent in all of this? I mean, I suppose it's plausible she didn't know what Lucas was up to, but it definitely helped her by keeping Cape Ivy on edge. Her entire job depends on crime." Gemma looked toward the front door.

"I doubt she's guilty, but I guess we'll never know. She wrote me a letter telling me she was too busy right now to focus on my case." Margot frowned. *I wish you well in your endeavors.* The signature of Dr. Williams' email continued to play in Margot's head.

When she'd read her words, she was gutted. Her hopes of having Dr. Williams' expertise were dashed. "I'd like to think such an accomplished professional woman wouldn't be associated with a man like

Lucas. However, we know criminals can railroad even the strongest people," Margot said. "But I still have Conway on the case." Margot rolled her eyes.

"Has he uncovered anything? I haven't heard any updates from you or the news," Gemma said.

"No, nothing. In fact, I have to call him when I have an issue. He's never called me first. Last I heard, he was still looking to connect all the murders, but no *one* suspect has stuck out."

"I guess Travis is off the hook for good?"

"I would guess, but I have no idea. Maybe Loni Smart will tell us on the news. She seems to get the latest scoop before I do." Margot sat back in her chair, crossing her arms.

"She'll probably find and interview the killer before Conway knows who he is." Gemma laughed.

Margot gave a half smile. "It wouldn't surprise me. Something tells me the killer is laughing at his good luck at having Conway on the case."

After they arrested Carter, Margot found a quaint bungalow house near downtown Cape Ivy that was much more spacious and had a much better security system. After her interview with Loni Smart and her speech with Dr. Williams, she had become a media darling, and they sought her out to discuss true crime cases as a victim specialist. "I don't know if I'm the right person for this, but I definitely have the will to keep victims' stories out there so they're not forgotten," Margot had said in her latest TV interview.

Margot's new backyard had a garden started by the former tenant that she hoped she could keep up with. She'd never had a green thumb before, but she liked the idea of picking up gardening as a hobby. The best part of her new house was its close proximity to the river. She could take an evening stroll, often taking Nadine's old camera along and snapping pictures of beautiful sunsets, imagining what Nadine used to see through that same lens on her evening bike rides. Most of the time, she could now think of Nadine without a tear coming to her eyes, but every now and again they formed, especially on those lonely nights when she wished she could hear Nadine's voice one last time. When she died, Margot thought she'd never forget Nadine's face or voice, but after a while the memory had blurred. Margot hated she couldn't remember every single thing about her aunt.

Once she arrived home from brunch, she leashed Pepper, who immediately charged toward the sidewalk, ready for his walk. Pepper, the ten-pound rescue dog she'd recently adopted from the local shelter, had given her as much unconditional love as she could ever want. This black and gray ragamuffin was her best friend right now, and nothing could make her happier. Pepper's kisses and snuggles were exactly what her heart needed after all she'd been through. Margot had learned so much since the awful July day, and although she wanted Nadine back, she'd grown to be proud of the strong woman she'd become.

Grief was the thing that never left her body, like the regret of missed opportunities she passed over. She hoped that with each passing day it would get better, and it did, but then something would strike her out of the blue, and she'd find herself shielding her swollen, crying eyes from onlookers. Nobody can understand anyone else's grief journey, even the ones that began on the same starting line.

She and Pepper had a date to watch the latest episode of *Survivor*, so she popped some popcorn and settled into a comfy position with him on the couch. Everything was falling into place. Almost everything.

CHAPTER 46
2021

"Well, look who's back! Hey Clara. What can I get ya?" the curly-haired brunette bartender said, smiling as she took the order of the much younger and hotter patron.

"Mims! I'll have a Cosmo. I finally had a night off and I had to come back to see my favorite bartender," Clara said, clearly trying to act sophisticated, as this was the best gay bar in Cape Ivy. Actually, it was the only one.

"What a shock. You're my favorite customer," Mims winked.

"Oh, I'm flattered. I may stick around, then." Clara winked back and glanced around the bar, which was adorned in an art déco design, like she had stepped back into a Fitzgerald novel.

"Here you go, Princess Clara," Mims teased as she handed her a Cosmo.

"How much?"

"On the house." Mims raised her eyebrows. She was always a flirt, especially with the younger ladies. Clara was a regular that she knew well, both in and out of the bar. Mims kept her hair tied back in a ponytail when she bartended and wore cutoff sleeve shirts, revealing a four-leaf clover tattoo on her right arm.

"I'll definitely be back," Clara smiled.

Mims had never had trouble with the ladies since coming out to her aunt at fifteen, as she knew she was gay from the age of ten. Mims had always felt like an outsider until she found her queer family. Once she came out, she gave up her given name of Miriam, opting for Mims as her new name. Working as a bartender was never her "dream," but once she started at the bar, it just felt right. She loved the hours, and it was a great place to meet people, especially women. She'd had her fair share of relationships, but none were ever long term, as she was a self-proclaimed loner when it came to sharing her living space. Her friends thought she just hadn't met "the one" yet, but she doubted it. She really thought she would always live alone with her cat, and as long as she could go on dates, that was about all she wanted. Mims had been used to the solo lifestyle since her teen years, and it suited her then and now. The only thing she hated about her job was the loud techno music they played on some nights, which definitely wasn't her style, but it seemed to bring out the type of women she enjoyed spending time with, so there was that.

Clara came back to Mims several times that night and the winks turned into eyebrow raises and eventually more conversation.

"What time are you off?" Clara asked, a hopeful look on her face. It looked like her friends were ready to leave for the night.

"Well," Mims checked the time, "I have to clean up after close, but if I get a little head start, it might only take half an hour, and we could be out of here by 2 a.m." Two o'clock was only another hour and a half away.

Clara seemed to like that idea and stayed and waited. Mims promised her she'd call her a cab in the morning.

"Oh, I'm spending the night?" Clara teased.

"Hell yeah you are," Mims flirted.

Both women checked the time every ten minutes, ready for the second half of the night to begin.

Finally, when Mims was off, they walked to her apartment, which was only four blocks away. Clara, who wore heels, wasn't as thrilled about having to walk, but Mims put her arm around her waist and helped her along the way.

"Brandy will be happy to see you again," Mims unlocked the door.

"Oh, I've missed her!" Clara became very excited.

Mims called for Brandy, her calico cat, but she didn't appear. "That's odd. Usually she only hides when men are here, but she likes women. Maybe she'll come out by morning." Mims headed to the bedroom to look for her cat.

Mims turned on loud music that was more her speed than the techno bar soundtrack: country. But Clara objected. "Oh, no, I hate country!" They settled on soft rock, which seemed appropriate for making out. They enjoyed the feel and taste of each other, luxuriating in the pleasure of their bodies meshed together. Mims never knew how straight people enjoyed the comfort of each other, but she'd much preferred the touch of a woman.

Afterward, they smoked a cigarette in bed and laughed about the night. Clara's tipsiness seemed to wear off. Both agreed they needed a shower after their long bar night and enjoyable sex. Of course, for Mims, that was also code for more sex in the shower, which happened until the water turned lukewarm and they dried off. At nearly 4 a.m., Clara decided she'd rather make her way home instead of waiting until sunrise, which was fine with Mims, as she wasn't much of the cuddling type. She much preferred having her bed to herself, and she was still concerned that her cat, Brandy, hadn't made an appearance. Mims escorted Clara to the cab with a quick kiss on the lips, and they vowed to catch up at the bar again soon.

Upon her return to her apartment, Mims called and looked for Brandy in the usual spots under the bed and behind the couch, eventually finding her wedged tight behind the refrigerator where she had never seen her before. She eventually coaxed her out with the promise of treats. Brandy appeared unhurt, but it concerned Mims because the last time she'd hid like this was when her friend Hector had come over to help move her couch. But even then, she'd come out relatively quickly as soon as he left, and she'd never hid behind the refrigerator. She took Brandy to bed with her after she ate and drank, and they lay together and snuggled a bit before the sun slowly peeked through the windows. That was when Mims noticed a large shoe print on the floor. It was too large to be a woman's print, and it was leading out from the utility closet, which was always locked. She had tried to open it once because she wanted to store some boxes in there, but couldn't.

Mims knew she hadn't requested maintenance in quite some time —maybe several months—and she hadn't received a notice that they were coming for a routine check. Her mind raced and her body stiffened in confusion. *Why would maintenance come in without notice?* Between the way Brandy was acting and now the shoe print, she was spooked. Because Mims worked late hours, she always made it clear, even when Elite Living took over, that she wanted advance notice of any maintenance orders because she slept during the day. Plus, she didn't like random men in her apartment without her knowledge. She waited until the main office opened, holding off on sleep to make sure they knew how she felt about it.

"Thank you for calling Elite Living. How may I assist you today?" Jameka answered in a cheerful voice.

"Hello, this is Mims Scott. I'm calling because I wanted to reiterate my request that I'm notified about all maintenance requests ahead of time. I noticed that there was a man's shoe print leaving the utility closet, and I have made no requests for several months," Mims said. "When I came home from work early this morning, my cat was hiding, which is a clear sign that a man was likely inside. At least, that's the typical reason she gets scared." She spoke in a stern but balanced voice.

"I am so sorry that's happened. Let me just look up your unit in the system and see what might have happened." There was a pause before Jameka returned to the line. "I checked the maintenance folder, and I don't see any requests or reasons for maintenance to have been in your apartment. The last request I have on record was several months ago, much too long for a shoe print to still be present, and certainly too long for your cat to still be in hiding."

Mims felt her face grow warm and her blood pressure rise by the minute, believing Elite Living was falling short with their security.

"Mims, again, I'm so sorry. I hate to ask, but you're sure a friend didn't make that shoe print? I just don't see any reason maintenance would be there," Jameka continued.

"I usually hang out with women, and this is a very large shoe print.

Also, I just mopped my floor two days ago, and I would have noticed this before because it's right where the sun shines in the morning. It's very easy to see."

"I tell you what, I'll ask all the maintenance guys if maybe they went to your apartment by mistake. Do me a favor, don't disturb that print. I'll be back in touch with you as soon as I speak with everyone."

Mims waited anxiously as Jameka hung up to call her maintenance staff. A half hour later, the phone rang.

"Mims, I believe you need to call the police. It sounds like you may have had a break-in." Jameka sounded very grim and pressed Mims to make the call. "As you know, through our newsletters and the media, we have had some homicides occur in a few of our units. I can't confirm whether the print has anything to do with the recent murders, but I'd rather you be safe and get this checked out."

Mims agreed. Her eyes darted around her room, a wave of panic settling in her stomach as she waited to learn who had been in her apartment. She held onto Brandy. *Has the intruder been in my bedroom, touching my things?* Mims felt somewhat reassured that Brandy had come out, as she knew her cat would be in hiding if a man were still inside. She dialed 911 and told them her story.

Within ten minutes, her apartment was full of men in uniform, and Brandy went into hiding once again.

CHAPTER 47

2021

"Size eleven men's, boss," Officer Allen told Detective Conway as he walked through Mims' front door.

Same shoe size as Travis, thought Conway. Though this wasn't a murder case, the victim was like the other murders that had occurred in Cape Ivy. A woman living alone in an apartment building, but now they had a shoe print. A fresh case was inviting after the egg on his face, following Travis's release. He couldn't escape the nagging feeling that Travis was involved. Carter wasn't currently a suspect in the murders, but the media continued to hound the detective that he should look closer. Conway knew what they didn't; Carter was in Illinois during Nadine's murder and was with his family the morning after Becky's death, meaning he was three hours away. Although the timeline could work, Conway just didn't put much stock into Carter being a murderer. While Carter could be a suspect for Deb and Jamie's murders, Conway pushed him further down the list. The biggest reason was that the choke mask was exactly the same in all the other murders, but looked very different from the one that Carter wore at Margot's.

Perhaps he's trying to throw us? Time will tell.

"Dust everything for fingerprints and lift the shoe print with tape. I want every inch of this apartment dusted down and roped off," Conway directed the junior officers.

Conway turned to Mims, who sat on the couch. "My cat is hiding somewhere in here, so please have someone watch the front door to make sure she doesn't run out," she said.

"Shut the front door, idiot!" Conway yelled at another officer.

Conway spoke in a much more grandfatherly tone when he sat down next to Mims. "I'm going to need a full report of what happened tonight through to this morning so we can hopefully catch the guy who was in here," Conway flipped open a notebook.

"Okay, well, I was at work, working as a bartender. I brought home a patron, we had sex, we showered, she left. Then I found my cat, who had been hiding behind the refrigerator. When I saw the shoe print, I called Jameka and then you guys," Mims rambled off.

Conway barely jotted half of it down, asking for a lot more detail. He wanted to know the exact timeline of the evening and the name of the person she was with.

Mims refused to give him the woman's name and was vague about their relationship. "We're just friends from the bar who see each other outside of there from time to time," Mims crossed her arms. "I don't want her involved. I don't even have her number. It was just a casual meetup."

"Could it be her boyfriend spying on you guys?" Conway was trying to see if it could be a jilted lover situation.

"What? No way. We're gay, dude," Mims snarled.

"You said you two went into the shower after sex. Maybe someone snuck into your apartment during that time," Conway surmised.

"Okay, I'll play. But how did he get into the utility closet, then? That shoe print is literally coming directly out of that closet. The only people that have a key to that closet are the maintenance men," Mims said.

It hit him like a ton of bricks. Travis was the suspect he'd focused on, not an inside job. He hadn't considered that it could be someone from within the apartment complex killing these women. It made so much more sense; it explained how the killer could enter with no one knowing. As Conway sat in front of Mims, he thought through all the murders and how obvious it now seemed that it was most likely an Elite Living employee doing this. Mims stared at him with furrowed brows.

How could I overlook so much? Divorce. Drinking too much. Not FBI worthy. For the first time, Conway doubted his abilities.

Finally, Conway said, "Thank you, young lady. I think I have all I need today."

And with that, Conway instructed the officers at the scene to finish up their evidence collection so that Mims could have her apartment back.

"I have interviews with a few maintenance workers to conduct," Conway proclaimed.

On the drive over to Elite Living's main office, Conway replayed the various murder scenes in his head. There was doubt, yet he still clung to hope that this oversight wouldn't embarrass him. *Open-mindedness isn't always a value in police work. We have to be prejudiced when solving crimes. At least my training taught me so.* However, Conway couldn't shake the growing rawness that he was just plain wrong. That he was the captain of a failed mission that everyone knew led to doom. Betty always told him that his hard-headedness would get him into trouble and, as a cop, it had never been an issue because his superiors had always rewarded it. But now he had the eyes of the national media upon him because of this case, and he felt the pressure like never before.

Conway arrived at Elite Living's main office and greeted Jameka to update her on the investigation. She took Conway into a private conference room where he could see stacks of pamphlets for residents on "how to be safe in your apartment." He grabbed one and flipped it open to see tips like, "Always lock your door" and "Check your surroundings before entering your home." He considered all of it good advice, but if the killer was a maintenance person, these tips would be useless.

"After speaking with Mims, it's come to my attention that the murder cases are taking a new turn. I now need to interview all the men that work for Elite Living, especially your maintenance men." Conway tapped on the table for emphasis.

With a gasp, Jameka got up to grab a file listing all ten of her maintenance men and gave it to Conway. "Here is the list of all the maintenance workers. They have access to the keys to each unit in case there's an emergency. You think one of my workers is the Choke Mask Killer?" She stared down at their names and then back at Conway.

"Well, I don't want to jump the gun. But, based on some current evidence, Mims may have been his intended next victim, but she foiled the plan by bringing someone home last night," Conway reached for the list of names.

Jameka raised her right hand to her mouth. "Oh my God, that's so shocking. I hope this isn't true."

"Is there anyone in maintenance that you might have any suspicions about?" Conway hoped to narrow down the list, although knowing the perpetrator's shoe size was a great start.

"Well, I don't want to call anyone out or accuse anyone of being a murderer. But I get really creepy vibes from one of my men. But I don't think I want to say because if it turns out it's not him, I'd feel really shitty." Jameka rubbed her arms and reaching for her cardigan.

"You can tell me. I won't spread any of that to him or to the media. Sometimes we have to go by our gut. Sometimes it's right, and other times it's wrong." Conway was still reeling after he'd followed his gut with Travis.

"Honestly, I've always gotten chills when I had to deal with Jack Moore. But I just assumed it's because he's quiet and stares a lot. I never know what he's thinking, and when I first shook his hand, I immediately felt a tremor," Jameka recalled.

Conway remembered that name from a prior interview in Nadine's murder case. He tried to remain emotionless, to not give away his excitement, but he was doing mental gymnastics over the connection. If Jack's name was being brought up again, this could be his suspect.

"Okay, that's good to know. I see him listed here. I'll interview everyone equally, regardless of your reservations. But I appreciate your input."

———

Back at his office, he contacted all the employees on the list and told them he needed them at the station for an interview regarding an incident at Mims' apartment. Sure, he could have called them into Elite Living's conference room, but he preferred the comfort of his own precinct, and Linda at the front desk made the best coffee that would fuel him through a marathon interview session. Plus, interviewing potential suspects on his own turf gave him the advantage. All the men agreed to come down to the office within the next week.

The first subject to arrive was Gary, a white male, aged thirty-five, married with three children. He worked maintenance at the location where they found Becky. His interview didn't raise any red flags as he answered the questions that were asked and had an alibi, producing a movie ticket stub from the night in question. Next was Juan, a fairly quiet Mexican-American male, twenty-eight years old, who mainly worked at the location where they'd found Deb. He did not report having an alibi, so Conway placed him on the possible suspect list and requested his shoe print. However, it was not the same size as the one left at Mims' location, so he was easy to rule out. Craig, the maintenance supervisor, arrived next. A white male, aged fifty-five, provided the most information about the backgrounds of his staff.

"It would shock me if any of them were behind the murders," Craig told Conway. "I see my crew as part of my family."

But based on the answers his crew had provided, Conway wasn't so sure.

"I just want all of this negative publicity to go away. I know it's hurting my position as the supervisor. How can they have faith in me if women keep getting killed, and if it turns out it's one of my guys? It would have made my life easier if Travis were the killer, because then this case would be over and solved." Craig downed the last of his coffee.

Conway couldn't agree more.

Craig reported he was home that night with his wife and daughter, who was home visiting from college and could verify this. His shoe size was also not a match. Conway removed him from the list of suspects.

Pete arrived next—a white male, thirty years old. He was a very talkative guy, and Conway had to keep repeating his questions, as Pete would start telling stories about other maintenance guys, especially about the ones he didn't like. Conway learned Pete wasn't fond of Jack because they'd gotten into an argument once about how to fix a heater. He claimed Jack became so enraged he'd threatened to kill Pete. "I never want to work another shift with Jack Moore again. He's an asshole and a hothead, and it wouldn't surprise me if he was behind all of this shit," Pete said.

Conway took notes, but he also knew that coworkers often fought and didn't get along. Pete didn't have an alibi other than being home with his wife. His shoe print was of a similar size to the one found in Mims' apartment, so he remained a suspect.

Conway's nervous system remained steady for all the interviews he'd conducted so far. Next to arrive was Jack, and the excited butterflies in Conway's stomach were drunk with excitement.

Conway made him wait. He liked to make a potential suspect anticipate the line of questioning about to come his way. The longer people sat, the more on edge they became. And if what Pete said about Jack's quick temper was true, Conway couldn't wait to see it.

Conway walked up to Jack, who was bouncing his knee up and down, and watched him startle as he approached from behind. "Ready? Follow me," Conway directed.

Conway chose the interrogation room, which was much smaller and gave the feeling of being arrested or just on the verge. For all the other interviews, he'd chosen the large conference space. He asked Officer Allen to sit in on the interview, but told him he didn't need his input.

"We meet again," Conway sat down across from him.

Jack still had not said a word since he'd come into the waiting room and announced he was there to meet Conway.

"Let's see, the last time I met you was during Nadine Chastain's murder case. Looks like there's been a string of murders at the apartments you work for. Seems to be a lot of bad luck over at Elite Living, huh?" Conway took a mocking approach in an attempt to lure Jack's temper out.

Still, Jack just sat there. Of course, he hadn't been asked a direct question.

"Let's get to the bottom of why we're here. This weekend, there was a break-in at another Elite Living unit, specifically in the utility closet that only maintenance has access to. And they left a big shoe print behind. What's your shoe size?" Finally, Conway asked him directly.

"I believe it's… Eleven." Jack's eyes narrowed.

"Eleven. Well, that's very interesting. That's exactly the shoe print size that was left behind." Conway wanted to run around the room rejoicing. "Where were you Saturday night, into the early morning?"

"Hmm, I would have to say I was home… alone."

"I live alone. It's a shame if something happens and we don't have someone to vouch for us when we need an alibi." Conway toyed with Jack, hoping to get a rise out of him.

Jack sat there, glaring at the wall ahead of him.

"But I now have you being interviewed on two cases—two crimes involving an Elite Living resident. One being a murder and the second a break-in. Which means you are a person of interest, and we will search your car and apartment as soon as we get a signed warrant. We've requested expedited approval in light of the open murder cases and the recent break-in."

Conway watched for Jack's face to do something, anything, but didn't see any response.

"So, I can leave?" And with that, Jack stood, and the interview was over.

Conway followed Jack out. "You'll be under police surveillance. We aren't taking our eyes off of you, Jack."

He followed Jack out to the parking lot and they stared at each other through the windshield of Jack's car.

As Jack pulled out to leave, Conway knocked on his window. "You better get that headlight fixed. Hate to see you pulled over so soon." Conway snickered.

Jack sped off as Conway watched him round the corner.

CHAPTER 48
2021

The interview with Conway made it clear to Jack that he was their prime suspect, and the walls were closing in on him. Although he typically enjoyed the confines of small spaces, he wasn't keen on the enclosure of the law. Jack drove away from his interview with his jaw clenched and a stress migraine piercing his temples. He watched Conway eventually fade in his rearview mirror. *I'm fucked. I left my fuckin' shoe print. God damn it. I need to hide evidence before they raid my place. Fuckin' cops. I should have killed both bitches that night.*

Jack noticed that a marked police car followed him all the way back to his apartment. As Jack entered his studio, he punched a hole in the wall behind the front door. Pain radiated through his knuckles up into his shoulder, reminiscent of when he beat Paul to death. But he had no time to nurse his wounds. They had him trapped. There was no way he could take evidence out of his place now without that cop stopping him. Jack paced his rented 600-square-foot space and tried to think of ways to escape the bind he found himself in.

He had vinyl, rope, fishing line, and metal brackets, which were all used for his kill mask and were currently being kept in his utility closet. In a studio, there weren't many hiding places, and he couldn't flush them down the toilet. He had two windows, but both were visible from the parking lot where a cop sat watching for him.

I need to run. Just grab some shit and make a run for it and lose this cop outside. That fuckin' cop thinks he has me trapped. I learned from Louie; they won't take me down that easily. I fucked up, not wiping my prints off that bitch's floor. My rage got to me. That bitch brought someone home, which she hadn't done in months. I should have just taken my chances and killed them both, but I bolted when they were in the shower. Now I'm fucked with the cops up my ass.

Jack threw some clothes into a bag and searched his apartment for any last second items before he made a run for the front door.

CHAPTER 49
2021

Judge Grant signed off on the warrant within an hour. Between the evidence of the matching shoe size, Jack Moore being linked to the crime scene of the first victim, and the fact of his employment with Elite Living where the latest break-in had occurred, the judge ruled that there was enough probable cause to allow for a search and seizure.

After he received the signed warrant, Conway immediately jumped into action. He drove to Jack's apartment, which was only ten minutes away, knowing he needed to call the victims' families before the media got word of this. Upon arrival, he saw Officer Allen's police car outside, which meant that Jack was still home, since Allen's job was to follow Jack's every move. Followed by two police units, Conway walked up to Jack's door, a whiff of cigarette smoke greeting him, and met him face-to-face just as he opened the front door. He appeared to be leaving with a bag in hand.

"Fancy meeting you again so soon." Conway showed Jack the warrant. Stepping inside, unable to conceal his toothy grin, he let Jack know they could seize any items, including the bag Jack was holding when they arrived.

Conway quickly saw this would be a short search, as Jack's apartment was a studio, with only the bathroom and utility closet having a secured door. Conway immediately called Jameka at the front office, asking her to bring the key to the utility closet. He believed that's where they might find the evidence they needed. Once they entered the apartment, they asked Jack to stand outside to keep him from disturbing their search. It didn't take Jameka long to arrive at Jack's, and once they unlocked the closet, they found exactly what they were looking for: sheets of vinyl, rope, pieces of metal, fishing line, gloves, and, ironically, foot coverings… all the accoutrements of a serial killer, or at least of the Choke Mask Killer.

Conway turned to look at Jack, who had been hovering near the doorway, but he was gone. He walked outside to see if he could find him. That's when he noticed that Officer Allen wasn't in his vehicle, though his patrol car hadn't moved.

Seconds later, he heard Officer Allen over the radio. "I got him. He took off running, but those years on the track team paid off. Walking back to the squad car with the suspect."

They arrested Jack and would later officially charge him as the Choke Mask Killer.

Back at the police station, Conway attempted to suppress his glee when he pressed Jack on each of the murders, asking about his whereabouts when each victim was killed.

Jack gave a slight half smile, but he refused to answer. He eventually said, "I think this is the part of the interview where I tell you to speak to my lawyer."

Conway slammed his notebook shut and left the room with Officer Allen in tow.

Jack showed no remorse, and it was clear to Conway he would not provide any solace to the families—not that they expected it.

CHAPTER 50

2021

"We got him, Margot."

She could almost hear the smile in Conway's voice on the other end of the line. "His name is Jack Moore. He's a maintenance man with Elite Living, and he's responsible for your aunt's murder, along with the other victims. I wanted you to know as soon as possible," Conway said.

Barely able to catch her breath, Margot let out a stifled murmur. She fumbled for the remote and turned on the TV. A banner rolled across the local news channel reading The Choke Mask Killer Has Been Caught. The footage showed a crowd of reporters outside the police station, who were thirsty for news about Cape Ivy's latest serial killer. "Are you sure this is the real Choke Mask Killer? How can you be certain this time?"

"I am 100 percent sure. We found evidence of his masks in his apartment. We actually interviewed him after your aunt's murder, so he had multiple connections to the case."

"What? Are you telling me he was on your suspect list this entire time?" Margot was in disbelief.

"He wasn't a suspect back then because he was doing routine

maintenance. His alibi checked out, and we didn't have reason to list him as a suspect," Conway said.

Margot was stunned. "I just feel numb. I can't believe he's been hiding in plain sight. Women call him to their homes and entrust him to do work, yet he's in there casing it for a future murder. I don't know how to feel about all of this," she said.

"It's a process, Margot. You can finally put a face to the monster you've been searching for since the day you found Nadine," Conway said. "The Choke Mask Killer is finally unmasked."

Margot hung up with Conway and called her parents. They hadn't spoken in weeks, but this was an important development that she knew they needed to discuss. Per usual, Stella was matter-of-fact with her emotions and had an air of finality about the situation. She had moved on years ago, and the fact that they'd arrested Jack Moore was a technicality for her. He could now serve his time and women would stop being killed.

Margot needed someone who understood the emotions that death brought, so she called Gemma. "Hey. Have you seen the news? I'm not sure how to feel right now," Margot said.

"Yes! It's all over the news. I wanted to wait until you had time to process it all," Gemma said.

"How do I begin to process this face that never popped into my mind? The man who killed my aunt never revealed himself in my thoughts. He's a stranger, yet I know so much about him as he's been on my mind for years." Margot sighed, her eyes fixed on the news coverage.

"I think it's just one day at a time. Connect with the people who mean the most to you."

"Yeah. There are only a few people I can trust, and although my parents and I haven't been close, I think it's time I forgive them. I feel an overwhelming urge to have them in my life. I guess I can finally start the healing process now, and they're part of that journey."

Margot hung up with Gemma and called her mom back. "Now that they caught Jack Moore, let's start fresh. I want you in my life and I want to forget about the past." Margot teared up.

"Margot, I should have been the one to initiate our reconnection.

But I'm so proud of you. I know I don't tell you that often enough, but you've been the best part of my entire life," Stella said, and Margot could hear her unemotional mom finally shedding some feelings.

"Um, are you crying? This is a new development for you." Margot giggled.

"Onions, Margot." Stella laughed.

Margot wrapped her arms around her shoulders, giving herself a warm hug.

————

Months later, the families got to weigh in on Jack Moore's plea deal and whether they believed he deserved life in prison without parole or lethal injection. The Mays family were on the same page and agreed that Jack deserved to live out his life in a cell, where he could spend each day without his freedom. "These families have waited too long for justice and, through this plea deal, Jack Moore will be behind bars for the rest of his life. They can go on with their lives without having to deal with his many appeals," said April Smith, the district attorney representing the case.

The victims' families agreed to support the deal as long as they could read victim impact statements, but it caused some controversy, as some family members were vocal that they should sentence Jack to death.

————

Finally able to return to Nadine's grave without fear of Carter or CMK, Margot made the drive to the cemetery that she had made so many times before. She laid out a blanket and placed a bouquet of sunflowers on her aunt's headstone.

"Nadine, it's finally happened. They caught your killer! His name is Jack Moore. Maybe I'm in some kind of shock, but I wish I felt more relief or joy," Margot told her. "I think searching for him for all this time has become part of my identity. I had always hoped we'd catch him, but now that we have, it just doesn't feel real yet." Margot bit her bottom lip.

Margot watched the other cemetery mourners walk by, wondering what their stories were. Were they here because of a murder? Natural causes? Death had been a part of her life since she was twenty. Dying was a natural part of the cycle and, sadly, there were people out there ready to eradicate others in order to fulfill their own twisted fate.

But not if I can help it. If I can save someone, anyone, with my voice, then what I've gone through is all worth it.

CHAPTER 51
2021

uilt in the 1900s, the courthouse was a grand, three-story stone building that sat high on a bluff overlooking the Mississippi River. White columns lined the outside, which provided shade for staff on a lunch break or witnesses who needed a breather from harsh questioning. The floor design was art nouveau, with tiny rose tiles full of vibrant hues of red, yellow, and green. House sparrows and finches lined the wrought-iron fencing that led up the steps from the riverfront to the halls of justice, where lifetime fates were determined.

"Today we're here for the sentencing phase in the State of Missouri v. Jack Moore, but first, we're going to hear victim impact statements from his victims' families. I do not want any outbursts or talking in my courtroom. Otherwise, my officers will escort you out," Judge Grant warned the gallery.

Margot sat in the back of the courtroom with trepidation. She feared being so close to the killer, yet she had prepared her statement, swallowing back any nerves. She sat next to her mom and waited to listen to how Jack Moore had affected each of the families with his reign of terror over their city. Margot squeezed her mom's hand as Stella gave her an affectionate wink and squeezed back.

"The prosecution calls Kelly Jones, who will speak on behalf of her sister, Becky Conrad."

Kelly walked to the stand, with only the sound of her stilettos rapping on the floor. All eyes turned to look at the captivating blonde who'd put on her brightest red lipstick for the occasion.

She held her head high and began: "Mr. Moore, you took away my only sibling and living family member. Since our mother has died, I have no one left on this cruel earth, and I have you to blame. I now have to face the cold reality of dealing with life alone without the family gatherings we used to have and the loving bond we shared." Kelly held her hand to her chest with her eyelashes fluttering, holding back tears. "You took away my best friend, and I will never forgive you for that. She was a dedicated nurse and was getting her life back in order to start fresh after a terrible breakup with a man she thought would be her husband. I know all about heartache. My husband cheated on me, and that breakup was devastating. She would call me every night and cry, telling me how much she was hurting and wanted her family back in her life after shutting us out for so many years. Yet you took that away from us. I hope you rot in your cell and live a very long, miserable existence."

And with that, Kelly glanced over at Jack, who wasn't looking, only staring straight ahead. Kelly looked at the judge, her eyes pleading for him to make Jack respond to her words, but the guards came to escort her toward the back of the room. She left as she came in. The loud clicking of her stilettos on the tiled floors echoed throughout the beautiful architecture of the hallways that had seen so much misery.

I can't imagine the pain of losing a sibling, Margot thought, glancing at Kelly as she left the courtroom.

"The prosecution calls Judy Hamilton, who is here to speak on behalf of her friend, Deborah Taylor."

Judy walked up to the podium, refusing to make eye contact with the killer of her best friend. She stared down at her prepared notes, only glancing up at the judge. Judy cleared her throat and read.

"Your Honor, I would like to make a statement on behalf of my dearest friend Deborah. She was just beginning her new life here in Cape Ivy and honestly, I have a lot of guilt for encouraging her to move here. I don't know if I'll ever get over that guilt, because I thought she'd have more advantages here than in Zionstown. I never thought I was inviting her to her death sentence." Judy's hands trembled as she took a sip of the water provided for her. "She had a lot of fear about crime in the big city, but I had never experienced it and convinced her to take a chance. Now, she's dead because of it. I will never forgive myself for it, and I will never forgive Jack Moore. He took away my friend and my peace of mind. In some ways, he killed me that day, too. I will never be the same. I rarely leave my house, and I'm afraid of everything now." Judy wiped away tears with the cheap tissue left on the podium.

"Deb was the kindest and hardest working woman I ever met. She was a lady raised with manners and believed it was her duty to take care of her parents, even if it meant putting her life on hold. She gave up so much to care for them and finally, in her fifties, she began living for herself. I blame myself and I have nightmares thinking of her final moments." Judy's voice quivered as she described Deb's tenacious nature. "I'm not a family member, so I didn't get a say in the plea deal, but if they gave me a vote, I'd tell them, 'Hell no, he needs to fry.' He doesn't deserve the air we breathe or even the limited lifestyle a prison cell provides. He doesn't deserve taxpayer money to cover his living expenses. Just kill him like he did Deb and the other women."

Judy turned and left the podium, never glancing over at Jack. Head bowed, she wiped away a tear and left the courtroom.

Margot twisted in her seat and thought of her own guilt. *I hope Judy can find some peace. I know guilt is just as painful as grief.*

"We'd now like to call up Mims Scott, Your Honor," the prosecutor announced.

Mims walked into the courtroom wearing sneakers, black pants, and a button-up blue shirt, glancing over at Jack first before she walked through the swinging double doors that led to the podium. She reached into her back pocket and pulled out her impact statement, laying it flat, but turned her body to stare at Jack. "Look at me!" she yelled, but Jack just stared straight ahead, never obliging her request. Finally, she turned her attention back to her statement. She cleared her throat and began.

"You wanted me to be your next victim. Well, fuck you, I'm nobody's victim. And fuck you for killing those other women, too. You're a lowlife loser that had to sneak up on them. They didn't even have a fighting chance to save their lives, and that makes you a coward. You're lucky I don't believe in the death penalty, but if I did, I'd petition to be the one to flip the switch. But death is too good for you. You deserve to rot and sit in a cell every day, surrounded by other low-life criminals, where you have to watch your back, never experiencing freedom again." Mims turned and left the courtroom.

Margot found herself with a smile. *Jack Moore definitely messed with the wrong woman.*

"Your Honor, we now call up Margot Mays, who is here to represent Nadine Chastain."

Margot's breath caught in her throat when she heard her name echo through the chamber. As she stood to walk closer to where Jack sat, Stella grabbed Margot's arm, telling her, "Let me do this. You've advocated so much for our family, it's my turn."

Margot sucked back the tears that wanted to flow with a big sniffle.

"Your Honor, we have a change, and Stella Mays will speak instead."

Stella walked to the podium, clinging to a piece of paper she had meticulously written the night before. She averted her eyes from the large camera faced toward her and immediately looked at the floor, staring at the tiled pattern. Stella pulled down the microphone, which made a loud screech. She cleared her throat before she began.

Margot knew this was her mom's first time speaking about Nadine's death in public, and likely the last. *You can do this, Mom.*

"Your Honor, I'm here to be a voice for my sister Nadine. My words represent my family, and I hope to do them justice. Nadine and I had a strained relationship as sisters, and her death meant we didn't have the chance to repair it. One thing we had in common was the love of my daughter, Margot. Although we showed our love differently, it remained the same. I'd like to think it brought us closer, but I'm not sure. I'd also like to believe that if she were alive today, the three of us would be close and do things that other families do—dinners, shopping, and phone calls. I will forever blame myself for not facilitating a better relationship with Nadine when she was alive, and I'll always blame you, Jack Moore, for not giving us the chance to work on our fractured relationship. His actions put a deeper wedge between my daughter and me."

Margot's eyes welled with tears.

Stella turned toward Jack Moore. "I hate you. My sister didn't deserve this. She was a beautiful, vibrant woman who was making a name for herself in the world. She was a leading businesswoman in a field of men, a feminist in a town of traditionalists, and, sadly, an unwitting target in a city with a cowardly murderer. You may have taken Nadine's life, but her spirit will live on through Margot. I see her tenacity, her vibrancy, and her beauty in my daughter. I beam with pride at the fortitude my daughter has embodied at such a young age. Nadine's voice will live on through my daughter, while the bars of the penitentiary will silence yours. May you never enjoy a sunrise or sunset, a cool breeze on your face, or the joy of your favorite song ever again. May your days be long and miserable, Jack Moore."

Stella turned to walk to the back of the courtroom, met by a weeping Margot, who hugged her mom. It had been months, maybe years, since they'd last hugged. It was an embrace they both needed, and they didn't want to let go. As the two sat down together, they held hands and Margot flushed with warm tingles that faded into an immense radiance of love.

"Your Honor, for the last victim impact statement, we call Roy Holly, Jamie's dad, to the podium."

Roy slowly made his way toward the front of the courtroom. His mobility had slowed from a recent stroke. He leaned on the podium and turned to look at Jack.

"Judge, I have some words for my daughter's killer. You are a cesspool, low-life, piece of shit that doesn't deserve to live. You deserve the same fate as my daughter, and I will celebrate when I hear you finally died. I hope it's at the hands of a fellow inmate, as I'll delight in your pain. I hope you live the rest of your life dreading the damnation of hell."

After his statement, he lunged with his cane toward Jack, who continued to sit and stare straight ahead with a blank expression. The guards moved both Jack and Roy away.

The audience gasped, but reveled in the display.

"Order in the court," Judge Grant demanded, banging his gavel, unimpressed with the commotion in his courtroom. "Back to your seats or you can leave the gallery," he said as he stood up to survey the room. His furrowed brows were down-turned, just as his white mustache was.

The prosecutor walked up to the judge for a sidebar discussion with the defense. Margot watched as she twisted in her seat. She was numb from all the heartache she'd heard today. *Is this what closure feels like? It sure doesn't feel as comforting as they say.* The prosecutor's loud heels on the marble floor alerted Margot to snap out of her thoughts.

"Ladies and gentleman, we need a brief recess until our next speaker arrives," Judge Grant announced.

The whispers grew as speculations circulated. Margot looked at Stella with surprise. "Wait, who is this? Was there a victim we don't know about?" Margot whispered to Stella.

Her mother shrugged and mouthed, "I have no idea."

The prosecutor walked back into the room and announced to Judge Grant, "My next witness is here, Your Honor."

Margot felt her palms clam up. *Who could this be and why weren't we told about another victim?* Margot took deep breaths as she waited for the new arrival.

The sound of a door creaking open caused Margot to turn and stare as a woman walked in, moving her head side to side, taking in the courtroom. As her head swung towards Jack Moore, Margot could see the shiny glint of light hitting off of her hoop earrings.

CHAPTER 52
2021

Jack's thoughts raced nearly as fast as his knee bounced under the defense table. Although his face gave away none of his thoughts or emotions, inside he thought of grabbing the guard's gun and shooting bullets into everyone's heads.

Jack couldn't have prepared for the last person to speak in court. Although she identified herself and the family as victims, Jack had never gotten the chance to harm any of them. When she began speaking, Jack rose from his seat until he was eye level with the judge and attempted to bolt toward the speaker. He wanted to crash his fists into her mouth so he'd never hear that revolting tone again. He wasn't upright for long, as several guards forced him back to his seat with a hard plop into his chair. Jack felt the metal keys attached to the guard's belt dig into his back. Trying to move away proved useless as they held onto him even tighter.

"This is utter nonsense. I call for a recess." Judge Grant banged his gavel as he stood, surveying the disorder in his court, tugging on his mustache.

. . .

After a thirty-minute reprieve, the guards escorted Jack back to his chair with an admonishment from Judge Grant. "You will not behave like a wild boar in my courtroom, or I'll have you secured in shackles until the end of the proceedings."

All eyes in the court moved from the judge to Jack, then finally the speaker.

Jack's Aunt Kathy started her statement over. "Thank you, Judge. I apologize for my nephew's outburst and, as you can see, this is much of the behavior we have had to deal with over the years. His mother and I have done our absolute best to instill the Lord in him, but the Devil got hold of him. From the beginning, we knew Jack was cursed because of his daddy's genes." Jack twisted in his chair and began shaking with rage.

"We did our best to reprimand Jack, but we could not fight the demon that grew inside of him. His evil was clear from a young age and he turned away from God. It devastated our family when we learned what Jack had done, and we cannot believe the shame he's put on our good family name. His mother is heartbroken over the way Jack turned out. She is beside herself to know that she birthed a serial killer. She is still in disbelief and no longer acknowledges him as her son. It breaks my heart for these victims' families and what they've endured, and I only wish I could have done more." Kathy turned to look at the row of grieving families and put her hand to her heart.

Guards held Jack's shoulders down, but it didn't stop him from attempting to rise up again.

You fucking piece of shit. I should have killed you years ago.

"I want to finish by saying that his mother and I are in support of his plea agreement. We agree to whatever the families want, as we believe Jack should never see the light of day. He deserves to sit and atone for his sins, and we can only hope he turns his heart over to our Savior." Kathy turned to face Jack. "Jack, please pray while you're incarcerated, and I will pray that God forgives your soul for what you've done."

Jack pushed through the two guards that held him and made it past his sitting attorney before they tackled him from behind. The last thing he saw was Kathy staring back at him, shaking her head as she left the courtroom.

Another admonishment from Judge Grant quieted the courtroom as he began speaking.

"Now, we have the last statement from the defendant if he chooses to make one." All eyes went to Jack.

Everyone waited while the lawyer whispered into Jack's ear and then stood. "Your Honor, Mr. Moore has nothing to say to the court."

Groans sounded throughout the gallery.

Judge Grant beat his gavel and again yelled, "ORDER," which quickly quieted everyone.

"I have received and reviewed the plea agreement from the prosecution. Mr. Jack Moore signed this agreement in which he confessed to the murder of the victims identified in this case in order to forgo a trial. The prosecution has waived the death penalty, and Jack Moore will receive the sentence of life in prison without the possibility of parole. I will agree with this plea deal. Mr. Moore, I remand you to live out the rest of your wretched existence at the Bonne Terre Correctional Facility. Take him away from my courtroom." Judge Grant slammed his gavel for the final time.

The guards escorted Jack to his temporary holding cell. Round metal bars, chipped paint, sliding and crashing doors, scuff marks from cheap shoes, and the smells of off-brand floor cleaner. These were the new normal for a prisoner, and Jack was the most notorious resident at the county jail. Now that he was in the spotlight, the once overlooked and faceless man had become infamous.

"Jack Moore, time to head to prison," the jailer informed him. Shackled and made to walk past several other inmates who cheered him on, Jack felt like he was in a bit of a dream. He soaked in the drive and sights, as he knew this would be his last time in Cape Ivy—the city that had taken so much from so many, which he'd had a part in. In a twist of irony, the trip took them by Nadine's apartment: the kill that started the reign of the Choke Mask Killer. He craned his neck as far as he could to take in every inch of her place.

Jack glanced up to the top floor penthouse deck and could see a new tenant had decorated it with large plants and a patio chair, but he did not see a bike. He smiled. *Those plants would make an excellent hiding place*, he thought. He faced forward with the river behind him, and a grin appeared as he thought of the whimpering pleas of his victims.

They'd finally sentenced him to life in prison for being a serial killer. He no longer felt the anger of getting caught, but had resolved himself to living in a cement box for the rest of his life. His memories of butterflies and women would live forever within the concrete walls of his confined home.

Jack rather enjoyed listening to the victims' impact statements and having his crimes repeated back to him. He liked to hear how the murders still tormented them to this day. Jack felt such power knowing he had that kind of control over anyone. It gave him satisfaction to know that these people gathered to discuss him and what he'd done. He'd never had that kind of attention in his life—at least, no attention that didn't end in a beating.

Although he didn't like everything that was said.

Kelly is a fucking lying cunt and I only wish I found her on the outside.

Let that old man come at me. I like his style, though. I am a cesspool. Ask my mom. She'd agree with you.

It took everything in Jack to keep his composure when Mims came to the stand.

Lucky ass bitch, you're not alive because of what you did. You're alive because I got sloppy and couldn't kill two bitches that night.

As Jack arrived at his new home, he surveyed the cement exterior that would forever house him. The sound of metal bars opening and closing would never end. However, prison had its perks. He'd never have to see or hear Kathy or Sandy ever again.

CHAPTER 53
2022

Loni glanced at her image in the mirror, satisfied with the accomplished woman she had become. She'd long ago given up the dream of moving to New York to sit next to whoever the latest and hottest morning TV anchor was. Dreams could change, and she had determined that Cape Ivy was in her blood now. She wore a blush-colored sweater with black pencil pants, her outfit of choice for today's interview with Detective Conway. His recent book on the Choke Mask Killer has been making its rounds on the airways, documenting his prison interviews with Jack Moore.

Loni whisked into the interview space with a minute to spare. No time for small talk about the weather or the St. Louis Cardinals—she kept her eyes down on her notecards and asked for a last second makeup check when the countdown began for the live on-air interview. "Thank you for tuning in to *Heartland Matters with Loni Smart*. Today we're here with Detective Dan Conway, who is credited with solving the case of the Choke Mask Killer." Loni turned her face away from the straight angle closeup shot which then panned over Conway's shoulder to zoom in on her face. "Welcome to the show. Let's start by giving the public an update on where Jack Moore is today."

Conway cleared his throat. "Thank you for having me. You can call me Conway. It's my pleasure to say that Jack Moore continues to be housed at the Bonne Terre Correctional Facility and is serving life without parole. I'd have to say, all in all, he's had a decent time since moving there. No disciplinary infractions or loss of privileges thus far."

Loni peered at her cards and asked her next question. "Your book, *CMK: How I Revealed the Man Behind the Mask*, has moved up on the bestsellers list. What made you decide to write about one of the worst serial killers to inhabit Cape Ivy?"

"As the lead homicide detective, I knew there was a high level of interest in this case. Even after sentencing, people would stop me at the grocery store and ask about specifics. So, I filled in the blanks. You know, appease the masses with a bit of an insider scoop." Conway chuckled.

"Did you ever consider how this might affect the families? I'm sure it's opening up wounds they'd started to heal. Was there any consultation with them before publishing your book?" Loni narrowed her eyes.

"Well, I didn't talk to the families. I guess I feel like that information is already out there regarding their grief. I don't think my book is offensive to CMK's victims." Conway looked directly into the camera. "I apologize if any of the facts from this book caused any family members stress."

"You left the police force right after Judge Grant sentenced CMK in order to write this book. Consequently, there have been other controversies surrounding your tenure on the case. What do you say to those who question your handling of the murders?"

Conway shifted in his seat. "Well, I had considered retirement for some time. I wasn't trying to sensationalize this case, but I wanted to write what happened from my point of view. I suppose some people saw it as my trying to capitalize off of crime, but that wasn't ever my intent. As far as opinions regarding my work, all I can say is I did my best at the time. The city and police force were under considerable pressure to solve these murders, and it narrowed my focus and, sure, maybe I missed some clues. Naturally, there will always be people who think they can do better, especially in this day and age of so-called online true crime specialists."

Loni leaned back in her chair. "Let's get into the meat of your interviews with Jack Moore. Tell me, how did you get him to talk, considering he turned down the option to do so at his trial?"

"I knew that a lot of killers want to get their stories out there. He rejected his chance at sentencing to give a statement, and I thought after a little time in prison, he might be ready to speak. To give some reason why he murdered those women."

"We know that his home life was less than ideal. Was his hatred for his mom and aunt the catalyst for the murders?"

Conway sipped from his cup of water. "Absolutely. Becky Conrad resembled his mom, and he chose her based on that. Unfortunately, he chose the other victims at random. At least at the time, we didn't see a pattern with the other women. His hatred for women certainly started early because of his mom and aunt. He never had positive female relationships and even confessed to raping a woman at a local bar when he was eighteen."

Loni snapped her head away from her notes. "Although it's not completely surprising, it was another disturbing fact to learn from reading your book. As we know, many killers start out as sexual sadists before it leads to murder. Although, it is interesting that none of the victims were sexually assaulted. When you went to interview him, did he discuss any victim's final words or last moments?"

"No, he didn't. He described his own feelings of excitement and the euphoria he felt once he deemed it was time to leave the utility closet. But he never talked about any of the victims. He never viewed them as having any feelings or caring about what he did to them. Jack was self-centered in the way he talked, only focusing on how the murders made him feel. He offered no remorse, not once during my interviews with him. As you pointed out, the murders weren't for sexual gratification; it was all for control," Conway blinked away a rogue eyelash.

"We learn a lot about his affiliation with Louie Hendricks. He was a mentor to Jack, but we know Louie was a bad influence with a criminal history. Did the fact that he'd had former police officers as mentors make it easier for you to get him to talk to you?"

The room's silence briefly broke as Conway's stomach let out a small grumble from hunger. "I believe so. Plus, being a man probably made it easier. I don't know this for certain, but I suppose he may have always looked for approval from an older male figure and maybe he thought if he talked to me, I'd give him the attention he wanted. I took my time in building rapport and we talked a lot about his Uncle Louie and how their relationship formed. Jack never met his dad, but Louie fulfilled a fatherly role. Once Louie died, he became a martyr in Jack's eyes, and he no longer had anyone in this world to care about," Conway said.

"Did he ever discuss his feelings about Travis and his arrest?"

"We briefly discussed that once. He initially thought the guy was a loser for putting himself in that situation. But it wore on Jack that Travis was being called CMK—he really hated that. He hated how it delayed his next murder because of the swarming media. He needed to wait until we released Travis before he started killing again."

"This is where a lot of your controversy falls. Your critics say that you zeroed in on Travis because he had an attitude. They believe, and I quote, you 'misused your authority to railroad a man with a less than desirable demeanor.'"

"God, I love me some Monday morning quarterbacks!" Conway laughed. "Look, I'm not the best detective, but I'm certainly not the worst. I did what I could with what I had. Travis certainly looked like a plausible defendant, and I'll just stop there." Conway crossed his arms.

The TV producer motioned for time, indicating they needed to pause for a commercial break. Loni promptly stood up from her chair and spoke with the producer, reviewing her cards. Conway stood and stretched, chugging the last of his water.

Back from commercial break, Loni smoothed her sweater and began. "I think the question we all want to ask is, did Jack Moore say if he killed all the women he pled guilty to?" Loni stared back at Conway.

"Jack still won't go into detail about any of the murders. He refuses to say whether he is the actual murderer of Jamie, even though he pled guilty to all the charges. Although, his plea agreement was an all-or-nothing deal, so he'd have faced a trial and the death penalty if he hadn't entered a guilty plea. I still have my doubts that Jack Moore is Jamie's killer, but the case has been closed as far as the district attorney is concerned and right now, they consider CMK/Jack Moore as responsible." Conway paused. "But I will always have my doubts. The media and my detractors have scrutinized me over arresting Travis, but I just can't shake the facts or the feeling that there's still something there. I feel like I'm missing some key evidence, but it's out of my hands and I have to accept the case as solved." Conway shrugged.

"Did the interviews ever become hostile? You mentioned he hasn't had any disciplinary marks while in prison. Did he tell you how prison life was for him?" Loni rested her hands on her lap.

Conway straightened in his chair. "I knew I had to be careful with Jack. I felt like I had one chance, because there were many people who wanted to speak with him, and I needed to gain his trust. The FBI was involved and their profilers wanted to gain access to his mind. I know he spoke with them, but I don't know how much he shared. He told me he wasn't keen on sharing any more than he had to and would not talk unless he got concessions. So maybe they offered him something in return, but I never knew what that was. The last visit I had with him, he told me that in some ways, prison life wasn't too bad. He had made a name for himself out in the free world, and guys respected serial killers in prison. He showed me several letters he received from women who wanted to visit him, but when I pressed him about whether he was going to do that, he just changed the subject. His anger toward women was quick to come, and I knew if I pressed too much, he'd end our interview."

"Did he ever talk about getting help or stopping the thoughts that he said gave him the urge to harm and later kill women?"

Conway shook his head. "No, he never sought counseling and once he started murdering, that was it. He knew it was what he wanted to do. According to him, it was the best feeling he ever experienced. His first thoughts of murder were when he was twelve years old and wanted revenge against his aunt and her boyfriend, but after Louie wasn't able to help him, he suppressed those thoughts."

———

Back at home, Margot watched the entire interview, recording it so she could watch it over again later. Conway wasn't her favorite person, and she definitely felt let down by the police department. *They interviewed the real CMK right after Nadine's death.* It had shocked her to learn this information, and time only made her angrier over that fact. Her aunt was gone, but they could have done more to save the other victims.

As Margot watched the interview, she felt like cheering Loni's questions. Conway had never been questioned in a forum like this, and when she started watching, she didn't think she'd get any answers. However, the longer she watched, the more satisfied she felt that now not only Cape Ivy but the national media would understand the incompetence she'd been dealing with.

Margot compartmentalized her grief, and she found she could talk about Jack Moore like she did any other serial killer. Margot no longer allowed him to control her feelings. Now she was in charge, and the only emotions she still had about the case were found in her memories of Nadine. And that's just how she wanted to keep it. She wondered if another cop would have noticed the signs much sooner? If they would have seen Jack Moore as the killer in front of them when they interviewed him after Nadine's murder?

Margot felt she had come so far—what a few years it had been following Nadine's death. She'd lost and gained so much, including herself, not only in the stress of searching for CMK but because of Carter, who they sentenced to five years of incarceration. She was not the same person she was when she'd moved back to Cape Ivy, and she was okay with that. Margot could see her growth when she looked in the mirror, and she was proud of herself. She just knew Nadine was beaming for her.

As the CMK case wrapped up, Margot made plans to take a long overdue summer break. This time, she would travel for relaxation.

Miami, here I come!

CHAPTER 54
2022

Jack didn't mind prison life. He had his own shed, or utility closet, all to himself, except that they called it a prison cell. He rather liked the small size and confinement it provided. Jack's desire to kill didn't end because he was in prison. When he'd see a female guard or prison official, his rage would come boiling to the surface and he'd imagine the type of home they lived in and how they would sound with a mask over their heads. They had segregated Jack, so he would never get that chance. "For your own protection," a guard had informed him. Now that Jack had been unmasked as the Choke Mask Killer, he was somewhat of a celebrity on his unit, which put him at risk of being killed. "You'd be a trophy kill for an inmate," the same guard told Jack. The only time they allowed Jack outside of his cell was for a daily shower and an outdoor break. As he walked the halls of prison, other prisoners heckled as well as praised him. In some ways, he'd finally earned the respect he never had in the free world.

Jack hoped that Cape Ivy still felt on edge, as he hoped they still feared the memory of him. Soon Cape Ivy would be back on the map with another killer's moniker following the Choke Mask Killer in the history books as the next murderer to hit the fault-line city. They're born every day or they're just waiting for their moment, like Jack had done. For now, Jack reigned supreme as the latest on the list of serial killers that had haunted the primal streets of his birth.

As Jack walked back to his cell from his hour of outdoor time, he overheard two officers looking out at the atrium making small talk.

"I never see butterflies anymore. Do you think they all just became extinct?"

"Nah, man. They're around. They just fly south this time of year."

"But I don't see them any time of year."

"They like to fly in the country, not in the city. They don't like people too much."

Jack just smirked. He knew where a few of the butterflies went.

CHAPTER 55
2022

Death can destroy and bond at the same time—with a murder, it's exacerbated. No matter how implausible it may have seemed years ago, Margot and Stella had become close. They'd made so much progress since that July day when Nadine's lifeless body had changed both of their worlds. For so long, Margot had focused on how it affected her, but she now realized that her mom was suffering, too. And now, they'd learned to support each other.

Margot tended to the garden in her backyard, letting out a contented sigh as a goldfinch fluttered by. She was trying to take a slower pace with life by caring for her plants and taking walks with Pepper.

"Margot, I'm here!" Stella announced before entering the side gate to the backyard with her own dog, Coco, in tow.

"Hey, Mom. I'm pulling some weeds. Come help," Margot shouted, shielding her eyes against the sun.

"Your yard is coming along nicely. I see the azaleas and tulips are blooming. It's going to be a peaceful sanctuary back here. You'll never get me to leave. You may just find me sipping my coffee and reading a book every day out here," Stella teased.

"Be my guest. Thanks to you, I have a beautiful garden. I suppose that the green thumb gene skipped me, but I'm trying to learn." Margot frowned.

Stella sat in a patio chair under an awning as Margot fetched a couple glasses of tea. They sat in silence, watching their dogs play as they sipped their drinks and enjoyed the cool summer breeze before Margot spoke.

"I really appreciate all the support you've been giving me. Since your victim impact statement, I feel that our relationship has really turned around. I think I didn't give us a chance sometimes, and I'm glad we've finally repaired it. I mean, it's still a work in progress, but I complain a lot less about you these days." Margot winked.

"I knew my ears weren't ringing as much." Stella winked back. "I couldn't be happier that my girl is back in my life. I know I wasn't the fun mom, but I tried my best. Margot, I wanted you to have your needs met, and it hurt that we weren't close for all those years," Stella's lips quivered.

"As I'm getting older, I understand that more. I'm also glad to be back in your life. Maybe we'll invite Dad next time," Margot said.

They looked at each other and simultaneously said, "Nah." They had waited to spend one-on-one time, so Charles could wait his turn to join them.

Margot discussed her upcoming trip to Miami, which she'd planned with Gemma. For too long, CMK, Carter, and Lucas had taken precedence in her life, so during her vacation, she wanted freedom from thinking of all of them. Stella was going to take care of Pepper, who she'd claimed as her "grand dog," which was another stressor gone for Margot.

———

Later that day, they went for a drive to Lorimier Cemetery to visit Nadine's grave, which had become fairly routine for them. While the three of them weren't able to do the things Stella talked about during her victim impact statement while Nadine was alive, the pair shared with Nadine all the recent events in their lives. Early in their visits, there were more tears, but as time went on, there had been more laughter and reminiscing.

As Margot sat next to Nadine's grave, she turned to look at the dusky sky. "I think this is the happiest I can be in a world without Nadine." Margot reached for Stella's hand and lightly squeezed it. "This is a much better trio than my previous one." Margot winked.

Stella squeezed Margot's hand. "I couldn't be prouder of how you turned out. I'd like to think you had some really outstanding role models in your life. Hopefully, I was one of them?" Her eyebrows raised.

"Absolutely, Mom. We've come so far, and healing my relationship with you means everything."

The two sat for another thirty minutes and laughed about old stories before packing up to leave home. A woman on a bike rode by with a bell ringing, which made them both turn to look at each other with tears in their eyes.

CHAPTER 56
2021

Spring was her favorite season, as it came with blooms and fresh scents, all displayed in a sunny bundle. Even the drive to the gravesite wasn't solemn because of the perfect weather. As she sang along to songs that were popular in high school, she reached to caress her growing baby bump. She enjoyed having her windows rolled down as she missed the smell of Missouri air. She pulled up to the cemetery, which was busy because of the holiday weekend. There were several renovations occurring, including freshly planted spruce trees and a new bush near the grave she was visiting. *What a nice touch. Now the birds can watch over her grave.* She saw a few dying flowers at the foot of the headstone and wondered who had left them. *Perhaps her sister? A friend? That's nice,* she thought. She needed to have visitors, and there was comfort in that thought. As she spread out a blanket next to the grave, she stretched out and pulled a few weeds that had formed.

"I'm sorry I haven't visited. As you can see by my belly, I've been quite busy!" she laughed. "I also moved away, and I don't get back here very much. Occasionally, I come back to visit my parents, but it's rare now that I live a few states away. I got married and we're going to be a family of five! Can you believe it? You can, I suppose. I know it was always your dream, and I'm sorry it couldn't happen for you, but life just worked out differently. Sometimes we fall for the wrong man, and I've learned a lot from some of that stupid shit you used to talk about, all that astrology crap. Turns out, Geminis and Libras are a much better match, so thank you for introducing me to that. Not that I put all of our relationship stock in the zodiac." She took off her shoes and rubbed her aching feet.

"There's more to life than fate and destiny. Sometimes you have to take matters into your own hands, and I'm really sorry, Jamie, but I had to do it. I tried to warn you about my genuine feelings for him, but you refused to listen to me. He was—excuse me, *is* my man, and I wasn't about to let you trick him away from me. Your little game of getting pregnant was the final straw, and if Travis wasn't going to break things off, I had to end things forever. But, hey, you're no longer miserable waiting for him night after night, wondering when he's going to come home or who he's giving his dick to. Now you're at peace, and I'm happy and pregnant." She rubbed her belly and gave Jamie's headstone a smile.

"Travis and I are married, and even though we don't see his other two children, we know they're out there somewhere. His whole arrest terrified him straight. It was the best thing for him, really. I mean, he seems a lot more faithful because he doesn't like to go out like he used to, but who am I kidding? He's still Travis. Believe me, I'm watching him. But he doesn't know our little secret. He doesn't know I was the one who killed you. I think he'd probably leave me if he knew. But he'll never find out—no one will. I planned it out pretty well."

Tiffany had gone by to help Jamie decorate and bake a cake for Travis's big reveal. They had been best friends in the past and were mending fences enough for Tiffany to show her support. At least, she hoped Jamie would think so. While Tiffany was there, she put melatonin in Jamie's drink to make her drowsy—not enough to knock her out, but enough for her to not pay close attention. Tiffany grabbed the spare key that was kept by the front desk drawer on the way out and returned later that night around one. A metal bat from her softball days did the trick of silencing the friend who impeded what she wanted.

"It was honestly my good fortune that we had a serial killer on the loose. I assumed they'd go after him, not Travis! But I was glad Travis got arrested after I found out he was with another woman that night. It was good for him to learn his lesson, and I think he has. But anyway, all of this crap meant we couldn't have a big wedding, even though we got money from his settlements. So we bought a house in the country. It's so beautiful, girl. White picket fence and everything! Anyway, I didn't come here to brag. I just needed to get this off my chest." She looked around, admiring the new spruce trees, watching a starling take flight.

"I probably won't come back to visit, but I also wanted to tell you about my pregnancy. I know you'd be so happy for us! If you couldn't have Travis's baby, I know you'd want me to!"

As she stood to leave, she took one last look at the grave and said, "Rest in peace, angel Jamie. I'm going to let the baby know you're his aunt."

And with that, she turned, leaving the pulled weeds in a pile next to the grave. She walked away, never turning around. As she buckled herself into her car, Tiffany sighed, thankful to have confessed the murder to Jamie, feeling a weight lifted, just like they'd taught her back in her Catholic school days.

Now was my soul free from the gnawing cares of seeking and getting, of wallowing in the mire and scratching at the itch of lust. St. Augustine.

As she drove out of the cemetery, she felt a little kick. She smiled and thought, *I'm glad you got to meet your Aunt Jamie, too.*

CHAPTER 57
2022

Black swimsuits, classic print T-shirts, shorts, and sandals were the perfect outfits for the beach. With CMK and Carter tucked into their prison beds and Lucas exposed as a troll, Margot's personal life was feeling much more balanced, and it was time for her to relax in the sunshine of Miami.

Margot thought about how her life had progressed since finding Nadine and eventually becoming a voice for victims. She didn't believe she'd done anything to solve Nadine's murder, but she'd certainly kept it in the forefront of the media, and she hoped that had kept Jack Moore from being able to murder more women. She'd take that win. Her local interviews and discussion garnered her a spot on the national stage, and she was fielding interviews and a future book deal.

Gemma came over before the two headed off on vacation. They were now bonded by their trauma, and Margot believed their pasts would keep their friendship solid. Margot was sitting on the edge of her couch admiring the prettiest red cardinal singing on her windowsill when the van that would take them to the airport arrived. The ride would take them two hours to the St. Louis airport, where they'd board a plane to the waiting sunshine, a treat compared to the dreary day in Cape Ivy. A Midwest storm dampened the ground—a true holiday for a robin, as she'd pick away at the dirt for a tasty treat of worm. The van driver had only scheduled one trip today, so they had to share their car service with another couple who were both in their late fifties. The woman wore her age better than him. Her graying bob covered her right glasses lens, and the various potholes in the road seemed to distract her as she tried to read.

A familiar notification ping from Gemma's phone snapped Margot's head toward her friend. *Death Toll* had an ominous ringtone Margot knew all too well. "You still have that app?" Margot questioned.

"Oh, yeah. I guess old habits die hard. It looks like it's back up and running again." Gemma fumbled.

"Leave me out of it. I want no part in *Death Toll* or the people there." Margot scowled and turned back to look out of the window.

———

Gemma's lit phone screen cut through the filtered light of early morning. As she shielded it from the view of those around her, she glanced over at Margot, who was drifting to sleep. Gemma never understood how anyone could sleep in a car with all the bumps and lack of comfort. As she logged in to *Death Toll,* she saw the usual chatter of those who were reminiscing about the good old days when Cape Ivy's killer was still at large. The excitement of his capture was long gone, and they all waited for their next thrill—a new killer who would satiate their attention spans.

Gemma began typing but quickly hit backspace. The van's silence was briefly shattered by the sound of the clicking text. *That was close!* Gemma logged out of TrollGod and into her original handle, onyx-heart. She hadn't made a mistake posting from the wrong account yet, but she told herself she could only hit send once she did a thorough check first. She couldn't let her identity get out since everyone still assumed Lucas was actually TrollGod. Gemma didn't feel sorry for him or the fact that he'd lost his TA position with Dr. Williams. *I had to do it.*

At times, Gemma felt Margot getting stronger and feared she'd leave behind her family-less friend. She couldn't risk Margot being unafraid and trusting of others. Gemma needed Margot to cling to her and believe that she was the only friend she could ever have…or want. She had Margot right where she wanted her: distrusting of men and content with the current state of her life.

When she and Margot had met for lunch a few weeks back, she'd looked up information on Lucas and the story about his sister, Sierra. Gemma already knew that the case was old and would require a deep dive, several pages into a search. She'd gambled Margot wouldn't do a thorough search, as she'd trust Gemma's report. Lucas was the pride of his parents for going into a field that could protect girls like Sierra. *I wonder what his parents think of him now? Do they believe his innocence or were they fooled by the story I created?* Gemma reserved the right to not feel sympathy for him. She knew he was a threat to her role as Margot's sole confidante.

Gemma could immediately see the elusive side of Carter—one deviant could recognize another. Maybe it was their eyes or the way they carried themselves. It was very easy to see who was psychotic and who the normals were. She watched as he pretended to care about Margot's well-being, all the while leaving flowers on Nadine's grave. Little did Carter know, Gemma also spent time in the cemetery—a great place for quiet contemplation.

Gemma clearly saw that Margot was painfully normal. She was just unfortunate enough to find her aunt dead. Gemma always wondered if she had passed by Jack Moore, but she believed she hadn't. She thought she would have recognized any killer by his scent, his stare, and his essence of death. She was glad Carter was gone. It only helped her own plan to have Margot trust her the most. Carter was too preoccupied with being a fanboy to recognize Gemma's own motives. Maybe if he hadn't been so engrossed in who Margot was, he may have noticed Gemma's deception. Carter was obsessed with true crime, and he'd come to Cape Ivy to ingratiate himself to its latest killer. By the time Gemma leaked her own identity on *Death Toll*, Carter was much too preoccupied with Margot to focus on her.

Gemma liked to think she was good at deceit. Maybe her dark side had formed during that ride with her dad. She would always have the overwhelming shame that she'd started all of this, as she was the one who'd told her dad about the affair. She was the one who didn't alert her mom or grandparents of the impending threat that was just seconds around the corner. Not even a scream or crashing lamp to give them a real chance. That day left her with remorse and the knowledge that she had destruction in her genes. She came from murder, and while she didn't want to commit murder herself, she felt closer to her dad than her mom. When she got into any predicament, she always wished she had her dad to guide her.

Gemma looked over at Margot, who was yawning and stretching, and gave her a terse smile. She'd learned early on how to act during the investigation of the Crimson Spree Shooter, which certainly made her skilled now. The Death Toll notification vibrated, alerting Gemma to more online drama. As she opened the app, she saw a chilling message: Murder Has Returned to Cape Ivy. Single Woman Found Dead with Knife Wounds to the Neck. Gemma couldn't have predicted the good fortune of another killer so soon.

Before alerting Margot, Gemma looked out at the rainy landscape, her eyes catching on a turkey vulture devouring roadkill with expert precision. She wanted to figure out the best way to tell her and how it would affect the rest of their day. *Should I wait until after the vacation? Margot knows I have Death Toll, so I don't want to raise her suspicions if she finds out and I didn't tell her.* Gemma took a deep breath and blurted, "Margot, there's been another murder." Gemma said it loud enough to stir Margot, causing the other couple to gasp.

Margot's body jolted with the news. "In Cape Ivy?" Margot asked as she rubbed her eyes.

"All I know is they found a woman in her Cape Ivy house with knife wounds to her neck." Gemma let out a slow breath.

The couple stared at the two women conversing so routinely about a homicide.

Margot's face was motionless, yet her eyes searched the van for comprehension. Margot shook as she rubbed at the forming goose-bumps on her arms. She turned to look back out the window as other Missouri towns flashed by. "This news shouldn't shock me, but it's bringing back some unpleasant emotions," Margot said, leaning her head against the window.

The van driver kept peeking in his rearview mirror at the silence killing conversation.

This wasn't part of the plan, but Gemma appreciated the new murder. It meant that Margot's fear wouldn't be going away anytime soon.

"I'm not in a vacation mood anymore," Margot said as she stared out the van window.

"Are you sure? I think it would do you some good to relax," Gemma said, hoping Margot went with her gut to return home.

"Yeah, I'm sure. I guess I was naïve to think that I'd be healed after CMK's incarceration, but this just brings up all those old feelings. The feeling of not being safe. I just don't feel comfortable going away right now." Margot wrapped her arms around her waist.

Gemma turned to look out the window. This time, she could see cows and cornfields passing by. The serenity of middle Missouri nature was a pleasant reprieve from their tense discussion. Once the driver dropped off the other couple, who quickly descended the van stairs, with their eyes wide from the horrific news, Gemma and Margot rode back with the driver to Cape Ivy.

Gemma much preferred her routine of home life. She could better control what happened, and the comfort of that was priceless.

The van sped past the Welcome to Cape Ivy sign, which dripped with rain.

As they arrived back at Margot's bungalow, Margot turned to Gemma, "Do you feel safe staying at home? If not, you're welcome to crash here." Margot pulled her full suitcase to her front door.

"I feel safe. I mean, aren't we used to this kind of fear?" Gemma shrugged. "Are you going to be OK? If you need me to stay, just tell me."

"I'll be fine. I feel safe at home. It has great security, both physically and emotionally." Margot held up her hand to wave goodbye to her friend.

Gemma turned toward her car, and a giddiness overcame her. She watched as fear spread all over Margot's face. Gemma couldn't have planned this any better. A scared friend clings to those she trusts, and Gemma knew she was one of those people.

Gemma walked up the stairs to her apartment, went inside, and landed on her couch, where she began scrolling through *Death Toll*.

There's no place like home with a murderer on the loose.

The End

A LETTER FROM NICOLE

Dear readers,

I want to say a huge thank you for choosing to read *The Final Sentence.* If you enjoyed it, and want to keep up to date with all of my latest releases, just sign up at nicoleannbury.com. I will never share your email address, and you can unsubscribe anytime.

I hope you loved *The Final Sentence* and if you did, I would be very grateful if you could write a review. I'd love to hear what you think, and it makes such a difference helping new readers discover my book for the first time.

I love hearing from readers! Send me an email at nicoleannbury@ gmail.com. You can also follow me on any social media platform of your choice.

Thank you!

Nicole Annbury

ACKNOWLEDGMENTS

There are several people I need to thank for helping me along this writing journey. First, I thank my editor, Meg McIntyre, with Phantom Pen Editorial for her phenomenal eye in helping make this book into my vision. There were many beta and ARC readers along the way that I couldn't have written this book without their feedback, to which I'm eternally grateful. The ladies in Quill & Cup were by my side as I wrote this novel, from notes to a completed manuscript, to which I'm forever thankful.

I'm grateful to my family for their encouragement and my parents for instilling my creativity. I'm especially grateful to my husband for giving me the encouragement to write. My writing life only began after I met him and I think he's been the catalyst for that.

I want to thank KFVS-12 in Cape Girardeau, MO. for providing background evidence and research on the Bandana Rapist.

To Stephanie, Lisa, and Bill, I will always remember your support of me and my writing. Though you're gone too soon, your encouragement will never be forgotten.

ABOUT THE AUTHOR

Nicole Annbury currently resides in Indianapolis, Indiana, with her husband and three cats. Although she's originally from Missouri, she spent part of her youth in California.

Nicole graduated from Southeast Missouri State University with a degree in human services and worked as a social worker for several years until chronic illness made that impossible. After being diagnosed with fibromyalgia and rheumatoid arthritis, she left her career and dreamt of the day she'd become a published author. It took her several more years to begin writing when the idea of *The Final Sentence* came to mind. Nicole is currently drafting book two, *The Signature Line*, with plans to write future novels.

When she's not writing, she enjoys nature walks, true crime documentaries, reality TV viewing and going on drives with her husband.

facebook.com/nicoleannbury

instagram.com/nicoleannbury

goodreads.com/nicoleannbury

threads.net/@nicoleannbury